INN-BY-THE-BYE
STORIES - 23

WILLIAM FLEWELLING

authorHOUSE

AuthorHouse™
1663 Liberty Drive
Bloomington, IN 47403
www.authorhouse.com
Phone: 833-262-8899

Published by AuthorHouse 01/13/2021

ISBN: 978-1-6655-1378-4 (sc)
ISBN: 978-1-6655-1380-7 (e)

Print information available on the last page.

Devotional

Some Reflective Prayers
Reflective Prayers: A Second Collection
A Third Collection Of Reflective Prayers
For Your Quiet Meditation
A Fourth Collection Of Reflective Prayers
Cantica Sacra
A Fifth Collection Of Reflective Prayers
A Sixth Collection Of Reflective Prayers
A Second "For your Quiet Meditation"
A Second Cantica Sacra

Directions Of A Pastoral Lifetime

Part I: Pastoral Notes, Letters To Anna, Occasional Pamphlets
Part II: Psalm Meditations, Regula Vitae
Part III: Elders' Studies
Part IV: Studies
Part V: The Song Of Songs: An Attraction

Exegetical Works

From The Catholic Epistles: Bible Studies
Paul's Letter To The Romans: A Bible Study
The Book Of Hebrews: A Bible Study
Letters Pauline and Pastoral: Bible Studies
The First Letter Of Paul To The Corinthians: A Bible Study
The Gospel According To Luke 1:1 Through 9:50
The Gospel According to Luke 9:51 Through 19:27
The Gospel According to Luke 19:28 Through 24:53

all published by AuthorHouse.com

Contents

Foreword

In the course of these late stories I found myself adjusting to the flow of things. These, like all the stories after mid-August 2003, had been kept on floppy discs, sequentially, and not produced in hard copy. At a point I can no longer identify, but during my tenure in the interim ministry I was performing between October 2005 and August 2007, I produced the stories in hard copy. That required some playing with pages, a process I had learned over the previous decade or so. But what happened was a general shuffling of order in the individual stories.

Of course, I sorted out what the issues were and managed to reconstruct the stories. I ended up finding that the numbers ran away on me – there being only twenty-four in this series rather than twenty-six as I have before advertised. I was afraid I was going to need to construct an ending to one story or another – but that difficulty was averted by sorting out what really was there in the printed text that I had at hand.

The stories, so far as my work was concerned, had run their course, at least with respect to how my work was evolving and happening in those days. I suddenly found that they were done. And so, I stopped.

I am glad now to have these ready for publication. I have certainly enjoyed the process of revisiting them in their more or less mature form. And I hope my readers find them enjoyable as well.

After the usual Appendix (now Appendix I) that lists the appropriate scripture texts that lie behind the stories, I am offering Appendix II: The Prequel. For these stories had a beginning that sought to establish itself between 23 December 1979 and 28 September 1980, ending a little less than a year before the other sequence began. For my purposes – and, hopefully, yours – I want to leave the Prequel in place here, as a completion of a trajectory in my ministry and writing that served me so well for so many years.

William Flewelling

MCI

With all of his customary dignity, Terzi made his most occasional visit to the Commons, emerging somewhat mysteriously from the Leaferites' Hill. No one noticed when he appeared; when Geoffrey did notice him, Terzi had all the aplomb of one who had always been there, consummately relaxed and at home. 'Good afternoon, Terzi' offered Geoffrey, good naturedly. Terzi nodded graciously, with a restrained, formal and polite smile. 'Good afternoon, Geoffrey' he replied.

By the time this exchange had happened, Geoffrey had moved so as to stand beside Terzi, not far from the Leaferites' Hill and looking across the Commons, today unusually populated with about everyone who would ever come to the Inn-by-the-Bye.

Clyde was pacing around over toward the Big Rock, playing his shawm – some lively dance tunes, to which Mahara was dancing, trying to involve Guerric in the dance even though she *knew* full well he was not a dancer: not at all. Others were watching, thinking about this dance but holding back. Nearer the Inn-by-the Bye, Thyruid was serving the good things that emerged from Marthuida's kitchen. It was, in brief, a party day.

'Did the noise bring you here?' asked Geoffrey. 'No. No. Not at all. We heard it, of course, but I came neither to complain nor to dance'. 'If not a dance, perhaps something to eat ... Marthuida has done a fine job today'. 'She always does very well'. 'True, true: today, however, exceeds her normally high standards. Taste and see for yourself!'

'You are tempting me, Geoffrey!' 'If you would be tempted, this is as fine an occasion to be tempted as I can imagine'. The two of them chuckled together and let it pass. 'I came with the hope of finding a moment to speak privately with Thyruid. I might find myself disappointed in that hope'.

Terzi wandered off, politely moving among the partygoers in search of Thyruid. But every time he drew near to the round Innkeeper, something or other would divert Thyruid to somewhere else, leaving Terzi frustrated yet consummately polite.

Hardly by chance, Carymba also noticed him and read the sort of brooding frustration that seethed just below the surface of his composed demeanor. She guessed by his movement that he was seeking to speak with Thyruid – a nearly impossible task on this particular day, given the events sprawling around the Commons and sponsored by the Inn-by-the-Bye ... and the Innkeeper in particular. So, with care, she moved herself so as to meet up with Terzi directly. She could tell he was able to move through the pleasing, mulling crowd with ease; no one was bothering him, and no one was in a position to actually encounter him either ... not since Geoffrey made his ploy with pleasantries.

'Hello, Terzi! how pleasant to see you join in the festive air' greeted Carymba with a calculated air of lightheartedness. 'Hello, Carymba. Actually, I came for other reasons than the festivities'. 'At least sample Marthuida's table!' 'I might need to do that yet' he replied, with something a bit more wry than any chuckle, though he attempted the chuckle, too, for politeness' sake.

'You seem to be seeking Thyruid'. 'Yes. You always did observe things well'. Carymba blushed slightly, glanced down ... then returned: 'If your business has nothing to do with this party, Thyruid might be too distracted to help you much'. 'I am beginning to think you are right, that I chose a poor day to seek out his counsel'. 'If it is wise counsel you desire, take a pot of tea, a cup for yourself and another, some scones perhaps, and go to sit in the shade with Missus Carney. A wise woman yet, and not met with all those demands on her attention'.

Terzi glanced at Carymba who gestured to where Missus Carney was sitting, in the shade to the side of the Inn-by-the-Bye. She watched him muse for a bit. Then, he nodded: 'That might well be good counsel in itself'. Carymba glanced down, again flushed – somewhat more than slightly, missing in the act Terzi's polite nod to her as he moved from her side toward the laden board.

At the board, he chose a teapot, a couple cups and was gathering a few scones when Thyruid interrupted: 'Here, use a tray to carry all that, and find yourself a place to sit, where you can enjoy it'. 'Thank you. That is a good idea, good counsel … to use a tray! So much better than fumbling with the whole collection awkwardly in my arms!'

Gathered, he carried his tray with all the composure and propriety, even dignity of a formal maître d', or of a gentleman's gentleman such as Geoffrey. with such formal graciousness did Terzi approach Missus Carney. 'You seem to be alone, and with nothing in hand. May I join you and share some tea and scones with you?' 'Why, thank you. I saw you gathering an arm load before Thyruid suggested the tray; I had thought the load would be awkward – but the tray transformed all those appearances. Ah … and here, I prattle! Please, sit down. I am honored to share in your kindness'.

Seated, then, Terzi poured a cup of tea for Missus Carney, one for himself. All the while, she was watching him balance the tray on his knees, albeit with great care. And Missus Carney wondered momentarily just how they were going to handle this! To the relief of both of them, Geoffrey suddenly arrived: 'I thought you might find the tray on the knees a strain, even if you were seated face to face, knee to knee, sharing two laps as a table for the tray. So, I brought this small table for you to share'. 'Why, thank you, Geoffrey' replied the very relieved Terzi, who had begun to recognize how delicate a thing proper dignity can be in a situation like this.

Finding the table arranged so that a corner came between them and the extending square readily handled the tray, the teapot and cups and scones, Terzi sighed an almost noticeable sigh. 'This should be most pleasant, don't you think?' 'Yes. I believe it will' replied the smiling Missus Carney.

3

Once their sharing in scones and tea had progressed a ways, as Terzi was about to steer the conversation from the lightly amiable to his reason for appearing here at all, Clyde meandered by, playing his favorite dance tunes on his shawm, with a following train led by the exuberantly dancing Mahara. Missus Carney leaned to Terzi: 'Is she not lovely, and *such* a dancer!' Terzi agreed: 'Radiant; exultant in her dance'.

At last, a lull gave Terzi room: 'Missus Carney, I came down from the Leaferites' Hill hoping for some counsel. I had thought to seek Thyruid, but he is overwhelmed. Carymba suggested you might offer a word'. 'I can try'. 'It is Walter'.

'Oh. What do you do with an irritant like Walter?' 'Precisely'.

'Your every need was met here'. 'Yes'. 'And, you see, nothing about this party was disrupted'. Terzi nodded. 'So, you see my counsel'.

11 September 2005

MCII

Dew lingered, richly layered along the grass, across all Hyperbia, long into the unfolding morning. Though the sky was a thorough blue, deep and radiant in the filling out of the morning hours, the cool remains sufficiently to hold the dew's drenching measure until the Sun itself could ignite in sheer brilliance and hastily vaporize that morning layer of wet freshness from the land. All that would come; but, for a long time, Jasper found the dew thick and full, slow to dissipate.

Where Jasper would normally have ended his night at work in John's Foundry by finding a place to sleep comfortably, his restlessness of this morning discouraged him from even *seeking* a place; he had simply meandered off once the usual shut down chores were complete. He did not bother to comment on what was on his mind – for one thing, he did not know, himself; for another, there was no reason to comment as John was concerned only that Jasper be ready for work that night.

Setting out, then, Jasper left the Foundry and began walking. He ambled along the Hills, passing quickly the Way Down: he was *not* intrigued with old matters. Rather … well, Jasper was not sure what it might be that was making him go on this way.

The path led him past the way up to Missus Duns' sod house; Jasper did not even pause. When the Fringe arrived, he walked along the rest of the rise, above the low-lying Fringe. His pace became resolute, measured, never wavering from that crest while brooding over the time he had spent wandering those clumps of reed-grass and low, narrow, meandering paths in the midst of the pervasive swampy water – and the stifling sort of silence there!

Meeting the Empty Area – he, like most, had never been there – Jasper stopped and gazed. *This* was a place that held Jasper back. He stared *this* morning, a fact that contradicted everything he *normally* did. This was not a place to fascinate the likes of Jasper. He figured Carymba had gone out there. He wondered a bit about Walter but figured *he* was too unhappy about everything in life to risk the sort of depression Jasper *must* be involved in such an abandoned place. 'And Malak, of course' he muttered under his breath, almost forgetting that mysterious one who simply approaches with a message – then vanishes – or so it seemed.

Before long, Jasper developed a creepy feeling, as if unseen things were creeping willy-nilly across him bringing a long shudder that bounded from heels to nape and back, and forth, again and again. At last, ending with a quiver all over, Jasper turned from his gaze into the Empty Area to continue his circle of the Fields, aiming over to the Spinners' Shop … meaning nothing more than simply moving along his established sweep around the Fields.

His feet had become wet, and his legs – past his knees. Yet, he had been so preoccupied with nothing at all that he did not even notice the wetness. Jasper continued not to notice as his route swung around again to lead down the path by Mary's Flower Shop, on near the Foundry where he started, and on toward the 'Y'. Jasper never paused.

By now, he was only *physically* aware that he was growing warm, to sweat – but paid it no mind. Only after the sweat had pooled beneath his eyes and the brine had begun to burn his eyes would Jasper realize how warm he had become.

But, for now, he came to the 'Y' and half automatically turned to go down the Valley Road under the thick green cover of the overarching, interlacing branches of the trees. The still air he had known on the Fields became even more still along the Valley Road.

Without a thought, he passed the Narrows and the roots steps up to the path into the Crossed Hills. Not knowing where he was headed, he had no inkling whatsoever whether Hidden Cabin would be his destination. Instead, without a thought, he ambled down to the Beach – where the Sun dominated, glistening off the Sea and warming the sand under his feet.

As if it were meant to be so, Jasper walked straight to the edge of the strand's wet sand. Having stopped, placing his hands upon his hips, he gazed across the regular pattern of the Sea as the waves lazily rolled in toward shore. Where the waves would gently lap up the strand, wash a ways and then retreat in a tumbling hurry back to the Sea itself, as if the waves ran out of nerve and had to sweep quickly back into the undifferentiated waters of the Sea, Jasper stared with a sort of measuring stillness.

Suddenly, Jasper dropped to one knee in order to loosen his shoe; with a certain effort, he pulled off his sock and stuffed it into the waiting work boot. At first absentmindedly, but then on purpose, he curled his toes into the sand and squeezed the granular grit out between his toes. For the first time all morning, before or since the Sun rose, Jasper grinned as the sand felt – he could not describe what it was like beyond being *sensuous* in this toes

Eagerly, then, Jasper switched knees and bared the second foot. He rose to his feet, curling *those* toes in the sand as well. This time, his foot had landed in damp sand, washed by some the waves flowing up the strand – the *more* energetic ones.

From standing once again, Jasper began to move toward the Sea – but then stopped, leaned over and rolled up his pants' legs. They were damp from sweat, wet from dew but he wanted to preserve them from the Sea. When the waves sloshed around his shins, half-way to the knees, he stopped, hands again on his hips. Jasper squinted into the morning Sun and breathed deeply of the scent of the Sea.

Jasper had not bothered to notice *time* all morning – but particularly since he stepped into the Sea and let that water circulate about his legs, his feet, washing over them all before carrying most of the water and sand

and all back into the Sea as the ebb of each rushing wave escaped into the great expanse of water. He had left his work boots, socks stuffed inside, on the Beach and forgotten all about them as he savored the feel of the Sea on his feet, his lower legs.

'Did you forget these?' The voice belonged to Carymba; Jasper turned head and shoulders – *not* feet – to glance her way. The waif held up the boots, one in each hand, with an impishly quizzical expression on her face. 'No, I left them there so I could enjoy this so much more. I think this is why I was so restless all night … and I did not know it'.

'Wading like that is fun. Here, I will join you, except I am going to wade down the Beach and carry my sandals as I go. She held out his boots at arm's length, a smirk on her face that made him wonder if she would simply drop them. 'Ok. I am coming for them now. Then, I can wade with you, down the Beach'.

25 September 2005

MCIII

Low greys accompanied the gradual pretending to be morning. The Sun, assumed to shine the other side of those dense, laden clouds, presumed to bring a muted light that masqueraded as day until the grey give way to shrouded black. Early on, the wind came swiftly, curling around the Hills and Crossed Hills, swirling down, around to taunt the Fields, the Commons and the Plain alike, whipping sudden rain around. Settled from gusts, the wind still whisked under that laden grey cover all day, whipping the showers around, pelting windows and siding, trees and grass, paths and those few foolhardy walkers who dared the day.

Among the wee folk of Hyperbia, the day invited little daring. Effie woke slowly as the grey lay uninvitingly against the window of her garret room.

Similarly, Mary found little energy to make for herself any breakfast, though she did lie sprawled on her bed pondering whether a pot of tea would be comforting enough to warrant spending the energy to ready the stove (by which time she might as well make up a batch of scones as well).

Eliza woke, remembering she had promised to make a meal for John, though the rattling sounds raised by the wind in the trees in the Hills, and the dimness brought about by the heavy overcast encouraged her rather to curl in her covers.

At the Inn-by-the-Bye, Thyruid was about his polishing chores. Every morning for more years than he wanted to count he had brought out the polish pot from behind his counter and polished carefully all his prized brassware trim in the dining room. As he did that chore, he would adjust his lamps as well.

Because the heavy curtains maintained a dimly lit ambiance in the dining room, Thyruid really had not noticed the overcast outside. *But* he could hear the wind and hear the riveting of the rain on the windowpanes behind the heavy draperies. He could feel the cool and the damp; he wondered about starting a *low* fire on the hearth of the dining room. At the moment, it might well *feel* good. But, he wondered, if it should warm just a bit outside, would that fire on the hearth become a problem? He knew the way this season worked!

Up in Hidden Cabin, Mother Hougarry was up and busy. She had her stove going. The tea kettle was heating and her old hands were mixing up the dough for a batch of scones ... all under the carefully, studying eye of little Anna. She was sure Mother Hougarry would do it right, just like always; she was giving her careful study so that she would know how to do it just right, too. Anna was attentive to details like that, and was quick to note the whole process as well as its parts.

Anna figured Mother Hougarry would see if she wanted to help some day ... and when she did, Anna would be most ready. Because it was a heavy day, Mother Hougarry brightened her lights; because the wind slapped rain around Hidden Cabin, Anna knew they would kept inside today.

Guerric never rose easily. Today, as always, he was teased from slumber by Mahara, by her urging and more by the tang of gypsie cakes cooking on the stove and the pungent aroma of the strong coffee she brewed for him every morning. With no more than the usual reluctance, Guerric sampled his coffee ... having her pass the mug beneath his nose and waving it there until he began to respond with some sort of visceral focus, and she would lead him to the table where breakfast and a little time served to effect his transformation.

Today was like every day. Guerric did not even hear the wind, or the rain ... not until he was gathering his necessary stuff. By this time, he *was* functioning enough to recall the necessities of his day at hand. As he reached the door, opened it to go out into the blustery rainy cool, he paused: 'The Inn-by-the-Bye for lunch'. Mahara smiled slightly, and nodded.

In all this stirring, and more, the tone of the day persisted. The grey never yielded – beyond recovering to a mere dull drab from the occasional periods of heavier cover and misted rain in all its ambiguity. And the rain – it came and went, riding on the wind's persistent restlessness. As the morning wore away like a yawn, there was nothing outside to stimulate any kind of excitement. Instead, the day came as if it intended to mute everything and everybody.

Gradually, Mary had made herself tea, and scones; she made the day unfold as it ought, bringing her touch to the Flower Shop and her plants even though she had to figure no one would be coming through her door.

And Effie had gone to join the Spinners in their common breakfast and then, downstairs, at their Spinning craft. It would be a day like most days, even as the wind could be easily heard outside, and the rain pattering on windows and doors.

Eliza, too, summoned herself to her day, though she was long having no fortune whatsoever in deciding what or how she should go about this dinner she was to prepare! Time was rushing away on her and nothing was done.

Up at Hidden Cabin, Carymba made an entirely unusual midmorning stop. She was, of course, wet; Mother Hougarry insisted she sit on the stool near the stove and dry some while the scones backed. The friendly waif agreed and sat to join in the talk. She made it a point to ask Anna what she had been doing; the young girl explained how carefully she had been watching Mother Hougarry as she made up the scones. Carymba commented that she must be learning well from such a good teacher and would be ready soon to be a helper. Anna's eyes brightened as she, speechless, simply nodded. Mother Hougarry pretended not to notice – but Carymba *knew* she did. And *that* would be enough.

Carymba explained she could not stay but needed to get to the Inn-by-the-Bye before lunch was too far gone. Mother Hougarry said it was such a shame she could not enjoy these scones with them ... *then* hurried to fill a basket, wrapping a towel around the scones, nearly all of them: 'Here, you take these to Marthuida, and have some for yourself, too!' 'What about you?' 'Oh, it is so cool: we can stir the stove and make ourselves some fresh ... *fresher* than yours!'

Guerric finished up his first jobs and swung himself around to Mary's Flower Shop, where he rattled at the door, feeling that this was also her home – so just walking in would not be quite right. When Mary arrived, she invited him in and showed him some options; Guerric chose and she prepared them for him, knowing he would be carrying the flowers in the wind and in the rain. (He told her as she worked that he was taking them to the Inn-by-the-Bye where he was to meet Mahara for lunch.)

Eliza came down the Way Down, a rain cover wrapped about her and covering her hair. She was miserable and wondered if she could find John awake enough to explain she could come up with nothing for dinner.

Gilbert told his spinners that they needed to get out of their gloomy shop. 'Let us go to the Inn for lunch, make a bit of a celebration in spite of the weather'.

Marthuida told Thyruid to put the basket out since Carymba brought it. 'Share it around the room'. When all were there and the room was full, Carymba told of the scones and of Anna. Clyde said in climax: 'Then let us eat them for the joy of Anna!'

2 October 2005

MCIV

Beginning from the closing door left latched behind him, Margent carried all his thoughts and all his troubles, all the many things that had cluttered his day — carried them in his worried mind down the long, narrow, *dim* corridor from his unimpressive office to the door opening onto the narrow lane. The cobblestones were shaded, as they always were; he stepped into that shade and drew the door closed behind himself.

Morning had run over on him, again, and Margent was setting out late for his usual café for a bit of lunch. In general, he felt he ought to get out of the office for lunch each day, particularly on those days when he had had no visitors. He figured the City on the Plain was not possibly running as smoothly as the quiet he met in his inauspicious office in his back-corner location suggested.

The problem was not that he was unknown: almost everyone in the City knew where to find Margent if they wanted to find him. It is just that no one thought to go looking when Osburn ran the City with greater ostentation from his big offices facing the central plaza of the City. With Osburn, there was no *point* in going; with Margent there was rarely much *need* to go.

Margent's route took him down the deserted cobblestone alleyway to turn into another street, then into an avenue … and to his favorite café lunch spot before arriving at the boulevard. Along the way, the preoccupied Margent happened *not* to meet anyone. Had he not been so preoccupied, he might well have been somewhat perplexed by the quiet, for usually he *did* meet someone. Wrapped in his preoccupations, however, he did not notice. He barely noticed when he reached the customary door, turning in more by reason of habit than anything else.

On his entering, Margent heard the familiar, affable voice call out: 'Ah! You *did* decide to come today! I had nearly given up on your arrival … figured you had been swamped by business or something!' Margent glanced his way, offered a weak grin and a little word: 'The usual, please'. Then, he slipped onto a stool at the counter while waiting for his typical sandwich and mug of coffee. Tired, the Manager of the City on the Plain held his face in his hands, elbows on the counter, and let those hands rub his face: it felt good.

'You look worn out'. 'A little tired: that is all'. 'O! Master of understatement, if you ask me!' 'There were simply a lot of things to be done this morning. 'So? There are *always* lots of things to be done, every morning. That does not mean you let them get under your girdle'. 'You mean that burr only gives a body a sore?' 'You got it'. 'Like you have the experience'. 'Well, you stand back here and see a bunch of sad mugs run past, hear a run of sad luck tales, one long series of hard luck woes. Not quite experience: but it does run close enough for me'.

Margent sighed and let his head droop, gazing through the counter into some unavailable piece of space. His friendly host stepped back to make up the desired "Usual" … a simple sandwich and a mug of coffee. Shortly, he returned and set them before Margent. 'There you go' he said and began to move away.

'What sort of tales do you mean?' blurted out Margent. The lunch counter manager paused and turned back to Margent; he had plenty of time as the lunch crowd had all come and gone long since.

'Oh …it is just the usual. People try to make ends meet. People find trouble at home … some do not handle things very well. Sometimes, people say they once thought they knew what they were doing. Then, they lost all their bearings and nothing at all fit together anymore. Frustrated … frustrated … frustrated.

'Yes: frustrated. And all we want is to have things fit together some way, ... some way that makes sense of all this malarkey!' Margent looked at his sandwich and moved to pick it up, raised it in both hands and punctuated his comment with a bite that filled his mouth past coherent stammering.

'Sometimes, I wonder, doing what I do, what I *can* do in the office, if it really matters'. The counter manager bent over, resting his elbows on the counter and watching his customer. He knew that Margent was the City Manager and that he *chose* his back alley, out the way office place in direct contrast to the ousted Osburn. He knew Margent had wide approval for his choice. And he knew the City on the Plain was administered well and fairly. But now, all he could do was nod. He agreed: this *was* the question.

The counter manager went on: 'It is like I cannot make any difference in the eyes of these folk who come to bare their frustrations here. They meet me as they would meet a bartender ... only more soberly, all the way around. I wonder how Osburn would have dealt with all of this'.

'Oh, you know very well that he would do nothing, then arrange for making a speech. At the speech, he would be like a peacock. He always gave a marvelous show ... surely you remember! ... And then he would strut back into his City Hall to disappear'. 'Yes: you are right. That *is* what he would do'. Margent spoke in the flattest of tones, even flatter than did his host.

The manager of the lunch counter stood and stepped back. 'Just think of that man, before he went up on the bluff, and the people of the City told him to stay there'. 'I was there'. 'You were in the middle of it'. 'Yes, I was. Was it worth it, though?'

The door opened. Margent simply sat in his slump. The manager looked up: 'Eh? You, too, are late today'. 'Too late?' 'Nah. I can get you something; it is not like you are a stranger or something'. 'Thanks'. The customer took a seat at the far end of the counter, paying no attention to Margent whatsoever. 'The usual'. 'Sounds good'.

'Do you know why I am late?' The customer spoke to no one in particular and did not pause at all for any excuse for an answer. 'I was talking with some friends … the usual, you know: griping. I swear, this griping is our national sport. We were saying how nothing was getting done, how the City seemed so stagnant. I am sure you have noticed … or, at least, heard those who noticed'.

Margent simply listened; the counter manager merely stammered and felt helpless.

'Then, you know, another friend comes up, caught up with what we were saying and jumps in, adding: 'Yea! And what is not happening gets things done where the bluster and show we had before left life adrift'. We started to protest, then stopped. He was right. You know, I ought to go back to that hidden office of his … wherever it is … and let Margent know'.

'You just did'.

9 October 2005

MCV

After her late breakfast in the back-kitchen area of her sod house, Missus Duns moved heavily, lumbering slowly to the front area, thinking of her overstuffed chair there, and its great ottoman. Along the way, she noticed how dry the walls were, and the flowers on the windowsill. But, for now, she would leave them, promising herself that she would care for them later. For she was tired, and the vision in her head was of sitting in that overstuffed chair, her feet elevated delightfully onto the ottoman, enchanted.

Directed by the heaviness felt in her feet, Missus Duns tottered carefully though eagerly around the chair – aimed herself so that she would flop successfully into its plentiful fullness. She landed, ignoring totally the swelling puff of dust laden swirling currents her descent occasioned. With some effort, Missus Duns squirmed herself into her seat and found herself *comfortable* in due time. There, with her feet up and her body eased down into a curl, her arms up on the high chair arms and her legs across the mass of the ottoman, Missus Duns let herself simply sink into the chair.

Anymore, managing breakfast and the routines of her morning have had Missus Duns wrung out. She jokes with herself that it is a good thing she has no need to go anywhere, because she is tired after breakfast and taking a spell in this overstuffed chair is *most* satisfying. Being here, in her sod house, nestled as it always has been in a secluded niche of the Hills, Missus Duns had not been *able* to leave for years, from long before she found breakfast and rising chores the occasion for a period of rest.

Having flopped into her chair and given that final sigh of relaxation, Missus Duns soon sifted into an unplanned, later to be denied, nap. This chair always nestled her delightfully, always settled her into place ... almost like an open face cocoon! In quiet, in her room, her sod house, her secluded little niche in the Hills, this place that was simply *home* to her nothing – disturbed her nor the gentle settling of dust.

Now, the movement of the Sun was the only marker of time's immediate passage. Missus Duns was *always* in a mood to say the day past had been full and she had been gratefully aware of *every* passing moment.

As he often, silently, would do, Malak slipped into the niche where Missus Duns' sod house set, nestled and quiet, just to make a brief check on her. She had never seen him come by; so, she had no imagination-generated hint that she was anything but alone most of the time here.

Every few days Carymba – and, maybe, Geoffrey – would come by; of late, however, she has found it harder and harder to entertain her guests properly. Though she is *always* glad to have them come she nearly dreads their coming, all on the issue of entertainment and energy. So, Malak's barely perceptible visits served her well, avoiding all the fuss.

Almost as a shadow, a subtle shade, Malak moved with graceful ease from the twisting little rise onto Missus Duns' open space – remarkably flat around two sides of the small space). Long strides brought him counterclockwise around the open area, along the back rise and then beside the sod house from the back toward the front – and her only door. Before the door – facing front and *not* across the place she used to use for out of doors entertaining – he passed the little window set in the sod wall which *did* face the spot one first appeared in Missus Duns' little place.

As Malak passed the window, he slowed and let his over the shoulder glance give him a quick survey of the room. As expected, Missus Duns was asleep in her overstuffed chair, her legs propped on the large ottoman that had been there as long as Malak could remember.

He paused, letting his eye parse the scene seen through the splattered pane. The pause was brief; Malak is rarely still more than a fleeting moment. But the pause was long enough to assure that she was dozing peacefully and in good health before slipping like a shadow back across to that sudden twist that bore him from the niche of the sod house and silently back into the Hills.

Sometime afterwards, Missus Duns simply awoke. She slid effortlessly from that peaceful slumber into wakefulness: a seamless transition by which she was fully convinced that she had merely closed her eyes for a moment before opening them again. Once more, she would tell herself how refreshing it was to sit for a minute and close her eyes – then open them again to assume again the run of her day. Should anyone contradict her, she would simply smile and explain how she could tell – and her wise visitors would never press that the Sun had advanced through the day far more than she might have expected. And Missus Duns would remain delightfully oblivious!

While she sat in her all-absorbing overstuffed chair, with her legs still draped across the expansive ottoman, the door rattled. Missus Duns started to fuss about the effort of getting herself up from her overstuffed chair. The rattle returned and she decided she was old enough now to remain seated when visitors admitted themselves. 'Oh ... com in!' she called with a slightly regal tone to her voice.

The door creaked open. First, she saw Carymba and greeted her: 'I am just too slow getting up these days. Give me a few minutes'. Carymba grinned, her face flushed rosy: 'Just stay as you are. We will not be a problem for you'. 'We? What are "we"? I see only you!'

Geoffrey, and then Clyde slipped around the door behind Carymba. So, Missus Duns said: 'Oh! This is your "we"!' The words came as a sheer relief for what she saw of "we" was familiar and manageable. The trio came to the side of her chair, standing side by side as a veil while the rest ... Mary, Mahara, Guerric, John and Jasper, Effie and Eliza, Yev, Vlad, Duns and Cons ... slipped silently past, headed to the back of Missus Duns' sod house.

Geoffrey asked: 'Did you have nice nap?' 'Oh, you know I do not nap. I did close my eyes for a moment – a sigh, a few deep breaths, a wish and a wink and I am suddenly so refreshed!' 'Of course! You realize I am only joking' said Geoffrey. And they all laughed together.

Missus Duns remained comfortable for some time, just visiting like this. But the time did come when she began to think of food. 'Oh! I do need to get up and throw something together for us to eat! It must be about that time now'. And, as she began to stir herself, Eliza carried out a tray with four plates and a basket of scones, a tub of jelly and another of butter. Mary followed after, with a tray holding two pots, four cups for tea. 'Let us eat here' said Carymba.

16 October 2005

MCVI

A mottled grey morning emerged before the Sun actually broke the horizon. A chill – light crystal glittering flecks in still morning air – left no doubt of the changing season. The wooded Hills were showing color and Carymba knew that leaves were beginning to fall from trees as the began to ready themselves for Winter.

Ambling along the Beach, soft sand yielding awkwardly at each stride of Carymba's syncopated gait, the waif was forced to concentrate on the twist of torso, shoulders, arms and head for holding onto sufficient balance – while principally looking over the Sea to once again watch the appearance of day and dawn over the undisturbed horizon to the east.

Already, the mottled grey marked the blurred horizon as the warmer Sea supported a thickness of fog above the calm roll of those waters. From the Beach, Carymba could see the thin clear layer at the bottom, just above the water, and then the denser fog layers that finally melted off into a misty film on the way to clear air above. The mottled grey could be seen lightening by stages above the fog while the fog itself seemed to become more luminous ... as if the Sun were giving cool light right in the middle of this low hung cloud. Below, what could be seen of the waves remained in the dull shadow of the pervasive bank of fog.

Pulling her shawl more expertly about her shoulders, Carymba shrugged it into position against those glittering crystals that still floated in the air. Once the Sun came over the horizon, she suspected, the fog would begin to fade away and these crystal needles would vaporize; shortly, her shawl itself would become unnecessary, even burdensome. But first would come that rising of the Sun, painted over the white fog and exploding into the sky, now seen to be cloudless.

This while, as the Sun could be seen emerging from the Sea – though delayed a bit in time and deferred a bit in intensity – Carymba pressed her pace beyond the amble toward something brisker, something closer to that standard steady syncopated gait that kept her going day after day – though the effect *also* increased the slide of her feet in the loose sand underfoot. The added pace, added effort, added struggle distracted her gaze from the coming dawn and the lingering fog over the Sea that marked *this* day as particular. Only half thinking of these conditions, Carymba pressed her pace up toward the Sea Road where she would escape the loose sand for far easier footing.

Once on the Sea Road, Carymba glanced back over the bank of fog; the Sun was fully up now. 'Once it comes, it is quickly done' muttered Carymba to herself, half disappointed that her inept timing distracted her precisely through that moment of transition. A half-sigh sufficed to reply to the realized disappointment as she saw the risen Sun. Only half a sigh: she had seen the rising before and expected she would see one again – yet there remains a particular magic in that protracted transition – and this fog over the Sea would have added its particular quality to the event. There was nothing to do now but to go on with this day.

Taking more occasional glances over the Sea now, Carymba led her syncopated gait toward the Valley Road. What she likely would not have noticed with a continual stare appeared in her sampled gathering of the fog: it thinned and melted into the air as the Sun warmed everything but the shaded Sea itself. By her last glance, just before turning down the Valley Road and leaving so much of the Sea behind, the fog had greatly dissipated; occasional holes appeared – but none great enough as to allow a sure sight of the Sea from the land.

The turn complete into the Valley Road, Carymba moved easily along, wondering what she would do next. When she needed to know, she would: such was always her unplanned motto. So, unknowing as yet, she adopted a light step, a lithe pace in company with an open mind and a habitual, causal taking-in of what was happening on this so-familiar Valley Road.

About the time she was nearing the Narrows, the notion settled into her head that it would be good to go up to Hidden Cabin, perhaps for only a little while. 'Mother Hougarry will certainly have more breakfast than ten of us should eat!'

With a chuckle, then, Carymba turned at the Narrow, hitched her skirts and climbed the root steps to the path up into the Crossed Hills. Here, more than along the Valley Road, she noted the fresh leaf layer made for swishing her feet through the crackly dry leaves, some of which crumbled under her feet as she climbed through them form the root steps to Hidden Cabin, well up in these Crossed Hills.

Delightfully familiar, long-term familiar – more so than anywhere else in all Hyperbia – these Crossed Hills always welcomed her. Sometimes, she had thought they *shouldn't* welcome her so; but today was not one of those days. Instead, she reveled in the sense of utter welcome; she could not miss its appearing as it was, for her, simply *there* – as much there in her bones as on the path, in the trees, throughout the layer of fallen leaves.

Thus was Carymba in an exquisite humor when she stepped from the ground up onto Mother Hougarry's porch. Had she glanced down, she would have surely seen the litter of leaf crumbs around the hem of her skirts … and shaken them free. But she did not glance, nor did she notice. She rather swept along to the door, and through the door, knowing she need not knock, not here at Hidden Cabin.

Anna was startled; not often would the door be opened like this, least of all in the morning. Looking to see, however, Anna *quickly* recognized Carymba and knew her coming with joy. Jumping up, the child ran to the waif and threw her arms about Carymba's waist, barely bothering to slow the headlong rush first.

Carymba absorbed Anna and her impetus – though not without staggering backwards several steps so as to keep her balance. Once falling was precluded, Carymba laughed over the enthusiasm while Mother Hougarry more slowly came out and beamed to have Carymba here. 'You must have some breakfast! There are scones ready, still warm. I will have fresh tea in just a bit!'

Mother Hougarry disappeared into the kitchen of Hidden Cabin while Carymba disengaged from the remnants of Anna's flying hug. She did take care to draw little Anna next to her, an arm around her shoulders as she led each other to Mother Hougarry's table – where they were expected, particularly Carymba.

Anna whispered hoarsely: I have already had breakfast. But I will bet you I can eat some more – just a little, because you came!'

23 October 2005

MCVII

Damp chill penetrated flesh even as the day rolled toward afternoon. Rain had ceased, though the low-hung overcast wrought grey upon the wet ground and puddle-paths. Hardly an inviting day, if an excuse could be found to remain inside, most wee folk used it, appreciatively. Even those who were out in spite of reasonable excuses found the gnawing damp enough to cause them to mutter, murmur about cold weather.

By this late morning hour, Guerric had been rummaged out of his sleep by the usual means of heady aromas and luring wiles. He had primed himself on Mahara's startlingly strong black coffee, the way he liked it, and the gypsie cakes he preferred first thing in the morning. He knew it was cool and damp – near the stove was the best place to be, now that he was awake and away from the now-straightened covers of the bed. More, he had no handy-man jobs lined up for today: he did not have need to go out.

No one came to his door, calling him to any as-yet unknown needs. If he wished, he could linger near that stove for as long as he liked. Guerric had, however, become restless. In his restlessness, the stove-warmed cabin he shared with Mahara seemed too restrained.

So, having pulled on his jacket and a cap, gathering his toolbox (in case he should have need of it – he *rarely* went out without it), Guerric told Mahara he simply needed to go out. He did not know *why* he was restless like this – only that he was. She had no such need and could find plenty to do around the cabin.

Then, toolbox in hand, Guerric went out, closing the door behind himself – but not before the damp chill took advantage of the open door to sweep haughtily across the floor, eliciting from Mahara a scowl and, from the stove, a sparking of the fire to a flaring brightness.

Guerric used his free hand to tug his jacket more closely about his torso, latching what he had imprudently left open to the vagaries of the surprisingly raw morning. Even before he had climbed the rise to the lip of the Commons, above the Ravine, Guerric was scowling over the weather, whose chilling effect was far more biting than he had expected. Most certainly, his strides up the rise were accompanied by thoughts of turning back to the stove in the cabin, and to Mahara. The east wind that come on him full force as he crested the rise increased the urge, taunting him with the folly of his restlessness.

Nonetheless, Guerric shrugged his body and bent into the really modest, if raw, wind; he leaned himself into the proposed trek. He remembered gloves in a pocket and found them, working one onto the free hand before shifting his toolbox to the now-gloved hand in order to glove the other as well. Once done, he admitted to himself that the extra layer cut the raw wind and eased the sting on his hands and the white cold to his fingers. In such a posture, Guerric strode his way across the Commons, bitingly aware he was not used to this raw nip yet this year.

His thoughts focused on this wind: raw and penetrating, felt deeply. But, in the face of this too immediate damp chill, memories of Winters gone by came to mind as well, times when stiffer winds than this drove a deeper cold and needle-snow against this same body with hardly any effect at all. Certainly, he knew, he had not felt this cold then!

As a result, he wanted to scoff at himself, cowering before this little wind and shuddering, shivering as if life were being freeze-dried from his body. On the other hand, he also reminded himself that he *was* cold. Maybe he had forgotten a layer of clothing. *Something* must be amiss!

The Inn-by-the-Bye neared. He had not intended to stop there as it hardly seemed an apt destination for one claiming restlessness as the reason to leave the stove and the cabin on the slope above the Ravine's gaping plunge. As he approached the Inn, however, he wondered if, perhaps, he might learn there of someone's need for his handyman craft. This offered a second thought, an answer to his chilled body as well. So, he turned aside, took the step and opened the door, following it into the Foyer, closing it against the low-hung grey damp chill wind with relief.

Inside, the dim space slowed him momentarily. But he knew enough to set his toolbox along the wall, under a place to hang one's cloak or coat or shawl. For now, at least, he felt he would keep the jacket; he did not plan to stay long. As his eyes adjusted, Guerric moved to the steps down into the dining room; at the edge of the steps, he paused to glance around. A fire danced on the hearth, invitingly. Aside from Carymba, only those who lived in the Inn were in the dining room. As inviting as the dining room was, and as easily had he – or anyone – anticipated this scene, the raw feeling wind was likely enough to keep folk away.

The prospects reduced to getting warm and, maybe, trying some of Marthuida's coffee, Guerric wondered why he was out, or out *here*. No answer came quickly to mind, other than the pragmatic suggestion that he might as well take advantage of the warmth for a while. So, Guerric stepped down into the dining room and ambled toward the hearth. As today there was a chair at the far end of the table Clyde shared with Missus Carney, Clyde sitting next to the hearth and Missus Carney across the table from him, Guerric went to take it.

Having asked if the chair were taken, and assured by Missus Carney that it was not, Guerric sat down. Seeing Guerric in a seat, Thyruid walked over to see if he could get anything for him. Guerric smiled up to the Innkeeper and said: 'Not yet. I am out looking for jobs needing a handyman'. 'No business yet today?'

'No: it is a quiet spell, but I was restless at home, and here I am … warming up by your fire from the walk!' 'I imagine the fire feels good to you, coming from outside. I have not been out, and it feels good to me *anyway*!'

Carymba, sitting with Geoffrey over tea at the usual corner table, easily overheard Guerric – he does not talk much, but when he does his voice tends to carry well, and he does not think to speak softly. Excusing herself, the waif rose and slipped her syncopated gait through the tables and their chairs from her corner to this hearth-side seat in order to respond to Guerric.

Guerric, of course, saw her coming his way and knew already that she was the only one here this morning, besides himself, who had been outside. He knew Thyruid had no list of chores for him, so he found now a tickled anticipation over whatever Carymba might have in mind.

'You are looking for something to do?' 'Some good reason to be out doing something – yes'. 'Have you been to the Gypsie Area lately?' 'Not for a while, I suppose'. 'Uiston?' 'It has been some time since I have been there, either'. 'How about Missus Duns?' 'You mean her old sod house'. 'Yes, there. I see things needing some attention in all those places. But, I believe, they do not. You will have to point them out and let them agree … then move right along ahead, quickly!' 'Good ideas. Thanks'. 'Sure'.

30 October 2005

MCVIII

Effie, awake anyway, found the brightness of morning bursting through her garret window. Especially this time of year, it would be some time before the Sun rose over the Hills to shine directly into her window. Nonetheless, the *brightness* of the morning filled the sky over Hyperbia, coming from that East toward which her window looked.

Though snuggled within her covers, wrapped in the every-morning disarray of her bed, Effie sought a more direct awareness of this morning light; she spun herself so as to extract her limbs from the tangling twists the covers had endured. At last successful, letting the covers fall aside, Effie sat up to look across the Fields in the morning's luminous delight.

Quickly, Effie realized she had been so drawn up in her covers because she was chilly. Warmed by them, she forgot their purpose. And now, sitting freely, the chilled air in her barely heated (by whatever manages to seep through the floor or across the connecting way to the Common Room upstairs, where the spinners would share meals and some free time), Effie felt the chill directly. With a sweep, she drew the free covers up, around her shoulders, settling a couple layers across her crossed legs, enough to cut the morning chill and begin to re-warm herself.

Inside, all was quiet. Effie was confident that Martha was not up as there was no sound to be heard. Gilbert might be stirring; he is rather quiet. But Chert is a slow riser and unlikely to be the first up on a chilly morning. Effie enjoyed the silent time, a time to sit peacefully and wrapped in her covers within the morning glow.

Gradually – Effie did not notice at all – her curled posture straightened. For one thing, she warmed within the blanket; for another, the glow illumining her room, diffuse as it was with the Sun still behind the Hills, began to *feel like* it was coming from within her. She felt herself illumined, *illumining* the room.

The Sun had not capped the Hills when Effie first heard movement in the Common Room. Most likely, it was Martha, Effie figured. And that meant it would be best if Effie exchange her night clothes for day clothes. With a nearly saddened sense, she gave up her blankets and began to adjust herself to change for the day.

At once, the chill was all too present; she *wanted* to huddle on herself; instead, she moved quickly to re-dress and do so for the day. And, dressed, the chill was not nearly so present a problem. Holding her posture straight came more easily with the warmth. And still, that glow seemed to penetrate her body so that it could as be as easily coming *from* her body as *through* it.

The obvious thing to do was to leave her garret room and go to help Martha – a task that would be not-appreciated less than would be her not going at all. First, though, Effie bent down to organize her bed so that she could start the next night on a solid basis, no matter how soon that would deteriorate once she fell into bed for another night's sleep.

Satisfied, Effie left her room and crossed the lone loose plank over open floor joists – the temporary arrangement made when she first came, *years* ago – to arrive with the others. Chert had not emerged yet, but Gilbert had applied himself to his assorted chores and Martha was present to assure her indispensability. Effie slipped into the chinks left over, to help arrange things for breakfast and for the day.

The Common Room is internal, relying on lamps for light instead of windows. In many ways, that helped keep it more even, temperature wise. But it also meant the light was subdued, free from that glow that had been filling Effie's garret room. Within this muted room, then, Effie moved and managed her tasks with an unusual smoothness.

Martha, antagonizingly anxious as always, did not ruffle Effie, at all. Composure, balance, detachment from that sort of distress that often afflicted her around Martha: with such elegance did Effie comport herself that she evaded that turmoil completely. Something seemed amazing, though Effie did not notice, nor could Gilbert label the effect with *any* accuracy at all.

Gilbert kept a discrete eye on Effie. He did not want to be obnoxious, nor overly obvious. However, she was not acting as he would normally expect her to be behaving: not unpleasantly so, though. Gilbert wondered about what he could see – and perhaps, what eluded his awareness. For Effie's part, she was aware of nothing special. And Martha is only aware of Martha, as at any time. Gilbert alone realized that Martha was not irritating Effie, that Effie simply rode through Martha's ever-irritating style – one that Martha would deny if she were asked, and disclaim if circumstances required her to acknowledge it.

As the day rolled along – breakfast done, kitchen straightened, move of the four spinners (Chert did get up in time to eat; he misses few meals) to their work room downstairs accomplished, the settling-in to the regular spinning of their threads done – Effie continued her poised aplomb. She did realize that she felt good today – not simply being physically well or not-ill nor not ill-at-ease – but being positively comfortable with life.

Lamp-lit, the work room of the spinners was a subdued place – with adequate light to see the work when more than feel was necessary; but it was not bright, not even after the Sun would crest the Hills and shine brightly on the Spinners' Shop. The lamps held a steady light for them, even on a day like this one, or one that turned overcast and glum before the Sun did crest the Hills: the light was always a constant for them. This was their technology of the lamp!

Martha could not help but notice that Effie was quietly happy. She, too, came to notice that nothing bothered Effie today, that she blithely kept to her work with a lithe ease: no pout, no sullen glances, no taut words. Martha was beginning to find her irritating, very aggravating.

31

Oh, Effie was not bubbling over with pleasantness; she was merely an overtly serene object in the midst of the usual irritants of the day. Martha could tell it was not that everything went right for her; Effie stopped to adjust and the like about as often as usual. Nor was it that the others were inordinately kind to her. This was a typical day among the Spinners ... except for Effie.

Chert had taken a brief break to adjust his work and walk around a bit (as Chert in particular, more than the others, had to do every now and again), and walked to the door, just to see what the weather was like outside now. 'Well' he muttered, 'it is overcast out there, and raining'. 'Really?' replied Gilbert, surprised as he remembered how clear and bright it had been early, when he first checked the weather-in-place for today. 'Yep: it is rather dark out there now. Looks like the sort of rain that has come to stay for a while'.

'Oh well' replied Effie. 'At least we had that brightness early-on, a real glow. At least it was that way in my garret, early -on'. Gilbert looked at her, listening. After musing a bit in the silence, he added: 'It must have been almost glowing in there'.

'The light was everywhere, as if it were coming from everywhere'.

6 November 2005

MCIX

The morning rain had swept across Hyperbia with intermittent severity out of that dense grey cover that obscured the dawn and left the morning slinking-in, almost unnoticed. After a while, that thick grey still scattering outbursts of rain, there came to be light, enough for Mary to see her way around her quarters and down the stairs, even through her Flower Ship – though *not* enough to examine her plants in any detail whatsoever. Light was ample, however, for a general examination and the routine morning watering.

So, Mary, wakened and stirred by the early showers, gave up on her hampered restlessness once the light had become enough to see her way around. That a particularly severe shower swept through about that time proved to be all the added stimulus needed to rouse herself from her covers. With a swirl, she wrapped herself in her robe and with relish she slid her feet once again into her aging fluffy slippers. After but a whimsical pass at a thought, Mary put off her breakfast for a troubling, abiding curiosity over the welfare of her plants. Oh, she knew it was not rational; nonetheless, the itch and twitch in her legs would not let her shrug aside this *demanding* instinct.

Having walked down the stairs with what she passes off as elegance, Mary was pleased to be standing on the Flower Shop floor, without any approximation of mishap. She even allowed herself, in this morning privacy, a smug grin of accomplishment on the way toward beginning her watering process. Plant by plant, table by shelf, Mary turned her attention to her flowers. She could see well enough what she was doing – but any close attention was simply beyond her ability in the given light.

Once her routine attention to the Flower Shop chores – at least the most important ones – was complete, Mary remembered she was still in her robe and slippers, the robe over her usual nightclothes. And, a moment later, remembered that she was hungry *because* she had neglected making breakfast before examining and tending her plants. There being no pressing reason to dally further in the Flower Shop, Mary left it behind and, wiping her hands on one another to brush away the dirt, she began to climb her way up her stairs to her quarters.

The stove was still cold. And the room had a damp tinge to it. But she could see that the early rain had parted, and the dense overcast was breaking up, allowing some sunshine to bathe her window. Mary smiled at the new brightness that was already warming her room. The stove may not be necessary for *warmth* now, but she still needed it for breakfast, and for tea. So, in the bright sunshine, Mary moved through the steps needed to ready her stove and then to get her fire kindled.

Whenever the need is not pressing, the fire in the stove seems to take off easily; so it came this morning, while Mary readied her tea kettle to set out toward bringing it to a boil. The stove was heating directly as Mary readied her scones for baking.

In her warming room, Mary quickly changed from nightclothes to day – then readied the teapot, hastily as the kettle was already knocking and sizzling, and she wanted the pot ready when the kettle was ready.

Of course, the kettle did not come to a boil all *that* quickly; but she knew it would boil *very* quickly if she were not ready! The scones likewise seemed slow; she checked, and everything was as in delay mode. Distracted easily, Mary began to dabble with other things in the process, as waiting on such as tea kettles and scones could not hold her attention well.

Of course, Mary had no reason to leave her room – to straighten her bedding and arrange the table, get her teacup and plate, butter and jelly in place. But then, another little chore, and another caught her eye. She need not go far to forget her stove ... until the smell of scorching scones taunted her with a rash reminder ... and she rescued her breakfast before snatching the kettle from the hottest part of the stove and pouring the boiling water into the readied teapot.

After the flurry, as the tea steeped, Mary found herself flustered, felt her face flushed: this morning has unfolded entirely by accidental whim, almost to the point of major inconvenience, certainly a minor disaster over the scones. As she placed the scones in a toweled basket, Mary could not help but notice that they were rather over-brown, giving evidence to sight and touch of bearing a very crisp crust. 'It would not have taken much more for them to be really burnt' she muttered under her breath.

The basket wrapped and the tea coming along nicely, Mary heard the rattle at her door typically caused by someone rapping upon it. Were this a regular shop, from which she went home – rather than upstairs – visitors would try the door, pull it open, and enter. Because she lives upstairs, most of the wee folk are politely reluctant simply to walk in. So, they knock and wait for Mary to put down whatever it is she is doing and come, answer the door. Knowing this, Mary hastened to the stairs and started to rush down the stairs; she held the railing with one hand as her stocking-feet slid on the worn-smooth steps.

Squawking while flailing, as she twisted herself around to grasp the bannister with *both* hands, Mary concentrated on this practiced maneuver aimed at keeping her body from plummeting down the stairs into a bruised and crumpled mess at the landing most of the way down.

Being successful in arresting her fall (though with a certain yelp involved), Mary gathered herself and more carefully wended her way to the door. Rubbing a sore arm and realizing already that she had strained some muscles in this little escapade, Mary opened the door to greet Eliza – and, with her, John. 'I am so glad to find you here' Eliza began. Mary motioned for them to enter. 'We … John and I … are arranging a party this evening at the Inn-by-the-Bye. I wanted some flowers for the occasion. Can you help us?'

Just as Mary was about to respond, she remembered her teapot, then her scones for the breakfast she had not yet eaten, and finally her lack of shoes. Mary's extra stutter-style pause brought Eliza's brows to an arch in question. Mary spoke: 'I have a teapot about ready, and some crisp brown breakfast scones prepared upstairs. Would you join me for some tea? We can talk over what you may want over a cup of tea'. Eliza shrugged: 'I suppose we could'. John hemmed and hawed, not sure of himself at all. Eliza sensed his reticence: 'Oh, come along, John. I will be there to chaperone!'

Mary led the way, allowing her smile its space before she would need to put it aside upstairs, when they joined her. Eliza followed, and John came last, a bit on the sheepish side. Entering her kitchen area, Mary went to draw out the table – a small one with only two chairs. 'Here, sit at the table. I will bring the stool over and use that'.

Two more plates, two more cups and saucers, plus the basket of scones to join what she had already arranged made things snug. 'All there' she thought. Mary poured the tea: 'a little strong' she thought, 'but not too bad. Not too bad'.

'Now, said Mary out loud as she took her seat: 'What is it that you have in mind?'

13 November 2005

MCX

After the early grey had over-lingered close enough nearly the entire morning, a soft drizzle began to fall, moistening everything, yet without enough force to drench anything. Through that tangible, light rain, Mahara quickened her pace over the last part of the way across the Commons to the Inn-by-the-Bye.

Once breakfast had been finished, Mahara had seen Guerric out the door; she knew well enough that once he had breakfast and coffee in him – and had made it out the door, he would manage reasonably well through his coming day. Then, and only then, had she turned to the regular chores, the ones that kept the cabin home. It was late morning when she was done enough and gathered a cloak – the day was cool, but not so cool as to chill much at all, she thought.

With her cloak about her, Mahara had set out from their cabin, sweeping along the narrow path across the steeply sloping slant that swept from behind the Fields down into the Ravine, taking the familiar if concentration-demanding route toward the rise to the Commons.

Having passed the crest onto the Commons, Mahara had let her easy, almost distracted gait flow her along the Commons. Bound slightly by her cloak, her arms and shoulders could not fully enter the sway of her customary stroll. The Summer-freedom flash of her sweeping gait, her graceful sway, as she was now wrapped, was significantly subdued. And the cool morning grey did nothing but subdue her appearance and her flair all the more. All this while, the cool grey merely hung over Hyperbia: when

37

the soft drizzle began its fall, Mahara found herself just past halfway to the Inn from her home.

As the drizzle began, Mahara at first barely noticed, then realized the land was getting wet and a light beading was appearing on her shoulders, and her lashes. So slight was the immediate effect that Mahara simply continued as she had been. Reflection on the fact that it was raining (albeit in but a drizzle) and that she was unprepared for dealing with rain led her to lengthen, strengthen her stride. Doing this required a more exaggerated sway in the hips, countered in turn through the shoulders even though the cloak-rapped arms were not free to swing easily, leaving her with a still stilted character to her pace.

With a stern, taut, concentrated countenance did Mahara come to the steps to the Inn-by-the-Bye. She took them both in turn and reached from her cloak to the door. Opening, she entered; the door closed behind her as she eased it to the jamb. It was dim inside, as always; she shook her head; her long dark hair swung free, nearly snapping at the end before settling to her shoulders, somewhat freed of the drizzle's markings. Slipping her cloak from her shoulders, she hung it on the nearest hook. Entering the dining room by the steps down from the Foyer, Mahara felt a shudder ramble her spine while instinct had her rub her upper arms for warmth.

Across the room, the hearth entertained a lively, low fire. Clyde in his flannel shirt sat low in his chair, legs stretched in front of him, along side the dancing fire, on the edge of the raised hearth. She thought him warm, lazy as his fingers stroked his chest-long beard reflectively. Missus Carney sat facing the table, across from the hearth – and from Clyde – sipping at her tea, balancing her cup in the fingers of two hands. Considering the chill she was feeling, Mahara formed a distinct attraction to approaching Clyde and Missus Carney, at least so as to visit for a bit, closer to the hearth.

Free now from the cloak, Mahara swept her way across the dining room, swerving among the tables and their chairs toward the table by the hearth. She knew she chose this destination for its proximity to the hearth and, with that, the prospect of being warmed.

She *liked* Clyde and Missus Carney, but *never* chose to sit in this part of the dining room; she and (often) Guerric, would naturally choose a place more toward the middle of the room – and, given the spare condition of the dining room as lunch time neared, they might well have chosen a spot somewhat closer to the corner Geoffrey *always* chose, where frequently he would be joined by Carymba. All this Mahara had in mind as she neared the hearthside table.

A little bit sheepish, Mahara neared the table. Swallowing, and finding the saliva somewhat sticking in her throat, making the swallow difficult and troublesome, Mahara rounded the end of the table so as to be face to face with Clyde and in easy sight of Missus Carney. She had to figure neither Clyde nor Missus Carney would have *expected* her to come there to sit as she never had; and she certainly did suspect they would know she came there *precisely* because of the fire on the hearth.

Missus Carney looked up to Mahara with a look of disarming sweetness. Having seen in Mahara the tension of her frame and the tightness of her shoulders, her neck and her face, Missus Carney spoke: 'Oh, pull up a chair here, near the heath. You look half frozen, in need of the heat. It must be getting cold outside'. Mahara thanked Missus Carney in stammering tones and moved to sit next to her, there being no seat at the end of the table.

Thyruid brought her a mug of coffee, knowing that was her preference. 'A basket of biscuits?' he asked. Mahara nodded: yes. She was still taken aback by Missus Carney's dismissal of any wry tones about her coming to this table today, as the fire crackled warmth from the hearth even though she had *never* come before. She could not imagine Missus Carney could be entirely innocent of this distinction; she must be aware. But there was nary a hint, not a ghost of a hint in her voice or in her expression.

'I had been sitting here, watching the fire dance on the hearth, reminiscing. When a body gets old and the legs work only a little bit, when (like you see me doing any more) most of the time is spent sitting – when it used to be that life was active, even energetic, full of challenge – memories are about all one has to think about!'

Missus Carney chuckled at herself and fussed with her fingers before reaching to pour a fresh cup of tea for herself. 'I was reminiscing about all the years I lived and did what I thought of as "my work" in Apopar. There was so much to do there … then. But I grew old, and I could not do it anymore; my legs decided to quit on me! So, I gave my work to a helper, Nova, and stayed home. She convinced me to come here, and helped me come'.

Missus Carney cast a winsome if saddened smile: 'Now, I rely on Clyde to do the stairs. I rely on Marthuida and Thyruid for food and housing. I rely on my friends to come by on occasion'. Missus Carney paused then, misty-eyed in her long-gazing way.

Thyruid appeared, tray in hand. Bringing lunch, he bore an over-laden basket of hot biscuits, an ample tub of butter and a dish of currant jelly. As he set them down, he suggested breaking open a biscuit, adding butter to melt into the flaking interior, cap it with a dab of currant jelly for melting into an oozing goo, sinking into the crumb … simply for the joy of it. Thyruid savored well in his imagination all his ripe suggestions.

20 November 2005

MCXI

Not able to sleep and tired of squirming and tossing in her bed, Eliza just got up. That it was before dawn – she suspected *long* before dawn – no longer mattered. That the house was cold, afflicted by a wind that, unusual in this event, curled over the crest of the Hills and swept along the surface, underneath the now-bare branch cover – *that* also was of no concern. She quickly removed her night clothes, shivered yet more violently, and *more* quickly dressed for the day that was yet to arrive. Eliza dressed warmly as the chill in the house meant the frost was biting outside.

Waking and rising like this bore no immediate intention or inclination to go out into the wind – she could hear the wind, even feel it as it filtered through her sound house. Besides, Eliza had no Carymba-like urges to go out somewhere to discover where she ought to be, often when she arrived. Oh, no: for Eliza, she was much more intentional about her coming and going. What works so mysteriously for Carymba seemed to her to be entirely out of line.

Only frustration with not sleeping roused her; only chill in the house dressed her for the day, and warmly at that, long before dawn arrived. Now, she was turning to her stove, to do just what is necessary in order to rouse sufficient heat from it.

The stove was cold. She thought there ought to be *some* heat left in it, some live coals buried in the ash. She found not even a memory of a live coal; the night had proven more demanding than she had expected. The wind was not normal, not here! So, with a disappointment-sigh, Eliza cleared the stove of ash and began to lay out what would need to be done to get some heat rising from this stove. Cold starting is always difficult – surely, she had been awake long enough to have prevented this!

After passing through the trials of getting her stove going, Eliza began to reap the benefits; her house warmed, slowly at first. With the warmth, she began to relax. And, as the muscles in her shoulders and back and thighs began to ease, she realized for the first time that she had been tense, a tension due to the cold she did not want to admit could bother her so.

Eliza loosened her cloak and settled herself; it was still dark and the time until dawn was unknown to her. She felt a little drowsy. But, she told herself, she was already up, already dressed: it was a new day, not one to be spent going back to bed. Should she unmake her bed, work herself into the covers in day clothes? revert again to nightclothes? Baffled and in a mood of reform, Eliza took to arranging her stove, arranging for herself some breakfast and pondering how she was going to handle this already-begun day, even the thought of daylight was yet some undetermined time into the future.

Breakfast done: daylight delayed longer. Eliza was entirely uncertain of what, if anything, she could or should do now. Her plans and considered eventualities had become exhausted, so that her possibilities were thinning down to going out and going back to bed. She had already squirmed away from going back to bed once or twice. That left going out, she knew not where nor why.

This unplanned "let's see what comes next" style was all Carymba's, not hers! She had always thought it odd, foolish, even ridiculous. Yet, it was the *one* option left after she had set aside all the rest. So, knowing it was cold, and the that the wind was oddly sharp along the slope of the Hills (and who knew how it was anywhere else!), Eliza pulled out her hooded cloak, shook it out and slowly pulled it around her shoulders, to fasten at her throat.

Swallowing hard, Eliza took up her next step: moving toward the door. As she opened the door, she took care to be gradual, anxiously watching the opening onto the dark night. At the threshold, the warmth of the stove behind her, the chill of the wind-whipped night before her, Eliza stalled.

The night did not invite as did the stove – except for the fact that she had cornered herself. No one knew; but *she* knew. Somehow, *this* knowing was quite enough to keep her from the crackling invitation behind her and daring to face, even to *lean* toward, the stark night, dark and foreboding before her.

Eliza pulled the door shut behind her. She started as the latch snapped shut, and the door held closed behind her. She saw nothing but knew her face blanched; she could feel the color vanish from her cheeks. A few steps forward and she would find herself on the Way Down; she knew she would.

Stepping slowly, carefully in the surprisingly thoroughgoing darkness, Eliza realized how much she did *not* know the way – except by sight. Timid under cover of darkness, Eliza slowly eased her way to the Way Down; she remembered that there was rough ground across the Way Down from her house: she would know for a fact when she had gone too far.

Gradually, Eliza picked up a little *realistic* confidence about where she was, on the Way Down. Suddenly, she stopped; Eliza encountered her first decision – to turn left and go *up* the Way Down, toward the Crest of the Hills – or to turn right and go *down* the Way Down toward the Fields. Without a plan, Eliza was *stuck* with following … well, she was not at all sure what she might be following.

Being logical, Eliza stood in the Way Down and tried to muster for herself some sort of criterion for choosing: none came. Nonetheless, she waited until she began to feel foolish, and a little chilled as that low, land-hugging wind knifed into her.

Turning to her left at the last, Eliza began to climb the Way Down, going toward the crest. The climb came as rather steep in slope, into the dark, over a much less familiar trail with the wind in her face. Against all the obvious rationales she might have taken for her choice, Eliza went toward the crest.

The exertion soon had her breathing heavily. Her feet would slip; she would stumble. Wind and dark and slope – each was relentlessly against her, forcing her to defend this choice to her own rational mind. Finding no rational success, Eliza finally told herself that she had to decide, and had decided to turn left.

Defying her own better judgment did not sit easily on Eliza's mind. Telling herself that she is going this way "just because" left her taunting herself with every slip of foot, and every slice of wind, and every heaving pant. Realizing this self-argument was, as it must be, a rear-guard action, Eliza simply shrugged and kept climbing. By now, the whole rationale was driven by overt curiosity which, she decided, trumped all inputs to the contrary.

Even with the nod to curiosity for her reason, Eliza was not sure; she merely kept going as a matter of … well, inertia, or stubbornness, though she would more likely claim "principle". When she reached the crest – by which time the Way Down had all but disappeared – she simply stood still at the sight. As the fractional moon was just then rising over the Sea-defined horizon line, Eliza saw the view before her was open toward the Sea, with the scant moon casting its light across the clarity of the open waters of the Sea: sublime!

27 November 2005

MCXII

In a surprising warmth – surprising because unanticipated – Anna played on the porch of Hidden Cabin. Mother Hougarry had insisted she wear a wrap, as she had; long before now that wrap had taken its place over the arm of a chair while Anna played. Even though the porch faced north and was ever-shaded, she was hardly chilled! Mother Hougarry, of course, was within, occupied or preoccupied with sundry matters of keeping house, leaving Anna to her quiet play on the warm afternoon.

Anna was carefully engrossed in her imaginative play, so much so that she never heard Carymba's syncopated gait rustling through dry fallen leaves along the path up from the Narrows. As Carymba then neared the porch – she had seen watching Anna and guessing at the sort of imaginative play she was observing – the waif asked: 'What is your friend's name?' This being Anna's first awareness of anyone at all being around, she jumped to her feet. Her first instinct was that Mother Hougarry was scolding her about the clearly unnecessary wrap, Anna grabbed it and threw it around her shoulders – all before thinking anything at all about the surprising sound.

Carymba spoke again: 'Hello, Anna: I did not mean to startle you like that!' Anna looked around; she had been concentrating on the door and the expectation of confronting Mother Hougarry and had not noticed anything about this world behind her, the one in which Carymba was standing. Seeing Carymba, Anna started, then burst into a huge grin and spun to greet her; the wrap fell unceremoniously into a heap on the floor of the porch of Hidden Cabin in her haste.

Disentangling from the immediate greeting, Carymba asked again of the friends. 'Oh, those are all imaginary!' 'Of course they are: I had my own imaginary friends, once upon a time'. Anna looked up, surprised; she had not anticipated that anyone *else* would have friends like these. 'Do you think you are the only one? Those are very creative friends, able to open unexpected possibilities for you'. '*Sometimes*, they do surprise me!' 'Naturally! Now, do they have names?' 'Did yours?' 'Oh, yes: Celeste was my bestest friend – but she also played with Camille and David'. 'One boy?' 'Yes, one. I did not need a lot of them!'

Mother Hougarry appeared at the door. 'Oh! I thought I heard voices out here. I had not expected you, Carymba'. 'You know me: I wander in and find it fits OK'. 'Yes. Well ... I am glad it fits, OK'. Mother Hougarry's excitement dimmed in her voice, masked slightly by a certain bittersweet feeling. Always, it is a pleasure for Carymba to be back in Hidden Cabin; for Mother Hougarry, the air is filled with electricity when this waif returns. Always. the coming back has within it the tinge of an inevitable leaving; tonight, she will give Carymba supper; but she knows she will be gone before breakfast. Now, Carymba comes and says she comes and finds it fits ... OK.

Looking down so as to refine her bittersweet mood more privately, Mother Hougarry let her eyes rest on Anna's wrap, lying in a wad on the porch. Gazing at the carelessly dropped piece, Mother Hougarry knew that the wrap was not over Anna's shoulders. It may be unusually warm today, but not on any absolute scale. To Mother Hougarry's mind, this wrap would be better on Anna's shoulders than rumpled and on the floor of the porch to Hidden Cabin.

A quick look up sought Anna, in order to correct her. But the eyes of Mother Hougarry first noticed Carymba; the waif caught her eye before anyone else entered her view. Mother Hougarry lost her aggravation in an instant, simply undone in the glimpse of Carymba's face – a pose of disarming peace. Mother Hougarry stammered, gathering back her own eager tongue from its thought to lash out. And she, fumbling her hands, shuffled her way in turning around, mumbling about some tea ... just clearly enough for Carymba to catch her intent. 'Some tea would be very good: thank you'. Mother Hougarry waved her hand, not turning again, nor speaking, but shuffling from the porch quickly into Hidden Cabin.

Anna started up again. 'Did you ever dance with your imaginary friends?' 'I had trouble dancing, so my imaginary friends never asked me to dance. We would walk in the Crossed Hills instead'. 'Where would you go?' 'I liked to go look down into Uiston, or go over toward the Leaferites' Hill, maybe halfway toward the Narrows ... never much farther than that – until I grew up, of course!' Anna nodded, pondering; she had always stayed much closer than that. Carymba continued: 'I came to Mother Hougarry when I was much younger than you were when you came. So, I had been here for some time before I started venturing very far. I think I was older than you are when I started to wander, too'. Anna was hardly satisfied with that result!

'I think Mother Hougarry will have tea about ready by now. Why don't you join us with some tea?' Anna was not real fond of tea – but the proposal of being included at the tea table with Mother Hougarry and Carymba felt a little bit like being considered important. After the briefest reflection, Anna replied: 'That would be nice'. With a brightened smile, Anna scrambled to the porch and to the door, picking up her fallen wrap on the way. She trailed Carymba through the door and into Hidden Cabin.

Inside, little Anna scampered to the table. Mother Hougarry had set out only two cups; the child saw and began to withdraw when Carymba spoke casually to say: 'Let me get myself a cup so I can join you'. Mother Hougarry was momentarily perplexed, but Anna understood and moved to the chair that was not Mother Hougarry's. When she saw that, Mother Hougarry wanted to tell Anna no, that the chair was for Carymba – but before her tongue could wag, Carymba returned with another cup and pulled another chair to a third side of the table, keeping near Anna.

With three cups to fill, Mother Hougarry worried a bit about having chosen her usual teapot, it being smaller than the other one, which was meant for company. The chosen teapot could handle three cups, but there would be no tea left for refreshing a cup – plus, the tea leaves were not much good on a second steep. So, Mother Hougarry refreshed the kettle and set it where it could come to a boil before very long. And then, she brought a packet of tea with her, to add later to the teapot for further steeping.

Realizing the occasion, a beginning and one that it was time now to freely acknowledge, Mother Hougarry began to pour the tea, beginning with Anna's cup. The child noticed. She sat in her chair, her feet dangling and with her fingers under her thighs while her face simply beamed. Mother Hougarry smiled and nodded – then moved to fill Carymba's cup and, lastly, her own. Before sitting, she took some fresh tea and added it to the teapot. When all was ready, she took her seat, sighed slightly and spoke softly: 'There … now, we can enjoy our tea'.

'Anna reminded me of how I played when I was little. My imaginary friends: I had not thought of them for so long! And then, I remembered how I could wander these upper parts of the Crossed Hills – always carefully' reminisced Carymba. 'Yes. And Anna must be just about ready to begin – like that – now' replied Mother Hougarry, lifting her cup to her lips.

4 December 2005

MCXIII

This cold night nestled close and sharp upon Hyperbia when Carymba slipped from the sleeping Hidden Cabin. The late-rising moon loomed behind a general cloud cover, giving only the hint that the night was not intended to be impenetrably dark. Even so, Carymba's syncopated gait slowed along the familiar path from Hidden Cabin to the Narrows. The deep familiarity alone guided her feet through the bare trees, along the night-obscured, leaf-littered path.

Carymba, as she moved further into the woods along the path, adjusted her cowl, drawing it further over her head. At the same time, she made more secure the cloak wrapped about her body. Though there was little breeze – in the woods, *very* little – the chill in the air made itself distinctly felt. Her thought was that it was early for such a nip: she had not really adjusted to the cold yet. In spite of the sharpness to her cheeks, the tearing drawn to her eyes, Carymba continued her careful trek through the familiar night.

Simply because she knew the land, Carymba knew when she had reached the root steps: there was no other indication in the darkness. Care: find the tree: stabilize and test the feet into the root steps so as to ease down the last bit without entangling the feet and tumbling awkwardly onto the Valley Road. Thus, Carymba found herself at the Narrows, standing unruffled on the Valley Road, still in the wrap of a so-complete darkness.

A little shudder, a shuffle of her feet, a gather of her mind – and a sigh: enough to settle herself while glancing in the night toward the two ways to go along the Valley Road. Nothing suggested itself quickly; Carymba waited. Her feet felt the chill in this darkness; they urged her to move, to go *someplace* … either toward the Sea or toward the 'Y', if the 'Y' then either the Commons or the Fields. It would not matter to her feet as simply walking in itself would stimulate circulation and generate some warmth. Her feet pressed Carymba to choose.

Restless and pressed this way, Carymba found herself increasingly aggravated by her weakness on the one hand and the lack of direction on the other. Almost as if she had to force herself against the situation, she felt her head swirling about in indecision until she took one step toward the 'Y', two toward the Sea – back and forth in mounting frustration until she finally turned fully toward the 'Y', muttering under her breath that she *had* to do something.

Once she was moving, Carymba felt reasonably decisive. At the least, that awful discomfort that was plaguing her at the Narrows disappeared! So, she walked ahead in her usual fashion, adjusted slightly toward caution because of the lack of visibility. Some extra sense served to steer her along the bending road, missing any opportunity to collide with a tree.

By the time she neared the 'Y', Carymba could tell about her feet better – but not so much better that they were not cold, still. And, as she neared the 'Y' the light from John's Foundry began to make itself a factor for her.

Indeed, the Foundry was warm. And it was light. No other place would be available – except the Fringe and other outside places. No shelter was available now, except the Foundry and Hidden Cabin from which she had lately slipped away. She paused; her feet were none too happy about that pause. If anything, there was more breeze here than at the Narrows. The breeze made the sharper chill slice deeper. Carymba felt a shiver ramble up and down her body. The light at the Foundry invited; Carymba began to move that way.

As she came to the place where the path veered from the Foundry, Carymba knew she would *have* to go across the Fields and its not-yet-Winter-matted grasses to reach the Foundry. This was the best place for distance; there was no good place for easy trekking. So, Carymba took off over the Fields. It struck her that she had considered the crossing, being concerned about it, at all. Normally, she would have simply gone. While measuring her steps as she was, Carymba mused about the strangeness of the movement she was doing.

Perhaps anticipation of the warmth found nightly at the Foundry urged her feet. She could think of no other reason-at-hand for the urgency she felt in her strides. Quickly, then, did Carymba sweep around the corner of the Foundry, to the open great overhead door. She found the brightness of the Forge immediately. Shortly, she also felt the heat on her face; her body responded with earnest. Almost automatically, Carymba eased her way into the Foundry, free of any particular invitation.

The thought that she was just walking in like this caught Carymba's sense of humor. She may well appear lots of places as a total surprise, but (save for the Inn-by-the-Bye and Hidden Cabin, of course) she was typically reticent simply to walk on in. Even at Mary's Flower Shop, even more at the Spinners' Shop, she felt odd inside when she needed to "walk on in". Nonetheless, here she goes, taking her strides openly and uninvited into the Foundry, nearing that blessed attraction: warmth!

Carymba thought her feet would be pleased; their first reaction was to throb. The longed-for warmth seemed to burn, as if she had been walking into the live coals on a hearth. The eager, urgent pace slowed; she hobbled, awkwardly. The waif was near tears and at an unaccustomed loss for what to do.

Jasper, in a brief lull in the night's work, noticed Carymba and her apparent distress. She never had been like this, not in his memory. Breaking from his post, he went and brought her a chair, setting it beside her and saying: 'Sit there'.

Carymba looked at him, glanced to the chair while processing his command. 'Yes. Thank you' she mumbled as her hand reached to the back of the chair. Jasper reached to steady her, grasping her two arms through the masking cloak and easing her to sit upon the chair.

51

Seated in warmth, the pressure off her feet, the sensation changed, becoming strangely diffuse, an indescribable tingling all over, running around her feet in waves rather than gripping them in tight spasms of agony.

Looking over, John saw Carymba seated on the chair in an open area of the Foundry. He glanced to Jasper. 'I brought her a chair; she was hobbling so. She has sat there like that, leaning forward, as if helpless, ever since'.

Work was in order; John could pause. Able to go over to her, John went. 'Let me see your feet' he said matter-of-factly. She looked at him helplessly. 'Sit back; I will loosen your feet'. She did, and he did. As he bared her feet of shoes and layered socks, he found the skin red. He touched them gently, expecting them to be cold. Rather, they were hot to the touch. Jasper brought a towel. 'Should I bring water?' 'Not just yet. Let her sit, like this, and settle some first. We will see ... then'.

Carymba whispered: 'Thanks'.

11 December 2005

MCXIV

Sophie did not want to get up; it was still the middle of the night – she was sure of it! Nonetheless, Nova persisted while dressing herself. She had already revived the fire in the firepit from the overnight banking – enough to heat the stones for making their breakfast of meal cakes. This renewed warmth in their yellow mud hut enhanced Sophie's grogginess. In turn, Nova became ever more insistent, to the point that the reluctant Sophie did change from her night clothes to those fit for the day. 'Remember to dress warmly! We are up early because we have some traveling to do'. Sophie remembered, grumbling anyway.

Breakfast done, Nova pulled on her warm Winter cloak and urged the unenthusiastic Sophie to do the same. The child, who would prefer to curl within her covers for a few more hours wrapped her cloak about herself, too. Slipping through the low entrance to the yellow mud hut, Nova entered the frosted night; the air was colder than she had anticipated, and she responded by bringing her cowl full forward and nestling the cloak securely about her frame. Sophie followed and winced so as to be heard when the crisp cold came fully upon her. As Nova before her, Sophie saw to the requirements for a modicum of warmth.

Having reached this point, Nova glanced back; Sophie lagged, in un-enthusiasm. 'Come along; walk beside me today. There is no reason to follow behind on this trip; we are going together'. Sophie responded, hurrying up beside Nova. She knew she did not often go with Nova, that this was unusual – the trip even more than the premature hour. Sophie wondered when it might get light, when this dark night might break for a Sun that might in turn soften the rime that stung her face. Sophie found no answers: night clung and Nova kept them pressing across the flat and open land, away from all her familiar world.

Indeed, Nova did not ease their pace. Sophie found herself tiring; she was not accustomed to long treks, least of all ones like this, under "forced march" conditions. She would go a ways often – but as a meander under condition of daydream fantasies – maybe breaking into a short run, just for the fun of it. But long walks at steady, urgent pace: *that* was something she had not done often enough to count. She wanted to protest that she was tired, complain that her little legs were weary, and the cold air was harsh in her lungs; but she knew that Nova would not be sympathetic, at all.

The Sun was just beginning to lighten the east, a crease along the horizon as Nova led them into a thicket. 'What out for the canes: those thorns are dangerous' said Nova as straight matter-of-fact. Sophie had just enough grey-light to see them, and shudder. She slipped behind Nova, figuring it would be better to proceed single file. They had gone far enough, and she was lost enough that Sophie had no intention of slipping away from Nova: none at all. The thicket merely made it all the more imperative in her mind, this staying close, no matter how stressed her tired legs might feel!

Suddenly, they were at the Great River. Sophie was surprised when they stopped so directly. She saw Nova bring her arm out and wave, a long-armed, sweeping, exaggerated wave while her eyes were directed to a house on a rise – one to which Sophie had to look thrice even to see. She could not imagine what was happening next.

Nova waved a second time, and a third. Sophie thought, and waved, too. After a little, the door opened and a wee man stepped out and began to walk away from them, along a path Sophie had not seen, traced along the top of the other bank on around the Bend in the Great River … and disappeared from sight.

Nothing: that is what Sophie thought. She was perplexed and a little concerned even as she half-way felt the rising anticipation in Nova. If the so-early rise, the long, frosty forced trek, the thicket were without any reference for her, this stop at the Great River and a little man's strange behavior was even *more* so. Nothing prepared Sophie for the next, unfolding, rapid sequence: a boat appeared, sweeping around the Bend, then floating up to the shore before them; Nova spoke: 'Come along: grab your skirts and climb aboard; be quick! The water is cold'. Suddenly Nova and Sophie both on this boat, the boatman cast it off and they were swerving by the current across open water; Sophie clutched the boat and blanched in fear. As suddenly, they were nestled to the other shore and Nova was climbing up the bank. 'Come along!'

Before them lay the Plain, though Sophie had no idea of any of the names or of the places or of anything. 'Come along!' Nova was again at this forced march pace and Sophie hastened after her. She would struggle to stay close, and then run to close that little gap that seemed always to reappear between herself and Nova. She was so intent on keeping up with Nova that Sophie did not notice the City on the Plain to her left ... nor the Gypsie Area to her right.

Breakfast, those meal cakes she had been barely awake enough to sample, lay long ago and far away by now. Sophie was increasingly aware that she was hungry. The hours and distance conspired as morning raced along at this exacting pace, continuing beyond relief – the conspiracy brought attention sharply to the weakened legs and the hollowing within the pit of her stomach. Sophie found her body complaining to her will. At the same time, she knew all too well that Nova would stop when she would stop – and, until then, Sophie was expected to continue, without complaint.

Keeping her grumbling subdued, her murmuring to her inner voice, Sophie sulked behind Nova with legs growing stiff from the unaccustomed exertion. And her belly was rebelling over its growing hollowness. Between the need of staying with the relentless Nova and the need to move herself around the nagging of her own tired-hungry body, Sophie hoped for a speedy completion of this morning march.

Having passed beyond the Plain, Sophie half-way noticed the closeness of the last part of the Wood on the right and the narrowing from the left as they neared what Sophie would learn is the Inn-by-the-Bye. Suddenly, the Inn was beside them; then, Nova turned. At last, she turned, thought Sophie. Sophie saw the Commons open before her eyes; she wondered how much more! And, at once, Nova turned to the door. Stumbling, Sophie came after her, thoughts of warmth, food, chair rumbling racingly in her mind.

Inside, the dim light seemed pre-dawn to Sophie's eyes. She found herself groping as she would not need to do in the dark hut she called home, even in the darkest middle of the night. Slowly, her eyes adjusted to let the strange fixtures of the Inn-by-the-Bye emerge as, first, looming, floating, haunting specters – then, settling into place, equally strange but fixed in place, at least. More importantly, her nose picked up aromas that suggested food – though food she did not know at home. At the moment, she did not want to quibble over anything: longing was her dominant feature.

Once their cloaks were hung, Nova led her into the dining room; Sophie thought Nova must have been here before. Through the odd scatter of tables and chairs they wended their way toward Missus Carney. 'Missus Carney' said Nova: 'tell us about your days in Apopar – so Sophie can know them wisely, and I can hear them again'.

'Oh! Nova! … And you have brought Sophie again! You both must be hungry! … Thyruid …!'

18 December 2005

MCXV

Frost painted curls of filigree around the corners and edges of her panes. Already, it was past midmorning. She had overslept, fairly coddled herself in her covers against the nip that came even in the room where she slept. The stove had gone cold over night and, lacking defense, the cold had crept into her room. Insufficient heat rose from the well-managed Flower Shop downstairs, resulting in a cold nose once Mary did rouse from her slumber.

As she woke, and became ware of the chill, Mary realized she had not been restless overnight, meaning that her covers had remained in reasonable place and that she had stayed warm – save for that nose.

Realizing that she *had* slept far longer than was judicious, Mary stirred herself. Out of her covers, a shiver rattled her body; she rubbed her arms, sandpaper with goose flesh against her cooling palms. Quickly, she flung her robe about her and stuffed her bare feet into the old fluffy slippers once more. Pausing long enough to stir the firebox on the stove, find it long cold, Mary went on to pursue the downstairs stove. It was not too cold in the room for her to delay on starting the stove – but downstairs would be different as the plants in her Flower Shop were far more cold-sensitive than she.

Certain relief came over the anxious Mary as she rushed down the stairs to find it remained *fairly* warm. If the fire were out in the stove, it had not been out long. With luck, it would still be live and easily refreshed.

Opening the firebox, Mary stooped down and peered within; there, a low flickering flame danced over grey ash with a hint of orange buried beneath. Adding a piece, the ash was broken away; a breath on the coals brought a brightened glow, a pulse of heat radiating into her face. Mary smiled and watched as the added piece settled on the coals and gradually began to smoke. She would wait on it to burst into flame before adding another piece to carry the warmth assuredly throughout the shop.

The fire readied, Mary shook her hair into some semblance of place and took up a quick, preliminary tour of the Shop. No frost appeared on the plants; no frost-burned edges gave their tell-tale signs of woe. The window was painted white, however, and Mary drew the plants on the bay window shelf back from the glass some distance, an act she was silently scolding herself for not having done yesterday. 'Well, better today than tomorrow' muttered Mary, under her breath. Then, she decided simply to remove the plants from the shelf by the bay window entirely.

One last glance around, satisfying her inspection-instinct, Mary became aware of her own morning hunger; the hour was rather past that of breakfast now. With a nod, then, toward the Flower Shop, Mary turned and climbed the stairs toward her own room.

Upstairs, the chill nipped even harder; her body had quickly adapted to the downstairs level of warmth, enough to rebel all the more now. Through the reflexive shiver, Mary began to lay the fire in her stove's firebox – a patient act on an impatient morning. Regardless, Mary set the pattern meticulously and, then, lit the fire and watched it grow – slowly at first, then cracklingly through kindling and into the more serious stuff. Warmth emerged and the cold stove began to take in heat toward becoming a radiant source for her room – *and* a source for making tea, baking scones.

Waiting on the fire to do its creative work, Mary readied the kettle and set it atop the stove. She began to mix up her usual batch of scones. Once ready, they must bake. And once readied, it will be time to ready the teapot before the kettle boils. In such a way, breakfast will appear at almost the right time and in about a common moment, all to maximize the weight of the morning's satisfaction. She had learned how to piece this bit of morning together. But *this* waiting, *this* morning, after oversleeping so, and dallying over the Flower Shop before breakfast – the waiting was accompanied by more than latent longing!

'Enough of that' Mary sputtered under her breath and turned to change from night clothes (plus robe and fluffy slippers) into day clothes, a warm variety against the painting frost. Mary's nose alerted her to hasten as the scones were browning early, needing to be adjusted in the oven so as to slow the browning, allow a more thorough baking to take place. She made the adjustment, still barefoot.

Immediately, a rapping came upon her door: a *most* inconvenient occurrence. She had little time to spare. Nonetheless, after breathing again, she ran barefoot down the stairs to the door, opened it breathlessly and said 'Come in! Come in! … And close the door, please' as she turned and raced up the stairs, her skirts flouncing as she held them free from her flying feet.

Mary had barely taken notice of who was at the door. She disappeared, nonetheless, and brought out her morning scones and poured her boiling water into the readied teapot to steep her morning tea. That done, Mary padded to the top of the stairs and called down: 'I am sorry to run off like that, but breakfast was nearly ready. How can I help you?

Her visitor, being out of sight and slow to answer, left Mary baffled. Curious in her bafflement, she took a step down the stairs and moved to the outside wall to increase her angle of vision. *Everything* was uncertain just now. She needed to know who was here, and why – but there was also the matter of the steeping tea and the just out-of-the-oven, not-yet-in-a-basket scones that were cooling on her, upstairs.

Awkward: that is how she felt. And a little aggravated as no reply was forthcoming. Another step: her breathing became deeper; her heart began to pound in her chest; a warm flush rushed from her throat, up over her face, her head. Another step, slowly; Mary felt wary now. Yet another step: she stood exposed, her bare feet set flat upon the stair.

'Hello?' spoke Mary to the cloaked and hooded back she saw examining a display in the middle of the room. 'Oh! I am sorry. I knew you ran upstairs and bid me enter. I did not hear you come back'. Thyruid turned around and tipped his hood back off his balding head.

'Oh! It is a surprise to see you here, Thyruid. I cannot remember *ever* seeing you away from the Inn-by-the-Bye'. 'I know. I have not been away in forever'. 'Could I retrieve my breakfast and join you?' 'Surely!' 'Would you care for some scones, some tea?' No. No, thank you anyway'. And Thyruid returned to his examination.

Mary basketed her scones, being wrapped in a towel as usual. She found a tray, muttering something about never having used that tray before. On it, she placed her basket, her teapot and *two* cups ... just in case Thyruid changed his mind. Then, she shod her feet and took her tray in hand and strode down the stairs – she thought of being elegant, but remembered she had never managed that act and, when she tried, her failures were always spectacular. So, she concerned herself with *not* tumbling with the tray in hand!

Successfully down the stairs, relieved, Mary set her tray on the empty bay-shelf. 'Thyruid, I often eat alone. Come and share some tea with me – perhaps a scone as well. Please'.

25 December 2005

MCXVI

Overnight, it snowed. There was nothing heavy, nothing to bother; but the land was mostly white ... only some greenish brown stubble sticking through the crust in some places. Yet the air was not really cold – just enough that, after a while, cheeks would look ruddled, slightly chapped by the crisp air.

All the wee folk *knew* this was not much in the line of snow; yet they would trudge through it as nearly knee deep. This snow was wet, apt to cling to them, packing easily under their feet, clinging to shoes and sliding under stress. For all these reasons, travel would slow considerably.

Effie woke in the early light and, glancing out her window, recognizing all these factors, she thrilled at the notion of this snow. Sitting up cross-legged on her bed, Effie studied the as-yet undisturbed white over the Fields. She remembered that Gilbert had spoken of a relaxed day, one that would allow them all a bit of refreshment, a little bit of distance from the spinning routine. 'Was it today he meant?' ran through her mind with a distinctly hopeful cast.

Inspired by hope-filled enthusiasm, Effie scrambled her way into her clothes for the day, somewhat warmer than is her usual custom. Anticipation helped her scurry across the plank between her garret room and the main section of the upstairs quarters at the Spinners' Shop. No one was there. Stopping, half-holding her breath for silence, Effie listened; all she heard was the pounding of her own heart.

Carefully, then, she eased her way in silence down the hall toward the rooms of Gilbert, Chert and Martha: not a sound … save for a soft snore coming from Chert's room. Her hope that *today* was the day for refreshment seemed confirmed; Effie beamed, then turned, bent and scurried back to her garret room to finish readying for trying out the new-fallen snow.

Warm and ready, save for her hooded cloak, Effie returned to the Common Area: still no one up; all was still. Rummaging a little, she found some left over scones from yesterday's baking: a little dry and hard, they yet supplied her with a sufficient breakfast before she turned and slipped down the stairs to her cloak, and the door … and outside. The door to the Spinners' Shop clicked closed as the latch fell into place. Effie was out in the snowscape that had enticed her so.

Because she always took the path, Effie began her walk in the snow along the same path. The undisturbed snow was as thick here as over the grass. Something felt normal about the path; of course, she took it as was her custom. She may be out alone on what she is reasonably certain is Gilbert's Day of Refreshment, but the daring is not rebellious.

While enjoying ploughing through the white snow along the path, heading toward Mary's Flower Shop, Effie found herself thinking about the Fields. She had not gone romping on the Fields for a long time, not even in the Spring, when fresh grasses are most inviting. She looked at the Fields, finding something effervescent bubbling up inside her. A yelp escaped and she began to run onto the Fields, away from the path, snow flying all around her.

Romping around the Fields, Effie whooped and shouted – a day for refreshment indeed! She was not about to settle for less. Panting, she drew up under Mary's window, made a snowball and heaved it on its way; it splattered at the edge of the pane, rattling the window and attracting Mary's attention (and irritation). As Mary scowled out the window, Effie grinned back, waving to encourage Mary to join her in the snow.

Mary's first reaction was to scoff and the tomfoolery she saw. But shortly, she began to sense a glimmer of impish fun in the sporting through the snow. The longer she thought on the bright expression she observed on Effie's face, the more inclined she was to join her. For all the care she gave her plants – and she *had* already made her rounds through the shop this morning – Mary *did* take distinct pleasure in open play.

With an erupting grin, Mary waved back, becoming agitated in her fresh excitement. Extempore gestures tried to convey that she was coming, would be there momentarily. In disarray, Mary fussed her way around her quarters on the assumption she could verify everything was as it ought to be. Of course, she could not. And so, she simply mustered means to wrap her feet and frame, her hands and head in warmth enough before she scampered out the door.

While urging herself along, Mary bent to gather a wad of snow and ready it to answer the one that rattled the pane at her window above. Rounding the corner to meet up with Effie, Mary found herself exactly in position to let the snowball fly ... and find its target directly. Effie was surprised, then bent to scoop her own reply as Mary had already mustered a second round the matter of surprise. Both in preparation, snow packed in hand and glint in eye, a rose upon the cheek and a carefree grin consuming every hint of guile, the two approached – squared off as if intent – and burst into laugher simultaneously. Mary waved her hands toward the Foundry ... and the pair spun off together in loping paces through the knee-deep snow.

Effie thought of her brother, Jasper, who had spent the night working with John at the Foundry. She knew he would be tired – likely was asleep in some warm, dry corner of the Foundry. They did not see either Jasper or John; without going in and executing a search they likely would not find them. So, as they ran toward the open big rolling door that faced the Fields, Effie raised her arm and flung her snowball into the room. It landed on the floor where it smashed into splatter for melting away. Mary did the same before they turned aside and slowed to a heady pace, stepping high through the snow.

63

There remained snow in the air, filtering lightly in the morning gleam. The pair kept their pace, long strides in rhythmic persistence carrying them with vigor through the now-relentless snow. In a sweeping arc, they brought themselves around to a point where they crossed their trail from their run toward the Foundry and went on to the path – as snow covered as the grass for that matter – and onward to the 'Y' and toward the Commons, around the Big Rock.

Soon, the two of them came up on Eliza – whose passage from the Way Down toward the Inn-by-the-Bye they had missed in their enthusiastic mirth – and swept around her on either side, arms circling her shoulders and waist. Eliza stumbled; they held her up and spoke: 'Join us on a romp about the Commons, laughing for the pleasure of it all!' Eliza would demure … but felt swept into their pleasure; she lengthened her stride, pulling arms about her companions and finding their laughter her own.

The circuit complete, the trio arrived at the Inn-by-the-Bye. Mary commented outright: 'I almost hate to leave this go for a pot of tea … but the tea would cap it all delightfully!'

1 January 2006

MCXVII

Belatedly, the sunshine appeared; it came only after morning had elapsed. Since what passed for dawn softened the starless, moonless overcast night to the soft, textured yet thick shadows of grey, day had protested it had arrived. By convention, no one had argued; but only now was anyone fully convinced. A warming came with the unveiling of the Sun, even this Winter Sun unhindered by wind, aided by a sort of presence from the South. The sunshine, capturing a sudden blue in the sky and a brightness about the wintering Hyperbia, brightened dispositions as well.

As arranged, Guerric was then hurrying to the Inn-by-the-Bye where, he was reasonably sure, Mahara was already waiting for him. He typically ran late, typically gaining a sullen pout and awkward adjustment. And, as always, he hurried to try to minimize the play of this dissention.

The handyman lugged his toolbox with him as he rounded the Big Rock, coming from the Fields onto the Commons. In his stirring mind – well awake by now though mornings were ever a strain to begin – Guerric mulled over the grey of the morning. For a long time, it had remained as an invitation to stay groggy. He was *feeling* grey.

From the cabin perched on the slope of the Ravine, Mahara was making her way to the Inn-by-the-Bye. She was already up onto the Commons and making direct progress, her cloak caught in the energetic sway her sparkling pace always induced.

Not Summer-free, of course, the flourish of hip-driven skirts pressed restively against the necessary weight the cloak applied which the counter-torque of swaying arms from twisting shoulders strained against the natural reserve a Winter's cloak presumes. The while, the cowl retained its presence, sheathing loose hung hair that willed to flash in Sun-lit ripples. She saw Guerric entering the Commons, pressed her pace to draw near.

It was as the pair crossed the Commons, headed to meet one another at the Inn-by-the-Bye, the morning grey suddenly began to break up. Someone of a more analytic attitude might reflect on how the cloud cover must have been thinning all along, or how there must be more wind up above than they register down here on the ground in Hyperbia. After all, to their mind, things had remained rather calm. And from the perspective of both Guerric and Mahara, the dull grey had remained rather uniformly dank until the Sun broke through and sudden gapes appeared in the clouds, opening to rich blue. For them, this appearance came as an ending of the morning's oppressive sway.

With sunshine, Mahara felt warmer. A hand rose and flung back the cowl, opening her head to the Sun and the air. Her long hair remained caught at the collar, restricting her head and inhibiting her freedom; two hands emerged, opening the front of the cape to its hasp while the arms rose, and her fingers lifted her tresses free. A shake of her head and the long dark strands whipped loose and wanton in the air. Sunlight gleamed from the flounce of the flung hair. Guerric smiled; his whole body responded in joy.

Guerric, having the shorter distance to cover, came to the Inn-by-the-Bye first; he waited, watching Mahara close the gap. She no longer permitted her cape to hamper her pace. Though the hasp held, she made no further effort to keep the cloak to herself. Free arms swung as the shoulders countered the hips, stride by stride. With such freedom pulsing, the cape caught the air and billowed, leaving the skirts to flash and shake in the sunshine. Her face – with a bit of warmth from the Sun amplified by the energy of her stride – glistened, moist over olive on rose.

Arriving, Mahara stopped before Guerric. 'With the Sun out now, you could almost want to stay outside'. 'Yes. Yet, the ground is wet, and the damp is chilling. There is not enough Sun to overcome Winter quite that quickly'. 'Oh, Guerric: you can find the dismal in the grand! We could stroll the Commons, circle the Fields, pass this Sun-blissed part of the day … and sup later rather than now'. 'So, celebrate the blue sky on an empty stomach?' 'Maybe you are only practical' she pouted. 'You never were much fun on an empty stomach'. 'And were you?'

A knowing, confessing sidelong glance was Mahara's only possible reply. A hint of a shrug and Mahara turned to enter the door. 'I suppose it is best for us to go on in'; the tone of her affect was purely flat.

Guerric pushed open the door and let Mahara enter. With a twitch of her skirts – just barely sufficient for the need – she swept her way into the Foyer. Guerric followed and closed the door behind, against the new-found brilliance of the day. They paused in the dim Foyer that their eyes might adjust. 'Without the sunshine breaking in, this adjustment would have been so much easier'. Guerric looked at the shade he knew was Mahara. 'It was worth it, was it not?' 'Oh yes, yes. Yes'.

Once they had decided that their eyes had adequately adjusted, Guerric deposited his toolbox along the wall and hung his jacket above; Mahara followed with her cape. Assuming an air of elegance – which no one would think to dispute – Mahara took Guerric's arm and the unlikely pair swept to the steps, then down into the dining room of the Inn-by-the-Bye. Thyruid noticed them at their entrance and waited for them to choose their place this afternoon.

Noting that Mahara aimed toward the middle-of-the-room table that they so often used, Thyruid ducked through the swinging door into Marthuida's kitchen. Shortly, he returned, bearing a tray with a mug of hot black coffee and a teapot full of steeping tea – the one for Guerric and the other for Mahara.

'May I suppose you came for lunch?' he asked as he set the tray and its contents on the table – then distributed them before his dining room guests. 'Yes. That is our intent' replied Mahara, never diverting her glance toward the round Innkeeper. 'Fine. Would you care for a basket of Marthuida's biscuits?' 'With the trappings … yes' she replied. Guerric added: 'That sounds very fine'.

As the voices were so disconnected from his inquiry, the while giving direct and apt reply, Thyruid merely nodded, held to a subdued grin as he discreetly turned away and bore his tray back to the swinging door behind the counter on his way to place the annotated order in the kitchen.

A glance around the kitchen did not find Marthuida where he might have expected, requiring a broader, more extended, searching glace that found her at the back door to the kitchen, the small one she normally would use and not the no-longer used great overhead door she had needed for so long for the feeding of Yves and Betsy, the not-wee children for whom she had cared. It appeared to Thyruid that she was rubbing her hands in front of her waist while she was gazing out the door.

Curious, Thyruid went to her. 'Isn't that sunshine delightful now?' she said. 'I hardly want to leave off the sight of it'. 'That must be what is on Mahara's mind – and Guerric's … that and the bright attraction of it all'.

'Oh: and they wanted some biscuits for lunch'.

8 January 2006

MCXVIII

Morning, still cool, shone bright. Already the shadows of the Hills had passed to the path along the front of the Spinners' Shop. With the trees bare, Carymba could watch the golden brightness creep from that door as she sat atop the Rock at the end of the Way Down. Peaceful stillness dominated.

She had seen John and Jasper finish off the night, having banked (she knew) the Forge toward starting it up again come evening. By now, certainly, the Spinners were about – and Mary at the Flower Shop; she had seen the witness to their morning firing of their stoves. Carymba herself sat, nestled in her cloak, arms wrapped about her shins, and her chin resting on her knees.

In this morning stillness, Carymba heard someone coming down the Way Down. Quickly, she decided to stand; so, she rose. Once on her feet, watching the bare path below her, Carymba quickly wondered why she would react this way; it made no sense to her at all. As she questioned herself, she still felt the stiff tension in her body, as if she were pretending to be ready for some unknown uncertainty. In her thoughts, Carymba scoffed at herself; in her composure, the waif remained unusually taut. Most likely, she heard Eliza, and the worst-case scenario, this would be Walter. She knew no other candidates for this sound she could plainly hear coming down the Way Down.

As probabilities would have it, Eliza appeared in a loping gait, coming down the slope, holding herself from going too fast while avoiding mincing her steps along the path. Carymba noticed Eliza's carefree style and let down her guard, nearly laughing at herself for her prior reaction. 'Hello, Eliza!' she called from her perch, surprising her friend.

Staggering to a halt, Eliza caught at her breath, gazed up with jaw agape and then recognized Carymba: 'Oh! You startled me! ... Well, hello, Carymba! I was coming down with a thought of breakfast at the Inn-by-the-Bye. Why not come with me?' Eliza extended her greeting with a flashing smile.

Having no reason *not* to go, Carymba easily decided she could do exactly that. And she did. She came back down the little path that led from the top of the Rock at the end of the Way Down. Eliza held her pause the short while until Carymba joined her. Setting off together, they assumed the steady plod of Carymba's syncopated gait. With an amiable ease, the pair turned at the path along the edge of the Hills, headed toward the 'Y', the Big Rock and the Commons, exactly as they had done an uncounted number of times before, either alone or together, with each other or someone else. This whole unfolding event came with the most ordinary aplomb, a matter of everyday offhanded happening.

After this most easy going of starts, Eliza turned quiet, such that her silence could be felt – even by one not nearly as aware of life's subtleties as is Carymba. Slightly awkward, Eliza fumbled in her steps; Carymba slowed to make it appear they were in unison, attempting to minimize the sense of discontent for Eliza. In all, the waif waited. Eliza steadied herself and held her pace; wanting to glance to Carymba, she was afraid. She kept her eyes to the ground, her head bowed and her body unusually taut. This was not going as Eliza would wish.

Past the 'Y', the pair swept toward the Big Rock. With Eliza feeling awkward, and Carymba trying to figure her way through the confusion, the pair balanced their silence with irregular discomfort. Eliza portrayed confusion, uncertain how to bring this awkward phase to an end.

Around the Big Rock, Carymba glanced down the Commons toward that place where the Sun shone on the matted Winter-grass. A peaceful hinted smile swept across her face. 'Look! Isn't that Sun on the Commons lovely?'

Eliza looked. She saw the bright stretch on the ground out beyond the still-extensive shadow of the Leaferites' Hill. She saw nothing really extraordinary as the Winter grass lay over, wet and drab – merely something bland with the Sun's light added, perhaps to give an accent to the blandness! Besides, this was not enough of a diversion to budge her off her morning preoccupation with Carymba – was the waif leading her to the Inn-by-the-Bye? Had the momentum of origination in this trip slipped entirely away from Eliza herself?

The pair walked, still at Eliza's stuttering pace, looking toward the Sun lit extremes of the Commons and seeing its plainness – the one with wonder, the other with bewilderment over whatever could cause this wonder.

As they walked, a voice called from behind them. 'The bright sunshine – glorious on the Commons: Yes!' Eliza was startled: a second opinion, and *she* still had no clue as to what they saw before them at all. Carymba turned her head, twisting her shoulders slightly to complete the turn: 'Terzi! It has been a long time! Yes, that sunshine on the Commons – it *is* glorious!'

Terzi approached: 'Do you mind if I join you?' 'Not at all. Eliza had invited me to join her at the Inn-by-the-Bye for breakfast. So, Eliza, do *you* mind if Terzi joins us?' Eliza replied: 'Of course not. Do join us, Terzi'.

Eliza was in a position of being polite, after all. Refusal would have her appearing churlish where she felt she could not afford such an appearance; she *was* like it or not, up against Carymba who always managed a gracious presence. Besides, she reasoned, this would divert her situation from this awkward, embarrassed impasse she had entered. The immediate smile modulated under reflection into increasing warmth. 'Thank you' replied Terzi.

'What brings you down from the Leaferites' Hill this bright morning?' asked Carymba with offhanded aplomb. Eliza had the same question in mind, though with more of a darkened ambiguity about it than did Carymba's easy innocence. For, though Terzi's arrival disentangled her from her perplexity, it also disengaged her from the direct share with Carymba at breakfast.

Terzi made it unlikely she would have an occasion to press directly her long held bafflement over the subtle draw Carymba had over everyone in Hyperbia. With such ease, *sublime* ease, the waif had all the wee folk in Hyperbia following her. Eliza did not understand – why, even on this walk, which she had herself initiated and on which she was leading, now she felt like she was following Carymba – as if the waif had the idea in the first place!

'I have some questions, I suppose' answered Terzi. 'What sort of questions?' replied Carymba. 'That is the problem; I have not been able to formulate them. They seem to float in midair, taunting me with their imprecision, their ambiguity'. 'I see'. While Carymba paused thoughtfully, Eliza half sympathized with Terzi: forming her own questions had long frustrated her. In fact, she had noted that one thing Carymba did was not to worry much about these questions or their answers. She, instead, provides a sort of welcome for the ambiguities that plague everyone else and blithely walks through their midst as if they would show her their own resolution. What silliness!

'Maybe we should relax over breakfast together, the way Eliza suggested to me back by the Way Down'.

15 January 2006

MCXIX

A necessary drizzle, chilled and driven by just enough wind to make it slice into whatever flesh might be unwary enough to be subject to the cold dampness, soaked into the soil of Hyperbia relentlessly. Even so, Wilbur was up early, ready for daylight as he was every day.

By the time of the first hints of morning cracking the monolithic darkness of the night, Wilbur was standing before the big window looking over the Great River just past the Bend; he could see the dark water, knowing its power in spite of its placid appearance, and the brambles across the way ... and, in particular, the pathways that emerge at water's edge. He was sipping at his mug of dark, piping hot coffee, and waiting for what the day might bring.

Daylight comes slowly when a necessary drizzle sifts from low hanging, dense clouds – though Wilbur bore his own deep sense of what is the time of the Sun's rising, a time he anticipates so as to be ready. Always ready: that is Wilbur's daily intent, carried over time even though the apparent urgency of the need he served had waned over the years he had been the sole ferry across the Great River. Thin light appeared, allowing the view across to the brambles to emerge in the grey of the morning.

Wilbur studied this view. The drizzle was barely falling, almost as a mist ... but slightly heavier in intent than a pure mist. Yet the fall was so gentle that he could perceive no rain-patterning on the laminar surface of the Great River below his window. The window provided a sense of chill. Distant from his kitchen stove, the cold seemed to seep through the glass and drop down around his legs. Even with the glass, the dampness of the

73

chill came as well and gnawed into him. Wilbur, in spite of his intentions, eased away from the window and its witness to the penetrating drizzle just beyond its somewhat sheltering pane.

'I never did like this chill' Wilbur muttered to himself. 'But my ability to *ignore* it seems to have deteriorated over time'. Wilbur heard his muttering and paused. Not often did he acknowledge in any form the passage of years, save as the building of a larder of experience toward the more capable handling of life. Age itself was ignored; time meant experience and, with it, a deepening perspective on his craft and upon his instinctive calling to do what he does. But there it came, taunted out of him by that damp chill he found he could no longer ignore this morning.

Aggravated with himself, Wilbur soon found himself brooding over the talisman of age. After all this time of successfully ignoring these matters, now it has to crop up in him, and in a shiver-shudder over his old distaste for gripping damp chills. He had always thought of age as a tally on growth: time brought experience; reflection over time's experience offered a bit of wisdom, enhancing how life got lived – always helping him master what needed to be mastered as he went along. But today he could no longer ignore the damp chill. That is all.

Wilbur refreshed his coffee mug and continued to meander around his house – passing near the window repeatedly so as to cast a glance across the way, to the bramble on the other bank and to the openings at the shore, where eager customers would appear from time to time. But Wilbur found his restlessness bringing him back toward the kitchen and the stove over and over again. He would scold himself and mope out toward the big window once more. But then, his self-scolding would grow mute and his window time dwindled in favor of the stove, more and more.

Finally, on one of his fleeting and irregular passes to glance out the window, he stopped and looked again. This time, he saw, standing along side the edge of the Great River, at the end of one of the openings in the tangled bramble, a small, somewhat huddled figure in the necessary drizzle. As he watched this sole, still figure, he saw it as wrapped in grey, somewhat round and slightly ragged. From the dress, he figured it was an older woman, with pride, yet worn by her years. Wilbur thought quickly, trying to remember how long he had been away from the window, but could not say. This lack of attention disturbed him.

With a brow deeply furrowed and a concentrated frown on his face, Wilbur stood there, holding his steaming mug of coffee, gazing at this stationary, patient figure. Half non-believing, he watched; with his free hand, he rubbed his eyes – then waited as they re-focused: the woman remained in place. He sipped his coffee, blowing the steam away first, before finding his face engulfed in its dissipating wisps. The woman remained. As embarrassing as this was, most of all to his pride over his attentiveness and his responsive capacity, Wilbur wanted her to be a mirage. If she were imagined, however, she was certainly persistent about it!

Setting down his coffee mug and stepping into his own gear for rainy days, Wilbur took himself down his steps and out his door. A glance across the way: the woman stayed in place, waiting with all the appearance of one who is accustomed to waiting. Nodding, Wilbur moved directly up stream to the mooring place for his boat. Judging the current swifter than usual, Wilbur poled himself somewhat upstream, keeping close to the shoreline where the labor would be at a minimum. Once he felt sure he had even a fair margin for error, he shoved his boat from the shore, turning it around so as to catch the current and be carried forward into the Bend.

Using the current and sweeping across the Great River, Wilbur guided his boat near the opposing shore, coasting, slowing as he came along the brambles, drawing the boat to touch the shore just in front of the still-waiting woman. 'Climb in, quickly' he said in soft tones. She responded by stepping forward, grasping the edge of the boat and lifting one leg in. The skirts were a bother; she released one hand, almost by necessity, as the force of her actions had nosed the boat from the bank and into the catching current. As a result, she tumbled into his boat as Wilbur worked to bring the surprise under control and embark on the sweep through the current and the drizzle successfully.

Experience helps master surprises, and Wilbur made quick use of his many trips across the Great River and back to swing his craft smoothly and safely into one of the settled pools along the bank by the Plain. There, he announced to his quiet passenger that she could climb to the Plain and be securely on her way. The woman did not move; neither did she speak. Wilbur repeated himself; she did as well. 'I need to turn around so I can pole my way upstream along this sheltering bank'. 'That is fine' she replied in somber, sober tones. He paused; she did not budge.

'Ok' he said, a little puzzled but figuring it was time to get his boat back to its mooring and himself to the cooling mug of coffee. While poling the boat carefully upstream, keeping the nearly still edge of the stream, Wilbur concentrated – but remained curious about his passenger who did not disembark.

'Where are going?' Wilbur finally asked as they neared the Bend, where his following the shore was most nuanced. 'I am going to be a housekeeper' she said. 'Who needs a housekeeper?' 'You do. So, I am coming to keep your house'. 'I don't need a housekeeper!' 'Certainly, you do. If you did not, you would have been free to see me on the bank in the drizzle sooner than you did'. 'How long did you wait?' 'A while. … I was glad I had no emergency, though the drizzle was cold'.

22 January 2006

MCXX

Morning had come in dull greys, an overcast that muted everything. Carymba had been out for hours when daylight changed black to grey; she was by then walking down the Sea Road, musing on the fragments of notions haunting her mind. All those notions came in snippets, bits and pieces, none of them fitting together at all; she always thought they did not fit together *yet*. She would be patient, for often they *had* come together – many of them, some of them – to form something profoundly real.

No light shone; the Sea rolled under a chill breeze, surly and dark. Carymba held her cloak close around her, her cowl forward to shelter her face.

In Hidden Cabin, up atop the Crossed Hills, Anna was up though Mother Hougarry would have easily been pleased to remain within her covers longer. Once the child was astir, however, Mother Hougarry felt responsible for being up and attentive and aware of the doings in her house. As every morning, Mother Hougarry wondered where Carymba might be; it was her resolute opinion that morning as evening should find the waif in Hidden Cabin. That rarely happened – had not happened for years, nearly as long as memory served. Last night fell and Carymba was still about, several nights having passed since she shared at Mother Hougarry's table. Although Carymba was elsewhere, *somewhere*, Anna was at home, and up for the day; Mother Hougarry could sleep no more this morning.

While Anna was about her play, Mother Hougarry knew enough to go to her stove and get it started. Once that was done, she could get the tea water to heating and begin to mix up he scones for the day. In the middle of these morningly necessities, she was quite capable of keeping an ear tuned to whatever Anna was doing – simply for the sake of a gentle oversight and a bit of responsibility. Maybe, she thought, had she been more careful with Carymba, the waif would not be so prone to wandering at all hours of the day and night.

By now, of course, Anna knew Mother Hougarry's anxieties and how to keep them in line. That meant being quiet, but not *too* quiet. In return, she found the assured Mother Hougarry most kind and generous.

The day continued overcast; it seemed that there was no thinning of the weighted grey pall stretched from horizon to horizon. Carymba, rather at ease as to the span of vision provided, chose simply to watch the restless Sea for some time.

Carymba had long since slowed her pace to a rather quiet amble; being in no rush to go anywhere, her quiet amble came to a simple stop – she stood, somewhat huddled, on the Sea Road and watched the thrashing rollers come to wash up on the strand. There was barely light enough yet to allow her to discern the coarse wildness of the Sea. She knew it took no light at all to feel its chill sting penetrate her warmest cloak.

After a while, she retreated to the far side of the Sea Road, away from the Sea, and sat for a spell on one of the larger stones piled there. She was more comfortable, seeing that she was a bit removed from the spray of the Sea.

Carymba did little but watch the steady roll of the Sea. For such a moving mass, the overall scene gave the impression of violence within the unchanging throes of the water under the wind, buried under thick overcast. Something about that hinted rage – a strangely *controlled* rage – enchanted her, holding her attention to the point that Sea and soul seemed to merge, and that eager Sea enlivened the typical balanced calm that Carymba always knew in herself.

By late morning, the thick overcast had begun to darken and lower – even to hover (rather, *loom*) over the Sea and the Beach and beyond – most certainly over the lone waif seated above the Sea Road.

The change came gradually, accompanied by a slow freshening of the wind. A new bite rode the breeze – at first a dampness that moved at last into a legitimate mist, blown by a stiffened wind at a cooling temperature. By the time that mist would slap up inside her cowl and taunt her cheeks, Carymba had already thought of moving along; the cold mist merely confirmed her sense of time.

Carymba rose from the stones with a sigh, stepped down to the easier going of the Sea Road and then turned her efforts toward the Valley Road. Once her decision to move along had materialized, Carymba paid little more attention to the Sea. Waves gave evidence of the Sea's basic throes, but no longer to her eyes. They were attentive to the Sea Road while her mind turned to the path chosen and the anticipated relief to be met on the Valley Road.

By the time Carymba turned into the Valley Road, Anna had long enjoyed the warmth of Mother Hougarry's stove in Hidden Cabin. Since she had not gone outside, Anna had grown accustomed to the warmth, giving the matter no more thought whatsoever. Mother Hougarry, however, heard the rise of the wind – a certain moan through the trees giving a rueful response to the blow. She sensed the chill in that wind and her body told her of the dampness in the air, the penetrating nature of it all. Her mind mused over the unknown: where Carymba was in all this *looming* weather. Preoccupation took its place with Mother Hougarry while Anna settled for the already settled warmth of Hidden Cabin.

As the wind's freshened nature held and the mist cooled further, the effect on Hidden Cabin was to cool the edges, away from stove in the kitchen – which was their warmth. Anna gradually moved closer to the kitchen, noticing along the way that the warmth to which she had grown accustomed retreated from windows and outside walls.

The child, now in the kitchen, mused out loud: 'I wonder if Carymba will come by today. The wind sounds wild in those trees'. Mother Hougarry looked at her; after a long pause, she replied: 'I do not know. You never know with Carymba. ... But, yes: it does sound wild in those trees'.

Mist gave way to drizzle, moving through those stages bit by bit: mist to drizzle, drizzle to a regular rain, to a wind-driven, hard rain. Carymba wondered if the end might not be a simple deluge! As it was, she had reached the Narrows and turned to the root steps while her cloak was growing wetter all the time, offering less and less protection. The mist had filtered into the felting. Now, the rain seemed to have gained easy access into the fabric, making it all heavier and heavier on her slight frame.

Hardly a thought now appeared to her mind concerning climbing the root steps and gaining the path up into the Crossed Hills and on to Hidden Cabin. She simply clamored up the steps, sliding and catching herself as things were already wet … and wet clay makes slick mud.

Mother Hougarry heard steps on the porch; she listened. The door opened, letting a damp draft scurry across the floor voraciously; her ankles cringed. The door closed and the draft settled as the last eddies of the wind disappeared from around her feet. 'Hello!' she called. 'Hello!' returned.

'Ah – Carymba! We had wondered about you'. 'It is wet out there'. Carymba took off her cloak to let it hang and begin to dry. 'I will find some dry clothes' she said. 'Yes, do. And the scones are still hot. I will brew us some tea'.

29 January 2006

MCXXI

Martha's morning had started miserably. Although the day was bright and inviting and the rest of the Spinners were in a reasonable mood, nothing could quite suit Martha. She was never the happiest of persons, even at her best; but today, it seemed that nothing could satisfy her: nothing at all.

To start with, she overslept. For most people, this oversleeping would be an inconvenience and a momentary irritation. Martha, however, found this oversleeping a matter of grave concern as it meant someone else would be starting breakfast for the Spinners. Someone else would *make* the breakfast in fact. Even though she inevitably complained that the work always fell on her, allowing someone else to actually do it was the devastating fact that this morning has witnessed first of all.

Even before she dressed, once she realized she was late, Martha feared it would be Effie who settled into *her* kitchen. Gilbert would be bad enough – Chert would not be a factor there, ever – but Effie, that intruder – *she* was the disaster.

After throwing on her day clothes with great haste, neglecting her hair in all but the most rudimentary of ways, Martha swept out her door in unaccustomed awkwardness. She found Gilbert and Chert seated, Effie taking her seat, having just set on the table a steeping teapot. They looked her way, a lode of wary expectation on their faces. Effie broke the unsettling hush: 'Good morning, Martha. I managed some breakfast for us as you were delayed'.

Worst of all, Effie was pleasant. Martha found no tone of gloating in her voice – not then nor (so aggravatingly) as she mused over the event as the day wore long. A glance at the table: not a thing to disdain … except that Effie had prepared it. Martha could tell it was Effie's work in little points that some might not notice – not openly at least – at all; but Martha noticed as her already crumbling morning disintegrated a bit more.

Sitting down, Martha had to eat some breakfast although she certainly did not *feel* like eating breakfast. Not *this* breakfast. She was hungry, of course. And she was having a good deal of difficulty dealing with the somewhat noisy longings in her stomach. Obligation met resentment; need met determination: Martha sat down, and Effie poured a cup of tea for her.

Dull eyes gazed at the cup; Gilbert passed the basket of biscuits, still warm even though Martha was late to breakfast. Martha took the basket, opened the wrapping towel and looked at the few remaining biscuits. She took one – still warm, but by no means hot – and set it on the plate before her. Hungry and under full view, she ate at her biscuit, dry. She never liked them dry; she had to have something to complain about, even if only to herself.

While Martha was eating the biscuit she did not want to eat, the others dallied with her so she would not have to eat alone. Or they almost dallied – Effie eased off the plates to clean them up while Chert and Gilbert sat at the table and sipped tea with Martha.

They all attempted small talk; Martha was taut and terse, however, and what responses she *did* offer came with a felt (though usually masked) edge, dampening their efforts and confirming her misery as they sipped at their tea quickly in order to escape. Indeed, both Gilbert and Chert drained their teacups and found reason to excuse themselves – something about readying matters downstairs, where they would all soon be.

Alone with Effie, Martha was hardly pleased. After all, Effie had taken her chores and made breakfast, even good (if dry) biscuits. Effie had shown Martha to be replaceable. To Martha, it mattered nothing that everything came with a kindly edge. In a way, it made things even worse. The kindly crew had insisted she have breakfast, then deserted her at table while Effie was cleaning up – without even the decency to be tart, hurrying Martha along, to catch up.

Also, Martha glowered, Gilbert and Chert were downstairs setting up the day for spinning. This was usually Martha's task as well ... and she was absolutely certain that no one could do that chore properly – except her.

Martha finished her dry biscuit, stewing inside over how impossible it had been to enjoy, and rose, muttering that she had to go downstairs to make sure Gilbert and Chert did not louse up her pattern of preparation. Effie smiled and cleaned up Martha's barely used dishes: no butter, no jelly as the others had enjoyed. A wipe and a swish on the tea cup – then wash the teapot – and she was done.

Downstairs, Martha examined the setup, sticking her hands in to re-settle the lots of wool slightly – but even she had to admit to herself that there was no reason to do so, none whatsoever. Gilbert spoke, with distressing pleasantness: 'Up to your usual standards?' Martha was forced, *forced* to reply – there being no polite way to ignore it now that Gilbert had lifted the issue, and done wo with such a dastardly good-natured tone: 'Why, yes. It looks quite alright'. Her voice was trailing off considerably by the end of the brief conversation.

Nothing had been going right for Martha today. She knew it all started because she overslept; she consoled herself by noting that she *rarely* overslept and was therefore regularly able to be present, in charge, making sure everything was done right. As it was, she was hurrying, trying nearly desperately to catch up with the day – a seemingly impossible task. Under such a burden as this, she knew in her heart, *anyone* would say that this had begun a miserable day.

By the time lunch break neared, Gilbert, Chert and Effie were about ready to believe Martha, that this *had* been a most miserable day. They were all beginning to feel sorry for themselves – after all, it was difficult to feel sorry for Martha, whose way through the morning they had tried – maybe even *conspired* – to make easy in spite of her having overslept.

Effie, however, remembered the bright morning that greeted her as she woke in her garret room. Of course, the Sun was then still behind the Hills, but the blue sky had been cloudless and bright – a light blue, high and airy, and bright. She was not going to let Martha cloud it over.

Lunch break was almost upon them. Martha likely had something in mind, thought Effie; but *she* wanted some cheer. 'Gilbert', spoke Effie, 'do we have time to go to the Inn-by-the-Bye for lunch?' "I am not sure'. 'We could work a little late to make up production if need be'. 'True'.

Martha interposed sourly: Don't be silly. I can get us a lunch up quickly enough here'. 'What do you have in mind?' asked Chert. 'Nothing as yet. But, give me a few minutes, and I will'. Martha was threatened; Martha was terse. 'I would really like to get out in this day – it started off so beautifully' replied Effie. Martha scoffed.

'As I consider it … and look over how well we have done this morning, I think we could do that: a good idea!' commented Gilbert, looking around at the others, beaming. Chert grinned and nodded: 'I think so, too'. Martha once more glowered; her day became more miserable yet.

Normally, the Spinners would walk the path two and two. But when Gilbert and Effie started off in the lead, Chert came up and took Effie's other arm, leaving Martha to grumble along behind, lagging on the way to lunch at the Inn-by-the-Bye.

5 February 2006

MCXXII

The night hangs suspended above the Plain, moonless as the stars scramble the entire cloudless sky. This was not a time for travel as the stars sparkled without illumining even the most open of spaces on the land. Few would be out so late at any time, not here in Hyperbia; fewer yet would risk such a swallowing night as this for fear they be devoured as eyes were useless and broad spaces gave too few places for correcting touch. It was *also* a place for careful presence, but only for the most daring, or the most desperate.

Nights like this, cold and clear, dark and dense, enfolding everything within its strange complicity with lost dimensions, did admit a few whose thoroughgoing familiarity with Hyperbia – the Plain in particular – allowed them freedom: Carymba and Walter and Malak come to mind. The only sound in this night grown late would be the crunch of frosted grass; the wind was still, and all was a hush.

Coming from the Wood, from the secretive and unusual-laden Wood set between the Plain and the Sea, Uiston and the Gypsie Area, moved Malak. He had seen no one else about, nor heard them. Malak was accustomed to moving in shadows and seeming to simply appear – and disappear – with rare stealth. This night, late as it was, Malak was concentrating on his singular mission – he was always sent, always carrying a message. Often, no one really understood where Malak came from – only knew that, by his voice, he carried a message of impelling, if unusual, wisdom.

Malak's trajectory emerged from the mysteries of the Wood and began to trace its way across the Plain. Had careful ears been listening attentively, they might have heard his light step on the frosted grass. And, if those ears were unusually perceptive, they might have traced his direction as toward the City on the Plan.

Now, it is likely that more ears could tell he was headed toward the City on the Plain, or beyond it, at a slightly different angle, toward the way to Wilbur's house and his ferry service at the Bend of the Great River. Perhaps, more would recognize he was moving away from the Inn-by-the-Bye and the Commons. It takes great care to figure out the destination marked only by the soft crunch of frosted, stiffening grass. And, of course, someone would need to be listening.

Swallowed in the silent night – except for the soft crushing of whitened grass – Malak moved purposefully across the Plain, directed toward the City on the Plain. Rather, the path was nearly directed toward the City on the Plain, for even a refined, knowledgeable instinct like Malak's was not exact; most nights were not quite so thoroughly dark as this one, and redress to stationary stars would require him to turn around, making them somewhat more approximate. Malak figured he would be close enough that little clues along the way – mostly nearer to the City itself – would clue him in on his corrections soon enough.

The Plain is a level area; but it is not strictly table-top flat. Malak long had been well aware of the nuances of the topography – the rises and falls, the creases and the subtle depressions: these told him where he was. So, when he neared the City on the Plain, Malak found himself about the place of a convenient lane.

The City still labored under the City plan of the former ruler, Osburn. Because he liked grandeur and feared intrusion from the outside, the City has small lanes coming to the outer limits of the City. These lanes form a sort of always-disrupted web to follow on the way into town. Once sufficient progress had been made, lanes converged into alleys and then streets, streets join into Avenues, Avenues into Boulevards, Boulevards lead into Plazas. Changing the access would be painful, something every neighborhood resisted.

Malak toured the narrow lanes, discovered the alleys and the streets, followed into an Avenue and moved with confidence to another narrow street, jutting in another direction through the sleeping City. Acting as if he knew exactly where he was and where he was going, as if, had there been any uncertainties in his mind, Malak had sorted them all out while touring the lanes as he entered the City.

Malak slipped directly to an unlit door in the unlit side street on this still moonless night. The door was exactly where he expected it would be: he rapped against the solid door; the echo sounded behind the door, fading into silence. Malak waited, confident. Time passed; he listened for the stirring behind the door. The stirring finally came, and the rustle of activity until the door was opened.

A low lamp burned in the hallway, backlighting the thin figure before Malak. 'Hello. Come in'. The voice was soft, reserved yet welcoming. Malak stepped inside; his host closed the door on the silent darkness outside. 'You have a message?' Malak nodded. The message itself was brief, pithy, obscure: 'The night awaits the coming of the light'. 'Where?' 'In the face of reminiscences and under looming shadows'. The nod returned to Malak, a sign of understanding. Malak immediately turned, moved to the door, opened it just enough to slide his narrow frame through, and left. The door closed noiselessly behind him, leaving Margent alone in the hallway, thinking.

The message being well in mind, Margent went quickly to his room, where he promptly dressed for going out into the dark. On the way back through the hallway, Margent extinguished the lamp, stood, settled in the dark before opening the door and going out into the street.

The night was cold; he told himself he should have known that! He had worn his warmest cloak – and now he pulled the cowl full over his head for warmth. Margent shivered; he would be fine, but at first nip, the cold caught him by surprise, half overwhelmed him. None of this held him back; once he closed the door, he had begun his trek.

While passing from his modest quarters, down the side street on which he lived, Margent found himself reviewing his stewardship of the City. His work had always been that of managing the City. Only on occasion had it been necessary for him to stand in public and rally this City on the Plain beyond anxiety and into the vision that ha brought them to where they were. Everything that Osburn left was changed – and yet his charismatic squandering of the strength of the City would return every now and then to disrupt everything. From Malak's message, Margent knew that nostalgia for what folk thought they remembered about Osburn's style of leadership was likely at the heart of the issue.

Making his way through the dark, empty streets, Margent passed through the night and pressed his feet from street to Avenue, Avenue to Boulevard, Boulevard to Plaza – the old center of the City on the Plain, the place where he knew charisma was the molten force. The Plaza was empty and dark. Margent ambled around; the place felt strange. He glanced to the Bluff hanging over them all; it was dark and silent, too. Margent puzzled: this was where he most naturally understood Malak's words to indicate.

Margent ambled along, slowly, reflectively. He retraced his steps for some time, thinking over Malak's words all the while. At last, he muttered to himself: 'If I am going to accomplish anything while the night awaits the coming of the light, it will be at my office. I will go there'.

12 February 2006

MCXXIII

Mary woke; it was dark, sometime in the night, and she was cold. Her room was cold, and even her blankets did not suffice to hold her body heat. Such a wakening was a total event. She found herself already curled in her blankets, wrapped up completely on herself. Her thoughts turned toward her stove, which must be cold ... and then to her Flower Shop downstairs.

Against instinct, Mary forced her legs to straighten – still within the covers; the chill made her jerk violently in her bed; but Mary resisted the instinctual reflex to draw back close on herself. Considering the likely places she would have dropped her robe, deposited her slippers when she came to bed, Mary sifted memory to know where, exactly, she would find them quickly. For, once she abandoned her covers, the issue of the cold *would* really impinge upon her body; haste would be a major issue for her.

Once she had satisfied herself that she had a very good idea where to find the necessities, Mary forced herself out of her covers and onto her feet. Cold slapped the soles of her feet, compressed her body; a massive shiver rattled her frame. Her hand reached to the anticipated place: the robe squeezed in her fingers and her arms wrested the piece around her body as they stuffed themselves into the sleeves: relief!

With her feet inside the old fluffy slippers and the robe around her body, Mary set out in the dark for the stairs. She found them by feel and began to ease herself down the familiar steps to the landing: turn, take three steps and be on the floor of the Flower Shop itself. And so she did. Cautious in spite of familiarity (for the darkness was not yet relieved by the late-rising moon), Mary let her fingers search for what she knew was there, using the difference to provide the necessary connections on trajectory that eyes normally provide automatically.

The table: a bit further than she anticipated. Move along that edge until the corner; move along the next edge, trailing fingers gently on the surface until the end. Then angle about so, and step off into the dark, tentatively and feeling the way through open air. Finally, long after she was sure she should have found her place, she reached the next table. She reached the table – *almost* where she expected to find it.

Pausing in the nearly cold room realizing the chill was sharpening on her, Mary wondered at her not lighting a lamp to bring with her. Of course, most often, *enough* light from moon or Sun or *something* would be around to soften shadows and allow her to see the gross outlines of the room – quite enough for these purposes. *This* night was both darker and colder than she had expected. Mary shivered, then thought of her plants – and proceeded toward the downstairs stove, knowing that only the best of good fortunes would find there any memory of a coal sufficient to rekindle the fire and allow her to easily establish the stove for the run of the night.

Arriving at the stove, the iron held only a hint of warmth. The fact that it was not wholly cold inspired a hint of hope. Finding some light stuff, the makings for kindling for a start, Mary opened the firebox. No glow shone through – and only the hint of warmth, maybe only a fading memory of the last coal from the last remnants of a fire. Regardless of any chance that any live coal might still be around, she would need to start with the same sort of a basis. So, it would be the most fire-susceptible stuff first, then the light kindling, slowly heavier stock until she had the fire going and the Flower Shop warming again.

Having the first layer in place, Mary sniffed, hoping to smell the precursor of fire in the mix: nothing but stale ashes rewarded her hope. Nodding with a slight sigh, she placed the lightest kindling in place; that would be the readying before lighting the arrangement. A poke with the sticks and the whole ash base shifted; she heard the rustle but ignored it in following through her process of readying the fir in the dark. Suddenly,

Mary started at the scent of smoke, followed quickly by a flare of yellow light in the belly of the firebox. At least one buried coal was live enough to begin the fire again.

Mary grinned broadly, readying in mind to respond in such a way as would help this fire become so well established that she could return to her bed (after firing the stove upstairs, too) and sleeping out the night. While sorting things out in her mind, Mary was also accustoming her eyes to the brightness amid the dark shadows. By the time she could review the fire without wincing for the brightness, Mary could tell it was time to nurture the fire. Her practiced hands added to the fire bed bit by bit as the crackling blaze built for itself a bed of coals and a framework for perpetuating itself and warming the stove ... and then the Flower Shop itself.

Some time later, Mary saw the fire going well, and banked against the hours she would be asleep. Adjusting for a slow, steady burn in the stove – for the sake of her flowers, Mary took a lamp, lit it and took it upstairs in one hand. Not only was the night unusually dark but her eyes had also become accustomed to the brightness of the fire in the stove downstairs, forcing the night to appear even more impenetrable in her sight.

With lamp in hand, Mary returned to her stairs. Up in her room, the chill that woke her was still very much prevalent. Mary moved into the cold, leaving the stove downstairs – and its warmth – behind, gone but not forgotten. This stove: there was no mistaking – it was thoroughly cold, with no buried coal to be unwittingly tapped for the increase of the fire and the spreading of her warmth. Instead, she lay the fire as before – aided by the lamplight's soft glow in her room.

Once she was convinced that she had it ready, she lit a piece from her lamp and brought it to the readied kindling and watched as the fire gradually took hold and grew on the kindling. Adding as before, she made the fire in the firebox of her upstairs stove grow that warmth emerge into the stove, into the room. Mary set the fire for the next few hours and felt ... satisfied.

Figuring it was time to return to her covers and sleep through the night, Mary turned her attention that way. In her chilled state, she had torn the blankets all free; she took time now to straighten them, re-make the bed.

As she readied to step from her robe and fluffy slippers, put out the lamp and settle back into bed, a rattle came at her door, giving her a start; this was no hour for visitors! Mary took her lamp and went out her door, down the stairs to the Flower Shop, to the front door. 'Hello?' she spoke tentatively. 'Are you all right, Mary?' The voice was Carymba's. 'Yes. I had to tend my stoves against the cold'. 'Good. I was afraid something was wrong as your lamp shone at such an hour'. 'You must be cold out there! Come in and warm up. I will make us some tea'.

As Mary opened the door, Carymba was rather constrained to come in, even though this was hardly the hour for visitation, *nor* for tea. 'You should not do this, not at this hour'. 'Well, we are up and wide awake anyway: what matters the hour?' 'The cold stoves must have been a trial'. 'Actually, there proved to be one coal downstairs live enough to ignite the kindling – and provide the fire there, then to my lamp, and then to the upstairs stove'. 'What fortune!'

19 February 2006

MCXXIV

The day had become bright and surprisingly mild, the wind brisk enough to keep anyone aware as Jasper woke from his slumber. He had not slept well in years, not since he began working with John at the Foundry. When he started, Jasper had figured he would get used to John's schedule – working all night and sleeping come morning. At first, he fell into whatever place he could find and dropped into a deep sleep that would last a few hours – but by noon he would be awake. Over time, he did get used to the schedule, but never so as to get more sleep out of it all!

Awake now, Jasper knew he would not go back to sleep. He had *never* managed to be comfortable sleeping long during the day. And he half-suspected he would have a real hard time shifting to a more "normal" sleep-at-night pattern now, were he to try.

With resignation to all that this time had wrought for him, Jasper roused himself from his chosen corner of the Foundry and fashioned himself before migrating to where he could see outdoors and discover what this day he had been sleeping through was like. The day was bright and surprisingly mild as Jasper stepped into the brisk wind and caught his loose jacket about his torso.

Asserting his presence to the day, Jasper leaned against the wind and stepped onto the Fields. The Sun, high overhead, warmed so that he soon let his jacket lie open over his chest, to be not so thoroughly, suffocatingly over-warm. As no one was in sight or notice, Jasper shuffled across the Fields, headed toward the path leading to the 'Y' and thence around the Big Rock onto the Commons and toward the Inn-by-the-Bye, where he anticipated finding a lunch to assuage this hunger that accompanied his rising. Shuffling along, Jasper allowed himself to become preoccupied with vague suggestions to his mind – all of them meaningless, really.

In this shifting, preoccupied condition, Jasper paid no attention to his general environment; he was concentrated on these vague suggestions, as his mind supplied them – and the relevant meaningless tenor of it all. As a result, he was totally surprised by the sound of his name ringing in his ears by a voice not his own. Had he even suspected such an encounter, he would have long since put aside his shuffle for the far more agreeable swagger – or at least a *hint* of the swagger – so as to convey in intimation a direction and purpose, rather than the all-too-obvious disconnectedness of his mien. His *only* purpose was gathering a lunch to allay his hunger: nothing more. But now, this voice not his own planted his own name in his ears: "Jasper!"

With all that needed readjustment in his mind, Jasper continued to shuffle along across the Commons … slowly, perhaps even a bit more slowly, though any change would be at most barely perceptible. He had been alone disconnected, vaguely drawn onward simply by the hunger in his belly. To call that focused would grotesquely drain such a term of nearly all meaning.

He had entered the sunshine, experienced the surprisingly mild day, leaned into the wind, adjusted his jacket to the warmth he was feeling – and none of it really registered. He simply, merely shuffled along. He had glanced and seen no one when he first left the Foundry: that is true – and that was his last flicker of awareness. And now, the sound of a voice not his own came calling his name yet again, struggling against all that massive internal inertia.

Jasper did slow; he sighed while sifting awkwardly through this disruption. In a tardy response, he lifted his head and eased his glance in the direction of the voice. Even though it felt familiar in his ears, he had not yet begun to identify it for himself. Jasper looked: it was Carymba, coming from behind his pace. Her cloak floated on the wind, a billow rising, thence flapping behind her. Her hair blew back, away from her face. She smiled as her syncopated gait pressed to see him face to face; he wondered what she wanted. He waited.

'I saw you round the 'Y'; I was coming down the Valley Road' she explained as she arrived even with him. The exertion and the wind together brought a flush to her face – and her breathing was heavy as she let the appearance of her pleasure in having caught up with him carry it all from her.

Jasper's naturally cynical perspective rattled the entire scene, skewed it with a search for underlying motive. He was having no success. He had known Carymba for a long time, through all sorts of situations – and, at key moments, she had always provided a resolution to his situations. He had *never* been able to pin any ulterior motive on her; she was distressingly open and free.

Finally, after his lengthened silence, Jasper stammered out his intentions: 'I am ... just going ... to the, uh, Inn-by-the-Bye ... for something to eat'. Carymba replied: 'Do you mind if I come along?' 'No ... no... not at all. Why don't you join me?' 'That would be nice'. Carymba smiled brightly and the pair resumed their walk to the Inn-by-the-Bye, taking for themselves a mutually ambling gait. She asked after his work, how he was liking his continued involvement at the Foundry, the odd hours John insisted on keeping for his work. Jasper responded tersely, at first, then found himself relaxing and becoming almost jovial.

Jasper, of course, caught himself; he is *never* jovial! Never had he been jovial: it simply has never been in his system, not even remotely, in the most fragmentary, tangential way. Yet here he was, ambling across the Commons on a lovely day, chatting over the sort of stuff he always had stuffed inside and managed by a process of stewing over the aggravations of life for a while – and then dismissing the murmuring within as not worth the effort, and definitely unproductive of anything of value. He would – once he grew up and learned to control himself a bit – grind his frustrations away and leave them largely ignored. He never talked about them! Yet here he was, answering her questions openly and turning – well – *jovial* about it at that!

Jasper, with Carymba, arrived at the Inn-by-the-Bye. He reached forward to open the door, then let her enter before him. Inside, out of the bright sunshine, the room appeared dark until their eyes adjusted. 'This always takes too long' whispered Carymba. Jasper nodded, forgetting she could see his head move as little as she could see her – only after that exchange did either sense the vague shade of the other in the dimly lighted Foyer.

Almost at once, Jasper realized his foolishness and added a hasty 'yes'. After too long, eyes did adjust to the dim light of the dining room of the Inn-by-the-Bye so that the pair could safely resume their amble – no need for more than that! – to the steps and down into the dining room itself.

Taking a table not far from the paneled door in the paneled wall, the one to Thyruid and Marthuida's room, the conversation continued, and Jasper discovered himself increasingly at ease. A smile creased his face and he nearly chuckled … in spite of himself.

26 February 2006

Appendix I: Texts For Stories

MCI	Matthew 18:21-35
MCII	Philippians 2:1-13
MCIII	Matthew 21:33-46
MCIV	Exodus 32:1-14
MCV	1 Thessalonians 1:1-10
MCVI	Matthew 22:34-46
MCVII	Joshua 3:7-17
MCVIII	1 Thessalonians 4:13-18
MCIX	Matthew 25:14-30
MCX	Ezekiel 34:11-116, 20-24
MCXI	1 Corinthians 1:3-9
MCXII	Mark 1:1-8
MCXIII	Isaiah 61:1-4, 8-11
MCXIV	Romans 16:25-27
MCXV	John 1:1-14
MCXVI	Isaiah 61:10 – 62:3
MCXVII	Acts 19:1-7
MCXVIII	John 1:43-51
MCXIX	Jonah 3:1-5, 10
MCXX	1 Corinthians 8:1-13
MCXXI	Mark 1:29-39
MCXXII	2 Kings 5:1-14
MCXXIII	2 Corinthians 1:18-22
MCXXIV	Mark 9:2-9

Appendix II: The Prequel

Before the Inn-by-the-Bye Stories began in their formal and developing form, the idea of something like them fomented in my mind for some months. It was the year 1979 and increasing comment rumbled around on the use of children's moments in worship. I was pondering just how I might respond to such a wish in my congregation, one which had yet to erupt, when the thought of Children's story came to mind. I played with it for some time and then began a first story.

I shared a copy of the first effort with a likely member of that congregation. The return comment was that she felt it was too heavily endowed with the use of metaphor for children to follow. I took her at her word yet played with the idea for several months. Having begun for 23 December 1979, I continued the next week and on through the end of September 1980.

These first stories were written late in the weekly process, after the sermon was prepared, normally on Thursday. I took the homiletic effort as the start and reflected it into the story; this differs from the eventual pattern which saw the story written before the sermon, usually on Monday before the sermon emerged on Thursday. Whereas, the original notion that informs this Prequel built from the sermon, the long-term result built from the text toward the sermon.

Any number of aspects of these prequel stories – geographical and otherwise – changed in the nearly eleven-month gap between the end of the prequel and the beginning of what proved to be the main run. Names appear in the Prequel that do not exist in the rest of the Stories;

names appear with very different people and situations involved. So, the prequel stories really run on their own basis while also nurturing hints of an imaginary, fairy-tale world that would so generously serve my needs for so many years.

Now I want to lay out the origins that previewed what became the Inn-by-the-Bye Stories that have filled the first twenty-two volumes of this series – and the opening segment of this, the twenty-third and final volume.

William Flewelling

This is the beginning of a trial development of a children's story pattern to go with the sermon of the day. It is to be expected that the story will be written after the sermon is prepared and that it will contextualize the major thrust of the message in the life in the land here introduced. This first sample is for the sermon of 23 December 1979, titled "The Offering", based on Hebrews 10:5-10.

I

There was a low glow a-coming, a dull promise of brightness which brought sleepy eyes to blinking themselves awake. There were two, looking at each other: 'Yes, I am here. Are you?' 'Yes, I am here, too. But where are we? The place is fair and there is a growing light; but which way is East? We seem to be sitting on the Sun, waxed green beneath us'.

Thus, Yves and Betsy entered the strange land of their adventures. Brother and sister, they found themselves in an unknown place, alone together. This was a green and glowing land, a rich and luxurious place which promised to become home. It might as well become home, for they were here and with so much to see, so much to find, so much to do; besides, there was no view of a way back to the before. 'But where are we?' Betsy's question hung out in front of them like an invitation, begging them onward. Of course, the world, this strange new world, lay at their feet; it was before them and behind them and on both sides of them – even between them: Yves and Betsey were there, wholly there; but where?

'Let us start looking around'.

'Ok, Yves. But which way do we go?'

'There is always a but, isn't there, Betsy! Knowing no better, let's go forward, facing from the way we came into this land'.

The land was fair, and the day was pleasant, just the best kind of day for a walk to explore a new place. Walking came easily in the flush of curiosity, and the new home unfolded itself before them. Everywhere, the waxed green glow of what must be day shone beneath them, casting their shadows into a cloudless sky. The shadows flew up, darkening the general green hue of the new world; Betsy noticed things like that.

No one was seen around them as they walked through the countryside; yet, they did not feel alone and abandoned here. Something was different; it was like magic and they could not guess what accompanied them. They did not even try.

'Walking is easy here, Betsy'. 'Yes, Yves, it is easy; but I am getting hungry'. 'Stomachs as well as eyes need nourishment, delights to fill their curious needs for passing on the means of growth'. 'Well said, Yves; I must agree'.

Around the bend they had not noticed coming – it was just suddenly there – a small Inn appeared before them. The Inn was far too small for even Betsy and Yves; but a largish if low table was set out on the green before the Inn. The sign read "Inn-by-the-Bye": a strange name, thought Yves. And a voice from somewhere bid sit themselves down beside the table. The two were startled – and not startled – all at the same time. They had not felt alone on the land so the voice being there did not seem so strange. But, from where did it arise? the Inn-by-the-Bye? They could not tell. They did, however, sit down for they were hungry and a dressed table, even one set so low, promised the possibility of food to address that hunger, properly so.

'I feel silly sitting here! Who do you think is speaking to us? From whence do we suppose that food will come to us? What sort of place do you suppose this is, Betsy?' For all his confidence, Yves was really uncertain about the way things were unfolding in this place. Even bends in the road just happen!

'I do not know. And I do feel silly, too. But, you know, sitting feels good; I was getting tired, and I did not even realize it!'

A short, squat, plump and matronly lady came out of the Inn-by-the-Bye and welcomed the two, offering mugs of drink – milk, really – to the tired explorers. Hers was not the voice they had heard. The mugs, though, were amazing; they were normal mugs for Yves and Betsy ... but they were almost as big as the little lady who brought them with a smile. Betsy and Yves said thank you, for they were grateful for the offering of their hostess. And they asked her where they were. 'What is the name of this land?'

'Hyperbia'. The voice was a man's voice and came from the Inn-by-the-Bye; this was the voice that had bid them be seated. Behind the voice followed a little plump man bearing what was, for him, an enormous platter with a luncheon spread for two. 'My name is Thyruid; she (waving grandly with his spare hand) is Marthuida. We are your hosts at the Inn-by-the-Bye. Eat well!' And, with that, he spread the lunch before them, bowed politely, and returned to the tiny Inn-by-the-Bye.

The gift land was spread before them. They blinked at the thought of the strange little host and hostess, and of the tiny Inn-by-the-Bye in the strangely named land of Hyperbia. Yves and Betsy looked at each other, at this suddenly present food – and, giving thanks, took up the offering, the gift of the strange people, and ate. And they became filled.

Rested and satisfied, Yves and Betsy set out across the waxen meadows of Hyperbia, wondering what sort of land they were now discovering for home and wondering more about Thyruid and Marthuida who came, seemingly from nowhere, to serve them in their need. The place was offering them Home, a great enough gift for any of us: we know it where we find it ... and let it find us.

For the sermon of 30 December 1979, titled "And Jesus Increased", based on Luke 2:22-40.

II

The day had been wearing along slowly as the pair, Yves and Betsy, walked their way from where they were to where they came to be – all about the spacious green meadows of their new land. The walking along, which had been quite spritely earlier, went more slowly now.

Betsy and Yves were seeing much – the land was beautiful and the undercast of the light set the flowers and the plants in a fresh perspective for their joy. Of course, there were not any trees around; with the light coming from below rather than from above, the trees would have no need to stretch their arms to find the Sun. Things were different here; they found it interesting to visit this new home; but, even with each other, both Yves and Betsy began to become lonely. Their living-people-world was small, too small to really know Home.

'Do you remember lunch time, Betsy?' 'Yes. That Inn-by-the-Bye was such a surprise!' 'Even more, there were Thyruid and Marthuida – they talked to us!' 'That is right! And we have not heard another voice, besides our own, all day long! It is a strange world we have found, Yves. Do you suppose that we are really all alone?' 'I have not thought so all day long – but now I am wondering. Perhaps we should try to find that Inn-by-the-Bye again – but, looking back, the paths we followed all crisscross and wind together: we would *never* find it again'. 'Well, Yves' said Betsy dryly, 'do we sit here, go on a piece, or go back?' 'All we *can* do, Betsy, is to on … and hope'.

A few steps down the path, a turn in the road appeared – it was not in sight just a minute ago – and the magic of the land appeared before their eyes, for they actually looked to see it sparkling before them. 'Betsy, it is the Inn-by-the-Bye! The sign is the same – I would recognize it anywhere. But the Inn looks different. Where are we now?'

'Still in Hyperbia, my children'. The voice was followed by the gruff friendliness of Thyruid, strutting out the door of his Inn. 'The great light beneath us here is fading for night and rest – just as it shines for day and the adventures of the day. The road always turns to the Inn-by-the-Bye whenever it is needed. Hyperbia always answers the cry of her guests – like you two, like Marthuida (who had come out behind them with great mugs of milk) and myself, like all the shy folk who do not intrude, but are always Come when there is need of them. We only arrive when we are needed'. With that, Marthuida set the mugs before Yves and Betsy so they might satisfy their thirst.

And, suddenly, there were with the Innkeeper and his wife a host of wee folk, Come – as Thyruid put it – to share themselves shyly, respectfully with Yves and Betsy. For the children were lonely and longed for people to share their lives with, longed for people to make this place Home. And, of course, they all shared themselves with each other as well; they just do things like that, inclusively.

The glow underfoot was fading away and the shadows deepened as the joy of togetherness was being shared among the many – a many which now marvelously included Yves and Betsy, the newest and most oversized visitors to Hyperbia's amaze-filled land.

It was Relax-time – we would call it evening, but we are only eavesdropping on Hyperbia – and everyone swarmed around a low, glowing fire. Thyruid and Marthuida were busy bringing out food and refreshments from the Inn, all for the helping crowd. They were all chatting and laughing with their fellow-guests in this bounty-land they call Hyperbia.

The fire lingered long as new friendships were born or renewed among the many, the host and hostess, and Yves and Betsy, the new visitors to this magic land. The children found everyone gentle and respectful as they sampled the untold riches of each other – and the children as well.

For Yves and Betsy, it all began that Relax-time as Hyperbia took another step toward becoming Home for them. They found this day complete with these caring wee folk who made them at home, and Hyperbia Home for them.

For the Sermon of 6 January 1980, titled "Of This Gospel", based on Ephesians 3:1-12

III

Morning was coming again. The glow, tinted green, which characterized the Hyperbian day, was just beginning its certain shine.

'Betsy'. 'Yes, Yves?' 'Do you remember last night, with the warmth of all those wee people about us, and the Inn-by-the-Bye?' 'Yes. It was good to find friends to share the evening with – and ourselves with them, too'. 'Where did they come from, then? And where did they all go now? Are we just dreaming?' 'A full stomach last night and all those good times are more than dreams, Yves; they are real. The food alone assures that, and the friendliness even more so!' 'You are right, Betsy; that sort of friendship is real for it met us solidly in terms we could understand – yet consistent with this magical land'.

Yves and Betsy were new to Hyperbia; the ways of this strange and new land were only beginning to stir within them. That there was indeed a difference here was eminently clear. They found broad expanse, open land properly enlightened for their daily walk, gently darkened for their nightly rest. They found fellowship and refreshment when it was needed. There was a senses of presence about them; their feet were guided in a time of wonderment; their eyes danced across the sparkling mystery of Hyperbia's faceted presentation of itself. They set out once more, bounding across the land, feasting themselves on the still and ever newness of this place. 'Betsy, I think that everything is new, seen for the first time and the forty-zillionth time – all at once'.

The specialness of the day rose to meet them, step by step. Those wee folk who had enchanted them with a mass of friendliness were now seen along the way, scattered at their tasks. Had they been there all along, present but unseen because eyes were not seeing? Betsy wondered. Their presence had been felt. They themselves presented the strange and yet not-strange feel of this place.

Carymba, the waif who danced the hobbler's dance about the table, over the frothy, pungent drink which sharpened the tongue and tickled the nose, refreshing and enlivening – the milk of the mugs of Marthuida at that Inn-by-the-Bye – she cried out: 'Wait! My Friends! Betsy! Yves! These little legs do not hobble so fast as yours!'

Surprised by the clear ring of her voice, the pair spun around, anxiously seeking the source of the call only to find her suddenly under their noses. 'Here I am' she bubbled in the triumph of having arrived. 'This hobbling about is necessary for me – and the pace will be necessary for you should you agree to come along with little Carymba'. The impish companion along the way brought a slower step and a broader smile as Betsy and Yves wandered freshly across the glowing green of Hyperbia's mystic light-underfoot.

'Even smiles look different, Yves, when the shine sends shadows up for the chin to the nose'. 'Yes, Betsy, but aren't we glad that food and drink are not swallowed *up* rather than the convenient, the familiar, down!' 'Oh, don't be silly!' chimed in Carymba. 'Ours are not a strange land. This is the way of life we have shown – and been shown. It rings naturally to us'.

'Carymba, walking at your pace, we will never get anywhere – but we sure do see more than I ever thought possible. I had not noticed all those little flowers, nor the friendly smiles hidden away behind – behind – … well, behind my not-looking-before!' Carymba laughed at Yves, an infectious giggle which rippled about the hills of new-home Hyperbia and tickled the heart as well as the ears. 'You must slow down to see what there is to see. Here in Hyperbia, there is much to see of Home; but you have to look, my friend. You have to look'.

About the sudden bend, just newly arrived before them, arose the Inn-by-the-Bye. 'We are here' bubbled Carymba, 'because I am hungry. Are you?'

'Yes!' 'Yes!' 'And here are Marthuida's giant mugs of pleasant welcome. And there is the booming presence of wee Thyruid'. 'There too another day of Home unveiling its presence before our barely seeing eyes' added Yves.

The fellowship of friends, new seen though there before; the mingled aromas of a feasting spread, newly smelled and inviting all the more; the fading lights of a new Resting time; and Home spread widely before the door of the Inn-by-the-Bye, beneath the careful, watchful stewardship of the master and mistress of the house, before their attending, filling eyes; the Inn-by-the-Bye, Thyruid beaming, Carymba dancing, Marthuida bearing mugs too big for her, and a host of hostlings – all these made special the unveiling days of Hyperbia, new Home of Yves and Betsy, oversized children … but visitors less, homebodies more.

For the sermon of 13 January 1980, titled "Wheat and Chaff: Pleasing", based on Luke 3:15-17, 21-22

IV

Yves looked at Betsy, his mug in his hand, a wide moustache etched clown-like across his face in dripping milk, and he smiled: 'This is coming to be Home, isn't it, Betsy? It takes a while sometimes for the heart to adapt to new places, new ways, new people – but this place, this Hyperbia is becoming Home. It *feels* good'.

Betsy smiled wistfully, remembering how they had begun this new adventure in Hyperbia. Setting aside her drained mug, she wiped away the tell-tale signs of her delight-filled enjoyment of Marthuida's finest. 'Yves, do you ever wonder what would have happened if we had gone down a different trail than the one we took?'

'No. I cannot say that I have ever imagined *that*'. Yves was horribly practical and was always impatient with Betsy's "what-if ..." questions, particularly about things that had already happened. 'What shall we do today?' he asked: anything was fine if it got Betsy off her "what-if ..." meanderings.

Marthuida, noticing that both children had finished their mugs of milk, toddled out pleasantly to retrieve them – the mugs, that is – and greeted them with her tender smile. 'Are ye finished now, my friends? Aye, and isn't it a lovely day'. The gentle mistress of the Inn-by-the-Bye prattled on in the relaxed tension of the morning. (The day itself was relaxed ... but the "what-if ..." mood of Betsy was bothering Yves, and Yves' huff was bothering Betsy, yielding the tension into which the friendly chatter of wee Marthuida entered.

'Marthuida, I was *just* wondering how things would have been different for us if we had taken a different start when we came here – you know, going down a different path at the first. And Yves always gets put-out with me when I wonder what our choices have made of us. Do you think that is fair?'

'Well, well, my child' said Marthuida, setting down again her giant mugs – they were each nearly as big as she – 'I think much too much is made of this. Of course, how you start makes a difference. But the start, in our land, was your coming to the Inn-by-the-Bye for the first time; it was not your first guessing step but your first greeting with the makers of this place. Then, the choice did matter'. And, hoisting again the great mugs, she toddled playfully into the Inn.

Betsy and Yves looked at each other … and kept looking at each other for a few minutes. Finally, Betsy spoke: 'It is light now; let's go walking, just to see what there is to see'. 'Ok. Let's go'. And together, side by side, they ambled off, exploring again their new Home, their new growing Home: Hyperbia.

The two walked slowly, more concerned to see the obvious – like those funny little white flowerets peeking shyly out of the green by the way and perfuming the air, and the wee folk now seen working along the way, busy but always ready with a smile for every eye which catches the sight of them … indeed, all the things Carymba had taught them in her hobbled gait.

They became more interested in experiencing the gracious place of life than in just getting someplace. And who knows where they had been hurrying, trying to get? They did not: that is for sure. It was just a habit … and they had not known.

'Look Yves, a wee man! Shh, though: I think he is napping'. 'I am *not* napping. Most definitely not, young lady' snapped a voice too large and too ferocious for the size and apparent dignity of the resting man. 'I am thinking. I think a lot. And closing my eyes, sometimes, helps. It cuts down on distractions, you know. Humph. Now, where was I?'

'I am sorry, sir' answered Betsy quietly and half afraid. 'We did not mean to upset you. It is just that you … you … you looked so dignified and important when I saw you lying against that leaf. I do not remember you from the gatherings at the Inn-by-the-Bye'. 'Of *course* not! I was not there. How could you see me there if I was not there to be seen?' 'Oh' was all that poor timid Betsy could reply.

Yves, just now finding his tongue in the muddle of the excitement and surprise, stammered out: 'W ... w ... w ... well, then, who, may I ask, are you?' 'I suppose you must ask' grumbled the wee man so neatly dressed, so proper in appearance and so vicious with his tongue. 'My name is Geoffrey ... Geoffrey of Cumberland, a gentleman's gentleman by trade and sorely out of work since coming to this place from my – uh – former home. I ought to go back but I have lost the way. And this place is so cold. Why, you two are the first who have said two words to me!'

'Have you given anyone else two words? or is it just grump when your fine suit meets them?' 'What do you mean, child? I have no place! A man, a gentleman *must* have a place'. 'Ah, my sir, you must first have a beginning. Marthuida told us that this morning – didn't she, Betsy?' 'Oh – yes indeed, Yves. And, if you need a place, come with us, around this bend you did not see before ...'. 'Come, with *you*?!' 'Yes. Be our gentleman, if you must, and a new friend, if you will'. 'Why, all right; and, perhaps, the two names will fit together, at that!'

The Resting time congregation appeared around the Inn-by-the-Bye. Their mugs – small for the wee folk, giant size for the children – were spread on the table. The talk as Yves and Betsy led Geoffrey near was all smooth and friendly-like. Yves called out: 'Carymba! Meet out new friend, Geoffrey of Cumberland!' Before she could speak, she heard: 'Um ... um ... hello, Carymba'. 'And hello to you, sir ... rather, Geoffrey. Shall we have a pleasant Resting time? Here, have a fresh mug!'

For the sermon of 20 January 1980, titled "No Silence", based on Isaiah 62:1-5.

V

Geoffrey of Cumberland hastily set down his morning mug upon the table at the Inn-by-the Bye and, momentarily forgetting his dignity in the rush of the moment, scrambled over the dawning land of Hyperbia after his new-found friends, Yves and Betsy.

'This is terrible' thought the ever-proper Geoffrey. 'I would never, ever have done this before. Never! It is a shock to a gentleman to scramble in such an undignified way after those to whom he is to be a gentleman. Once I was a gentleman's gentleman! And now I am to be a gentleman and a friend to a pair of lively children who eat too fast and take off before these poor legs can catch them'. 'Oh! Wait! Wait for me!' he finally panted to the children ... who did stop to wait for their friend and gentleman (though they had much to learn of the ways of a gentleman!).

'We are sorry, Geoffrey' chanted his new friends. 'We are not used to having a gentleman yet. Remember, we are not from Cumberland. But then, we are all in Hyperbia now; we might as well get used to that fact' bubbled Betsy.

'Yes. Yes. I suppose we must. But what *is* Hyperbia, anyway? There are you two, I know. But you say that you are new here, too ... and you are certainly bigger than the rest of us here. Even I noticed that!' Geoffrey blushed at the quickness of his words, a strangeness to him because a gentleman by profession would never, ever confess to not keeping his tongue in strictest and slowest control.

'Oh yes, there is also that hobbling girl ... Carymba ... and the Inn-by-the-Bye: I guess this place is not so bad. I guess there is promise here ...'. And Geoffrey wandered along, seeing nothing, absorbed in the thoughts racing around in his mind.

Geoffrey's mood was catching. Together, the three of them ambled slowly across the green-glowing meadows, watched along their way by all the wee people along their path. All three of them had slipped into reveries, recounting privately the paths that had brought them together here, pondering in long silence what sort of openings the future might hold for them. As brave and as brash as they like to appear – particularly Yves – before all the others, they were really very uncertain about this new place. And so the day went: They passed along, wandering aimlessly, going nowhere in fact, and seeing nothing but their own beclouded faces.

The wee people of Hyperbia sensed the unformed questions were brewing behind the tight-drawn brows of Yves and Betsy – and of their funny little friend, Geoffrey of Cumberland. My, but those names sounded funny to the natives of Hyperbia. But, in their own special way, the Hyperbians were glad to have this new company among them. There was felt to be a sense of promise in their bumbling – by Hyperbian standards – ways. The question scurried along the string and around the networks of the wee folk: 'How do we meet these three new friends in their thoughtful shift from the things which are real *here* – the hopes and the promises, the challenges of Hyperbia – to something else?' At the end of the line of questioning sat Thyruid and Marthuida, at the Inn-by-the-Bye. And, at the table in the corner, dreamed little Carymba.

'What do you think they are thinking?' mused Marthuida, busying her plump fingers with unnecessary details about the Inn. 'What do I care?' growled Thyruid; and, answering his own question, he muttered: 'a lot. That is what!' 'I really do not know Geoffrey very well. He is so … so … so different than everyone else around here. And he is new, too. Yet, he us a perky character and seems so comfortable about Yves and Betsy. Huh. He calls himself their "gentleman", whatever that is. And whatever those children might need a gentleman for, and one from the wee folk. The children are so nice, and they fit into the Resting time circle at the Inn so well – in spite of their dreadful size!' Thus did Marthuida ramble.

'Do you think they like us?' queried little Carymba. 'I mean, all of us here – do they like Hyperbia?' She stammered to complete her blush.

'Huh?' grunted the ever-preoccupied Thyruid. 'Why, yes. I suppose they do like us. Why not?' 'Why do they wander so bluely?' asked Marthuida, fumbling her fingers with more energy – and full of annoyance at her husband not paying any attention to what she was saying. Indignantly, the two gazed at each other while Carymba hobbled quietly out the door. 'I am going for a walk' she said. 'Fine. Fine' the Innkeeper and his wife muttered in unison. 'We have things to think about'. 'Yes. Good-Bye for now' returned the retreating Carymba.

The little waif hobbled out, full of concern that all the wee folk bore over the way the three newcomers were acting this day. The three were acting so preoccupied that it made everything seem black – even the characteristic green glow of day – for the wee folk. Their day was cold; it was like those three were all alone, abandoned by something important. Carymba felt it all closely.

Carymba looked about, and the whole land lay in front of her, nearly silent. It was ghostly. Carymba shuddered and hobbled her way along until she saw the three walking slowly, aimlessly about, their eyes glassy, unseeing and their heads bent, their feet shuffling along unwillingly, automatically.

'Yves! Betsy! Geoffrey! I need to see you!' she cried out, surprising herself more than the three friends now drawn back from their thoughts. 'I need you!' And all the wee folk along the way wondered: 'What now?'

Looking up, startled and suddenly aware once more of each other … and of Carymba … they smiled. The smiles were little ones at first; then, they grew to bigger ones, and bigger ones yet until their very biggest burst onto their faces. 'You need us, Carymba?'

'Yes' she sighed as she hobbled up to them. 'Let's go find the Inn-by-the-Bye and gruff old Thyruid and little Marthuida and her mugs. Let us go together'. 'Good': they all agreed.

The road turned again and they all came to the Inn, to the worried pair, Thyruid and Marthuida, and to the wee folk who were hurrying in, for it was time to be pleased and together.

For the sermon of 3 February 1980, titled "Fulfilled Before Us", based on Luke 4:21-30.

VI

Over in the corner of the hill, away from the always earful Inn-by-the-Bye, secluded and setting in the shade of the blanket thrown beneath them, huddled together several of the wee folk. 'Remember the way it used to be here, when life was quiet, and those troublesome newcomers had not yet come to disrupt our ways?'

The rumbled speech came from a wiry little man with a stubble beard, grumbling unhappily about the way things had been going of late. 'That is right, Orgello' affirmed another, a younger man who really did not remember anything other than the stories of the days of yore. But then, neither did Orgello, the oldest and leader of the unhappy crew.

Geron, the youngest, the one who responded, pictured in his mind a world, a Hyperbia as of old, where glory came to those who held to the old ways, the traditions of the favorite fathers. 'Orgello, tell us again what it would be like if we ran things our way, without the meddling Innkeeper and his overstuffed wife, without that gimpy imp – Carymba, without that stuffed shirt – Geoffrey of Cumberland, and without those overgrown pups, Yves and Betsy. Tell us again how great it would be, just as it used to be when things were done properly, and the important people were respected'. 'Yes, tell us again, Orgello!' returned the handful of the unhappy.

'Oh, yes' scowled Orgello. 'Those were the days! The old families received their proper respect; they took care of their friends, too, just as they should. It was my father's father Jorgano who ruled then. There were no strangers in this land, and everything went as it should. Jorgano saw to that. I tell you, we who inherited the place from of old made the decisions and nobody dared stick themselves into the circle of ruling fathers. The fathers would take care of their own and keep out disruptive voices from speaking about the decisions of the elders. Things should be like that again. *We* should be the circle of ruling fathers now. Then, we would not have trouble with these … these … these strangers!'

What Orgello said pleased the group, a sad set who felt they needed someone else to fall into order that they might find themselves important with an importance they could not find within. Geron reflected the feelings of the moment: 'Yes, then people would know we are important, just like our fathers under Jorgano'.

In all their huddling excitement, they had not noticed that another had joined them. This one, too, was from an old family, though not from the circle of the ruling fathers. 'I remember the stories of the days of Jorgano, too. Then it was that another man, Priastes, had said to the worried ruling fathers that things would be different some day. Instead of their bunglement would come a gentle hand to open a promise of a new day here in Hyperbia'.

The voice belonged to the great grandson of Priastes and his heir in spirit. It was Paranates, one of the wee folk, one who should not have been about this dark cloud of a blanket where so much darkness clung and so much cold stirred about with a sputtering wind.

Geron leaped up: 'We know your kind! You are the source of our problem! There is no respect for your betters in you!' Orgello scowled in assent to his pupil in hate. 'Things will be better when we rule as did our fathers!'

'Say what you will, my dismal, beclouded countrymen, but there is more light here – off the blanket – than there; there is more hope in the limp of Carymba than in your stomping rage'. And, with that, Paranates turned and left. The unsure grumblers watched him amble across the glowing fields, away from their darkened blanket spot.

As Orgello and Geron urged their attention, the grumpy group saw the happy skip of Yves and Betsy and the hustling Geoffrey, holding onto his top hat, the gentle giggle of Carymba as he fell down, failing to keep up, and the open smiles of the circle as those newcomers approached the suddenly-there turn to the Inn-by-the-Bye.

The heirs of the circle of ruling fathers looked from their gloom and saw a bright fullness. Out from their heritage of a narrow pride they stepped. There was one step; then another; then a walk; then a run; then a sprint to join the promise unfolding in smiles and laughter, open caring, sharing, living by the careful labors of Marthuida and her mugs, Thyruid and his booming welcome. Those old timers were becoming newcomers, finding a joy they had never known.

Back in the corner of the field, away from things new-fangled, the two remainders – Orgello and Geron – huddled on their shading blanket. They looked at each other and kept on their blinders. Distractions from the light would only hurt their gloomy fantasy of a bleak glory that never was.

'Have another?' called out Marthuida. The old-timers who were strangely new and happy here wondered 'Who?' 'You' she bubbled. 'Ok' they agreed.

For the sermon of 10 February 1980, titled "Of First Importance", based on 1 Corinthians 15:1-11.

VII

Two leftovers of grumbling malcontent lay huddled together, licking their wounds like a pair of soundly defeated cats ... even though they had never come to blows with anyone over anything. It only seemed as if they had after their old supporters had tried the comforts of the enemy camp, deserting the prisons of self-terror, selfishness and hate to which Orgello and Geron clung so fiercely. Their corners had become dark and dingy while they had settled into a habit of deep confinement. When eyes and hearts are accustomed to the dark, light hurts and, hurting, frightens.

'Some things are important' grumbled the habitually unhappy Orgello. Geron grunted in angered agreement: 'Yes, we are important. The heritage we have as sons of rulers – that is important'. And, gloomily, they squatted in their shadows, walled away from any new possibilities arising in a world happily different from that of old Orgello's pompous paternal grandfather.

Now, this grumpy pair did not spend all their time in huddled, grumpy secrecy. And by no means were they shut out of the rest of the land of Hyperbia. They would have been welcomed within the pleasant sphere of Thyruid's Inn-by-the-Bye, the gathering place of the land, under the bubbling hospitality of the "Mother Hen", Marthuida. A seat would have been found for them about the circle of friendliness at the Resting time – what we who are just occasional visitors, privileged to peek into Hyperbia's magic realm, call evening. As their former allies in Grump, they could have come and been welcomed in the chatter of Carymba and Geoffrey, of Betsy and Yves, and of all the rest. But Orgello and Geron preferred the walls of Grump to the circle before the Inn-by-the-Bye. They avoided that always sudden curve in the road, turning back instead to their preferred Grump.

Along the edges of Hyperbia, the Hyperbia of today which they did not like, Orgello and Geron moved. They did their work; they earned their pay. A man has to eat, after all, even if he is of the wee folk and lives in

Hyperbia. Engulfed in Grump, the two companions in misery sat back, out past the edges of Hyperbian wee folk, and watched.

It is not that they wanted to get involved with the likes of those they watched. No. No. They were far too important for such degrading activities as that! Those old fools who used to bask in their Grump may have fallen aside through the nonsense of Priastes, refreshed by that fool Paranates – but these two, Orgello and Geron: they knew better. They clung to their precious Grump which no one else had any interest in taking up for themselves. Orgello and Geron had no competition for their land of Grump. They watched, nonetheless. And they watched in disbelief. Those folk out at the Inn-by-the-Bye just made no sense at all! For here is what they saw from their kingdom of Grump:

Little Carymba, the girl with the hobbling gait and the broadening smile, limped badly across the meadow. She had a rough going of it and she was tired from her rounds. She could not do very much and had always been one to move about the others. She would give a little hand here and there, an extra hold and a giggling smile.

Somehow, no one ever really noticed Carymba's hobble because of her bubbling smile. She was not very important, but always welcome as she never took herself too seriously and, strangely confident in herself, she always pointed beyond herself – somewhere. Orgello and Geron certainly did not know where. 'Look at that fool!' sneered Geron.

'She is almost as bad as that newcomer – Geoffrey of Cumberland. Nobody should wear those clothes. He puts on such airs of importance; that is what he does! Exactly that! Humph! A gentleman's gentleman, indeed!' The scoff came from Orgello, the prince of Grump. 'Look. He is going to bother that worthless, hobbling imp. Such as they are, they deserve each other'.

Geoffrey gently took up the basket Carymba had been carrying and wandered along with her, pleasantly, at her speed, pausing to greet all the workers along the way, lending a little hand in a pinch He just liked to do it; that was quite reason enough. All the wee folk – outsiders to the kingdom of Grump – welcomed them both. Life was bigger than just today for them, and much bigger than yesterday or the day before.

Betsy and Yves ran across the meadow, stumbling and rolling as the children they are – only horribly large for this land of Hyperbia. In the laughter of childhood, they came to the always open Inn-by-the-Bye with the opening circle ready before it. The enormous mugs came out, carried by the same sized Marthuida. Geoffrey and Carymba came in to join them. And so did the others, almost all the wee folk. They came together happily, freely for what was important included them all and permitted them to come to the broad place.

'Humph. Fools. All of them!' And the citizens of Grump turned away, for they were too important for the likes of those who would come to the Inn-by-the-Bye.

For the sermon of 17 February 1980, titled "The Meeting", based on Luke 9:28-36.

VIII

The glow of Hyperbia seemed a little brighter today; the grass was a little greener, a little softer to the eyes fresh opened and the toes fresh wiggled in the soft caress of the little blades of green. The fragrance of the hills filled her nostrils; the green of the meadows overflowed her eyes in the expectations of the day; the quiet of the morning pasture settled upon her ears, a delight in the full absence of noise. The day and all about it responded to the touch of hope appropriately for Betsy. It was as if the day and her mood and her task had sprung together from the same benevolent hand.

Betsy remembered a very few days which had come so fittingly. There was the day when the warm, soft Spring rain dripped gently down the windowpanes in rhythm with her musing, nearly bright sadness. And she knew well the day the silent fall of Winter white freshened the world with a coat of jewels in harmony with the lively air felt in friendship shared. Today, too, was something special. But then, Betsy began to run out of days.

This was a day to herself; Betsy had planned it that way. As she ambled pleasantly along, she enjoyed the chance to be alone. Brothers and sisters are nice – and so are friends – and we need them, and to be with them; but there are times when there is nothing in the world like being alone. It is a matter of choosing those time, for there are other times when there is absolutely nothing worse than being alone.

This morning, for Betsy, was a day for being alone; it was right for today. Betsy felt like a free-winged bird as she wandered about the path-marked meadows of Hyperbia. Betsy mused to herself: 'What a day it is to retire with myself and my thoughts and my feelings. Things have been so busy lately – so busy – why, there has not been time to sort it all out for myself, all these things, all these people, all these places. A day of retreat for the sake of assembling myself and my experiences – that is what I have needed. Today had come and is cooperating gloriously!

121

'Now, where do I begin? … There has been *so much* packed into the last few days. It seems like dear Geoffrey is always near. He is never in the way and I am always glad to see him: that is true. Yet … somehow it is good to be away where it does not seem that he is behind every turn in my mind. The funny little man … why ever did he latch onto Yves and me? I should be glad, I guess; he is really a comfort and knows just what is right, all the time'. To herself, Betsy chuckled as these thoughts strung themselves through her memory. Her shy smile crept along.

'Yves, too. What would the world be like without someone like Yves? He is ornery. He is stuck on his own ideas. He is bossy – *that* is true! – and he does not like to hear any of *my* ideas. He is as terrible as can be … but what would it be like without his laugh and tease? What would I do without him to listen to me? or at least pretend to listen to me? or pretend not to listen to me?! He is the only one here who is *my* size. Besides all that, he is my brother; that ought to count for something, I guess.

'All those wee folk – they are dears. I love them all in their funny little ways. But today, I am finally alone and maybe this will let me get things straight for myself. I have needed this for a long time now – a day to myself, without the pressures of the people and the land, of the hopes and of the dreams. A day to myself – and it is just a beautiful day for such a meandering'.

'It is funny. Now that I am by myself, I feel less alone than ever before. This meadow – how it glows today. Strangely. It is as if the grass were on fire for me. Yet it is soft and warm, soothing to my feet. I had never noticed that before. Could it be that the land has always pressed so firmly and warmly on me? Hyperbia seems alive today, alive and close upon me. I want to roll in the grass and laugh and laugh as never before. The grass seems to call me to roll and rejoice in it. Does it always do that – and I just never noticed it before? Is anyone watching me? No. I do not see anyone watching. I will look again … no one. So, here goes!'

And so, Betsy plunged herself into the grass and rolled and rolled like a puppy at play. From deep, deep inside her rose a laugh; she rolled and laughed with her whole body, her whole soul. 'I hear the laughter of the meadow ... the grass is laughing with me. Was there ever such joy? or have I lost it all? Is nothing real, or is this more real than anything?

'I remember from before, before Hyperbia became home – it was old Mr. Clyde; folks said he was crazy, but he never laughed like this. Did he hear the meadow laugh? Did he feel this sort of ... of ... of happiness beyond happiness? He was different than the others, so maybe he did. I do not know. But I sure hear it and feel it. It is like being alone and not alone, all at the same time. It is like meeting myself and this grass about me for the very first time. It is so different that anything I have known. It is great! It is ...'.

Betsy's thoughts slipped off beyond the realm of words and she sat in the warm embrace of the green glowing meadow grass, the laughing grass of Hyperbia. It was warm and soft – and so right today. 'The grass, the laughing grass: it is all about me. It will stay. And so will all that unknown more. I am sure'. So she thought to herself, pleasantly.

Yves smiled to her from across the way, on the next rise. 'Are you ready, Betsy?' 'Yes! I am coming. It has been a good day'. And she bounced, newly met, to meet Yves and find the others, just around the bend that was not there before, at the Inn-by-the-Bye.

For the Sermon of 24 February 1980, titled "Thus Were You", based on Deuteronomy 26:5-11

IX

'Marthuida, we have a good Inn' confided Thyruid as he worked at his morning chores – polishing the brass, cleaning the Common Room, getting everything set for the next day. Right now, he was polishing the great brass balls which shone the announcement of the Inn's inner staircase. They were his favorite items, particularly when they shone just right. He was proud of them.

'Yes, this is a good Inn' said Marthuida, a bit more awake than her subdued husband as she worked along with him – leaving all the precious brass to *his* care, as he wants her to do. She teased him a bit: 'Yes, this is the very best Inn around these parts. The *very* best'. Her eyes sparkled at her dear Thyruid as his customary flush pushed back the lethargy of the morning. One could almost see the scales of sleepy laziness fall from behind him behind the rush.

'Of course', he bellowed in his new day's awake-ness, 'this is the only Inn around these parts. And, mind you, even if it were not alone in its class, it would still be best. After all', his tone softened to add, 'what other Inn could brag of my Marthuida and her giant mugs?'

Marthuida blushed appreciatively and turned aside, suddenly busy with her duster.

Some time passed before Thyruid spoke again. 'Well, it must be mid-morning by now; I want to take a break over a mug of Marthuida's special'. 'Pick a table, then, and I will bring us two mugs' said Marthuida as she moved her portly self into the kitchen to retrieve the treat for Thyruid and herself. There was no point in letting him sit alone; he would just feel bad if she kept on working while he was taking a break. Besides, a rest sounded like a good idea – and she always enjoyed sitting and chatting with Thyruid. She was funny that way. 'Here we go' came the call down

124

the hall as the mugs danced their way to the table in the sure hands of the mistress of the Inn.

After enjoying deeply a long draught, Thyruid wiped his ample face and sighed. 'Life here with you is good, Marthuida. But it was not always like this'.

'No, it was not. Things were hard once … back then, back there. Poor Papa, poor Mama! Their lives just creeped along. Remember Mama's hands, Thyruid?

'Yes, they were red and rough and sore all the days I knew her. She worked hard, bless her. But she worked for precious little in return – money or satisfaction. The harder she worked, the less she had. The boss saw to that'. Thyruid scowled at the memory, too fresh for the years.

'Poor Mama, I think that I could not bear up under that load of sadness and labor. If the people she worked for had just been nice …'. Marthuida's merely trailed off into the past.

'It broke your Papa, too. He hurt too deeply, and he could do nothing about it. I would have been stuck too, if we had not had our one chance!'

'Yes, our one chance … after all these years, it is still hard to believe. It happened so quickly. We were there – in the Jaws as Papa called them – and suddenly we were here in a very different Hyperbia. All we brought was ourselves and a shudder at the snapping of … you remember'.

'It cannot be forgotten, really. It was a night. What a terror the nights were! You could only feel the hot breath of the Boss then; you could not see him to defend yourself. The knock at the door. Oh, my, do I remember that knock; it rang through the house and echoed sharply in the fearful corners of our hearts. My insides felt like jagged ice: rough and cold. I was afraid to open the door – but more afraid not to open it. So, I did, slowly, carefully. There was a little old woman there … with rough hands and a gentle look. We were used to rough working hands, but the gentle look was not usual. Anything gentle there was strange'.

125

'You offered her a drink, Marthuida; no one greeted strangers there, but you did. There was nothing else to do there in the night. She drank. Oh, how long she drank from that cup of water! Then, she said to come. … She had work for us to do'.

'Yes, Thyruid, my hands trembled. My knees shook. But we went with her, anyway, stepping beyond the door into the night. We found ourselves quickly outside the valley … walking, walking, walking … climbing, climbing, climbing beyond anything we had ever known or even suspected'.

'Yes, yes. We walked into that cloud. I could see nothing, not even my hand in front of my face. And, at the end of the cloud, we were alone. The last words I heard were: Do not forget: The cup of water: Do not forget'

'Is anyone here? It is time for lunch; and I am hungry!' The big voice came from outside; it was Yves who never had smudged Thyruid's great brass balls with his hands – because he was too, too big to get inside the Inn-by-the-Bye, even a little bit. Thyruid bellowed: 'Of course! Make yourself at ease! Just a moment, please!'

By then, Marthuida was out with a mug of water and a mug of milk. The Inn remembers Mama and Papa and the strange old woman who sent them to work their Inn: a knock and a cup of water to the least of these.

For the Sermon of 2 March 1980, titled "In The Lord", based on Philippians 3:17 – 4:1.

X

'They do not understand. They do not understand. They just do not understand. That is all I can say about this situation, about this ... this mess!' So muttered Geoffrey to himself as he finished preparing himself for the day at hand. Things had not gone easily for him of late. Why, O why had he ever had to come from Cumberland, a far more sophisticated land where gentlemen had gentlemen to wait upon them. He, Geoffrey, had been a very good gentleman's gentleman, knowing when to pour the tea or port and when to wait, knowing when to go ahead and make the necessary arrangements and when to hold back, knowing how always to secure the gentleman's advantage. That was his trade. 'And I was good at it, too!' said Geoffrey out loud, startling even himself. 'Well, I guess I am ready for another day. Where shall those children go today? ... Imagine, I am now the gentleman to a pair of oversized children who do not know what a gentleman is, let alone a gentleman's gentleman'.

'Geoffrey! Are you ready *yet*?!' called in unison Yves and Betsy. The day was bright already, and they were more than ready to go about their travels for the day. They knew that they were bigger than all the wee folk; they knew that all those wee folk worked at their jobs every day; but they played more than they worked for they were young, just children. A lot like Geoffrey, they added spice and sparkle to Hyperbia; they lived here and were finding it more and more to be "home". And, a lot like Geoffrey, they had not yet really given themselves over to the openness of this land, as they found it among the not-so-recent newcomers such as Thyruid and Marthuida, and like Carymba and so many of the other wee folk. They had kept and carried with them the habits of a lifetime – no matter how short it had been until now – across the threshold into an entirely new land, a place as unique as Hyperbia. It seemed so little, this carry-over, like a tiny pebble on a road; but it wore itself on the inside of the shoe, wearing sore the stepping foot.

'Coming. Coming! Wait up and all will be well!' cried Geoffrey of Cumberland as he came down the stairs, almost too fast, before he caught himself on the pride of Thyruid, the freshly polished brass ball. He still thought of himself as Geoffrey of Cumberland – except for the problem that Geoffrey was not in Cumberland anymore. Not only that but, like the children, he did not really want to back, even if he could. To go back would be to lose too much.

'Finally! I wish you could go a little faster, Geoffrey. We get tired of waiting for you'. 'Then stop waiting. What is your hurry anyway? The day has hardly begun at all'.

'With such an exchange, the wee folk around here will think you have deserted to the "kingdom of Grump"!' chided Thyruid. This parting note, as Geoffrey tumbled out the door of the Inn-by-the-Bye in order to meet his young companions, rode on the morning gruff grumble Thyruid bore early on in the day.

'They have so much to learn of life here, in Hyperbia' added his busy wife, Marthuida with sympathy. 'Remember how much we had to learn and the gentle help of old Priastes who saw how things might come to be'. 'More than that, they have much to unlearn' finished the dreamy Carymba, waiting out the time of unlearning.

Yves grumbled: 'What does he mean "kingdom of Grump"? Those two old men only sit in their cloud of doom and dream about yesterday's tarnished glories. Let's forget them and just go – go anywhere'. And, so saying, they set out for they did not know where.

'Yves and Betsy' complained Geoffrey, 'I wish you would become more respectful to me. I have done this job of being a gentleman for a long time, serving both a gentleman and his son in the very most proper of fashions. I know what I am because I know what I have been. I like you both very much. But we need to be more correct in our actions'.

'Now Geoffrey: remember that we are children, not a gentleman from Cumberland. We have never even seen Cumberland. We want to play; we have always played; that is the way we know ... from before. We do not want to change. So, you need to do things our way'.

'Then, maybe I should find another place'.

'Yes. Maybe you should'.

'Tsk! Tsk! My friends, my young friends. What are you doing?' The voice, old and kindly, belonged to the old man, Sola, a retired craftsman who had been watching them while puttering quietly with his hands. 'You remind me of old, old men. Not old in body like me, but old in spirit. Some folk never grow old in spirit, though some are always old in spirit. Old spirits are never able to live new lives, just as old minds seem never able to think new thoughts. The grace of novelty is either alien or a dirty word to them. Do not forget who you are and where you are. Look!'

And so, the three of them looked: they were in Hyperbia, in a new life. And so, it was that another little step in the long process of unlearning moved them along, aided today by this nimble wisdom of Sola. Little by little, the Hyperbia seen in promise by Priastes, the old seer, stepped a little bit closer now, to be seen in the Hyperbia before the eyes of this new trio.

Yves and Betsy and Geoffrey walked toward the suddenly-there bend in the road ... together, appreciating each other and the fact that they were not in the old places, but in the new, in Hyperbia. Old Sola, young in spirit, watched them go around the bend. Little Carymba kept on waiting for the steps to melt away for Yves and Betsy and Geoffrey, her friends now coming homeward.

For the sermon of 9 March 1980, titled "The Turning", based on 1 Corinthians 10:1-13.

XI

'Geoffrey!' The soft voice cut through the air and landed gently on his ears, still muffled by his left-over morning drowsiness. 'Geoffrey! What are you doing today?' With a bit more firmness, the words penetrated the sleepy fog which was only beginning to stir as morning movements began to be felt – barely. 'Geoffrey! Are you still asleep?'

Carymba had brought her voice over to Geoffrey as he sat, befuddled beneath Thyruid's favorite brass-framed window. 'This brass widow frame is brighter than you are this morning – and old Thyruid has not even polished it yet today!' Little Carymba laughed lightly.

'Give a man a chance to get to his chores in the morning before you complain' returned Thyruid, embalmed in an unusually lousy mood. For no good reason, everyone seemed tired and crabby this morning. Everyone, that is, except Carymba. And poor Geoffrey was still too slow to realize fully what was going on; he always was slow to wake up, but today he was slower than usual. 'What do you want ... so early ... he finally managed to mutter.

'Come on, Geoffrey. It is a really beautiful day. I had hoped that we could just walk and talk and enjoy life a little bit. I wanted to show you something. ... Oh, come on: it *is* a beautiful day'. So did Carymba tease him ever so gently. And so did Geoffrey begin to move, ever so slowly.

Beyond the little glen – a tight little valley beyond the door of the Inn-by-the-Bye – spread sharply rising and vigorous hills. Geoffrey had never been to this part of Hyperbia before. It was a truly amazing view as he looked up ... and up ... and up, as a little path wandered its way along the hillside; it almost disappeared from view since it was so small, and the hill was so high.

'I have not seen so steep a hill since before I came here, when I was in the high places of Cumberland. Are we near a border here?' 'No, Geoffrey, we are not near any border. We are in the very heartland of Hyperbia. This is *my* country, where I lived before I moved out through the glen and to the gentler hills you know so much better. Come along and bring the lunch. I will show you Hyperbia, a land you must love, a land which calls for your sweat and rewards you with gracious heights. Come on, my friend!'

And Carymba hobbled forward toward the sharp path. Geoffrey watched her move carefully and gingerly yet enthusiastically and with a very distinct purpose. Geoffrey looked at her and looked at the hill: she was so small, and the hill was so big. He looked at the long and winding path; he looked at the steep slope of the hill; he wondered just how the one called the little waif, the one with a heart so big and legs so stumbly could mount that path. Why, it would be a challenge for a mountain goat!

'Wait for me!' Geoffrey cried, grabbing the lunch basket. He had suddenly realized that, in spite of his doubts, little Carymba was nimbly climbing that impossible path.

Panting with unaccustomed climb, Geoffrey caught up with Carymba. Her pace was not fast; it could never be fast, even on a downhill move. But she never slackened her resolve to keep one foot hobbling in front of the other. Geoffrey took her pace and marveled at her steadiness of climb; he was ready to stop and rest a bit and sighed in his weariness.

'Come on, silly' chided Carymba; 'it is easier to just keep going than it is to sprint and pause. Climbing *these* hills calls for patience; they will not let you hurry, and you will not have time to pause halfway. There will be time enough for that come lunch time. We should have met a good place to see by then'.

'Are you sure about that?' asked Geoffrey, his early slowness passing aside into later tiredness. 'Yes. I am sure. Home is on the heights. I want to show you that. From there, things look different, and the patterns of the lowlands take on a fresh perspective. We are about halfway there. It is easier to climb, even hobbled, when you know what is coming. Trust my knowledge for now, just for a bit more'.

'Whew, I am beat. How do you keep going? We will never reach the top; is halfway not far enough? We can see pretty well right here. Let us stop here; it seems enough to me'. So did Geoffrey plead. 'Let me carry the lunch basket' commented Carymba. 'We cannot eat until we reach the heights. Come along!' And she took the basket as she insisted that they climb ever farther.

All the rest of the way, Geoffrey wondered why he had ever left that shadowed mahogany table in the cool Inn-by-the-Bye for this. Gentlemen should not sweat – and he was definitely sweating, although I suppose that a gentleman's gentleman would prefer the term perspiring. But, alas, he was hungry, and Carymba had the basket; he was healthy, and she was hobbled; besides, he was proud, too proud to turn back and go down the hill while she went on … if not too proud to grumble.

Thus, they moved and, thus, they climbed until, finally, they came to a flat spot, a crest on the climb and Carymba beamed and waved her hand about, indicating the view, and said: 'There. See what I mean?' Geoffrey looked and looked. The climb seemed short now.

'It is a beautiful day, Carymba. It is …'.

For the Sermon of 16 March 1980, titled "Two Sons", based on Luke 15:11-32.

XII

'What are you doing, Betsy?' asked Yves. He had been unhappy with her the last few days – as brothers are accustomed to be with sisters. 'None of your business, Yves! Just leave me alone' retorted Betsy. She was now unhappy with him – as sisters are accustomed to be with brothers.

Now, this agreement to disagree had its beginning yesterday. Yves had been in a particularly disagreeable mood – the sort of mood that occasionally comes over all children and most of the childlike among us. He had decided in his moment of weakness that he was going to do what he wanted and would pay absolutely no attention to the thoughts and feelings of anyone else. Nobody but nobody was going to tell him what to do.

Oh, it was a tremendous fit of childish stubbornness that came upon him; but then, we must not forget that he, in spite of his dreadful size – by Hyperbian standards, of course – was but a child. Thus had Yves decided in his early waking hours that day. And he was well confirmed to himself in his decision by the time that the warm glow began to brighten the land, casting his gloomy shadow across the sky.

It had become a bright day, a day on which to be cheerful; but Yves had already decided against any such thing: he was set upon crossing his shadow against that of every person he met. A mood like that can really rule over a person if care is not taken – and Yves was not about to take care.

Betsy, however, was as bright as the under-glow that day – and it was an exceptionally bright day. Much like the moods in children, days in Hyperbia could be brighter or duller … and no one really knew why, for it all came upon them from underneath, in the unknowable reaches of their land itself. Bright Betsy was the first one Yves saw that day.

'Let's go and watch the shoemaker, Yves. He said he would try to make my new shoes today. He said he had to make a very special last – what is a last, Yves? – and maybe our bigger hands can help him'. 'Nah, Betsy. You can go if you want; but I do not feel like it. I have other things to do, important things.

Of course, Yves had nothing in mind except that he did not want to do what anyone else wanted to do. Besides, as he had said it in a nasty way, a spark of resentment began to smolder in Betsy. She left her brother to find her shoemaker and try to make something of the day.

Later, Yves, having wandered to the Inn-by-the-Bye, roused himself to be a nuisance. It did not take much; somehow, everything he did, every turn he made was in the way of either Thyruid or Marthuida. Yves easily managed to make their jobs – which they dearly loved and thoroughly enjoyed – wearisome. Thyruid is gruff but hardly unpleasant – except that that day Yves really tried his temper. Yves was so big, remember, that his bulk plus his peevishness made things rough for the wee Innkeeper and his wife. 'I wish you would find something else to do' scolded Thyruid, completely out of character. 'You are just in the way!'

Besides Thyruid, besides Marthuida, there were others whose shadows Yves' shadow crossed. The effect was ever the same: Yves proved to be a bother to everyone.

All of this was what Yves, in his own mind, wanted. His cloud became darker and darker until it was the deepest shade of black. That deepest shade arrived long before evening slinked in that day. Yves stayed away from the Resting Time circle at the Inn-by-the-Bye that evening. He pushed everyone away. As he grew lonelier, he grew hungrier. The selfish indulgence of his mood ate away at him until he came back to the Inn in the morning – this morning.

When Yves came back, he came politely; he came quietly. He came only to the outer edge of the circle. And no one noticed him; rather, nobody let on that he was noticed. As far as he could tell, he was still alone.

And so, Yves sat on the edge of the place, leaning on a little ridge on the hill. Only Thyruid and Marthuida were to be seen. Yves quietly watched them work. As mid-morning came, Carymba and Betsy and Geoffrey came for brunch. Only the quick eyes of Carymba showed notice of Yves ... and smiled. She hobbled over his way and invited him: 'Yves, have missed you. Come and join us'.

Now, Betsy had missed Yves, too. But she was not so ready to let him return. Not just yet, anyway. She thought her brother ought to have to suffer some snubbery first. That would be a taste of his own moodish ways.

But Carymba, as always, was ready to be open ... and Betsy was denied the luxury of gloating. She could only bear her anger in silent protest within. And she did. This is how we got to our angry spat this afternoon – back at the beginning of the story today.

So ... Betsy wanted to be left alone. It was her turn to pout. She thought to herself: 'If only Carymba had left well enough alone ... if only ...'.

Yves was not ready to leave her alone. He had suffered his own silliness already. 'I am sorry about yesterday. How did your shoes come out? May I see them?'

Betsy just looked at him; children have not learned to stay angry very well. So, she smiled, too.

For the Sermon of 23 March 1980, titled "Behold", based on Isaiah 43:16-21.

XIII

'Yves, I wish I had never let you bring me out this far. I have never been so lost nor felt so alone, not even when we woke up and first found ourselves in Hyperbia'. Betsy was moaning. But still, Yves had brought her out on an exploratory expedition for two. They had not been prepared for a long journey; Yves, like many young children, had not thought past lunch time. At the start, all they had had was a bare sandwich apiece plus a few cookies borrowed from Marthuida's special kitchen. And those meager provisions had disappeared long before lunch time had even been thought about.

'Oh, Betsy' assured Yves, 'we are doing just fine. Quit your worrying. It only wastes energy and spoils the day for us. Come on'. Yves was proving not to be all that convincing anymore, largely because he was beginning to doubt his courage himself.

The adventure had begun simply enough; they had wanted to see what was beyond the ridge that the wee folk called the End Ridge. If it really were the end, they would quickly know it so. And, if it were not the end, they would be able to see what was there to see.

Much of the morning had been spent climbing to the ridge ... which is why they were so hungry and ate their lunch too early. This ridge was away from the steep hill country that Carymba had shown Geoffrey. Further, it seemed that everyone was afraid of the End Ridge, as they called it, and that no one had ever gone beyond it before. All this added to the children's curiosity, luring them even more to go and see.

Well, when Yves and Betsy reached End Ridge and looked across, they saw what appeared to them to be a mirror land. It was new and quite different in its look; so, the children looked at each other, drew in a deep breath, and stepped across, boldly entering this strange land on the other side of End Ridge.

This place did not seem too bad to begin with. But, as they moved along and one hill began to look very much like the one before and the one coming up next, and everything became more and more desolate – barren, bleak, bare, bone-dry – where they had known gentle warmth, they now found hot heat, hot pressing heat. Where they had known a soft glow of green, they now found a sharp glare searing their eyes in bitter brightness. Where they had known a land which softly welcomed the foot, they now found hard, hot, sharp ground, repelling their every step. If only they could fly! But they could not; they had to walk.

And, worse, they were lost.

'Betsy, I am sorry, but I think I am lost. And, if you are lost, too, what shall we do? I only know we cannot stop here'. 'Yves, I know we cannot stop here. And I know I do not want to walk any farther. What can we do?' So, they did what they guessed they could do: they looked at each other, lost and alone and bewildered.

Other things had been happening that day, all of them back around the Inn-by-the-Bye where Carymba was concerned about her big and young friends. She knew their childlike lack of attention. She even was the only one who suspected that there was something beyond End Ridge, although she had never mentioned such a thing to any of the wee folk around her. 'Sola', she asked, 'do you suppose that anyone can come back from over End Ridge?'

The wise old man with the young spirit looked deeply into Carymba's gaze, thought thoughts beyond the Ridge and answered slowly: 'Only if someone leads them back'. 'Ok' said Carymba. And she hobbled off with purpose in her heart – which really was her greatest resource; no one ever guessed just how big that heart really was.

By the time Yves and Betsy were beginning to feel lost on the other side of End Ridge, Carymba was climbing the other way, into the Hill Country, toward a little workshop there. 'Ribbert. Are you here?' she called into the dim shop. 'Yes. Can I help you? … Oh! Hello, Carymba. It has been a long time since you came up here'. 'Ribbert, I need your help. Are you too busy to go on an adventure – beyond End Ridge?' 'Let me get my boots. … Now, what is the problem?' 'I will tell you on the way' answered Carymba. So it was that Ribbert, the craftsman from the hills and Carymba, the wee waif with the hobble, came toward End Ridge that day.

'All right, Carymba; here we are. You stand on that side, the Hyperbian side, and sing across End Ridge until I get back'. 'I will, Ribbert. And thanks …'.

Ribbert stepped across and began to walk, dragging his stick in the increasingly rough land behind him, leaving a small, scratchy trail from the song of Carymba to himself. And Ribbert walked on, looking, dragging his stick and listening to the trailing melody. Finally, he found them – Yves and Betsy – afraid and weary, hungry and thirsty, and sure that they would never see anyone again. Ribbert came to the two big children. As he came to them, the song of Carymba came to them, too; and they knew the voice of Carymba. 'Come with me. My name is Ribbert. I am your friend. Follow me back to the Hyperbian side'.

Now, neither Yves nor Betsy knew Ribbert. They were frightened enough to follow him anyway. It helped their confidence, however, that he came with the song of Carymba, flowing to them like a river. So, they followed Ribbert following the song, feeling afresh the roughness, the cutting sharpness of this land beyond End Ridge.

It was not long before they came to the approach to the Ridge itself once again. As they came near, they were full glad that they were coming to it again and would soon see the gentle slopes of Hyperbia welcoming their feet again.

All this while, the song Carymba sang rang in their ears – and with it came a strange sense that they had been sung to in a different way by the rough and cutting land they were now ready to leave. There was, it seemed to them now, a singing there, too. Only now were they aware of that singing – if you can call it singing when the ears are not used in the hearing. The children paused, just for a moment, to listen.

Ribbert, noble Ribbert, crossed back into Hyperbia in his special craftsman-like manner. But Carymba, looking across End Ridge, saw the pause the children took, and she smiled. Her smile came from the realization that she now shared with Yves and Betsy one of her secrets – for, years ago, she had been to the Other Side once, too. And it was Ribbert and the singing of Ribbert's old, old grandmother that had led her back. She knew that even Hyperbia's land, gentle and steep alike, is made different by the unheard singing of the Other Side of End Ridge.

For the Sermon of 30 March 1980, titled "This Mind", based on Philippians 2:5-11.

XIV

Geoffrey sat on the top of the little hill, all alone, head in his hands, thinking. This was not the sort of thing Geoffrey normally did with his time. He was more of a doer thana thinker, as one might expect from a trained gentleman's gentleman from Cumberland. And, really, Geoffrey was doing more than just thinking; he was watching and thinking about what he was watching. For, from his vantage point, perched as he was on the crest of his small hill, his glance could take in all the activities of the valley's meadow-craftsmen and women, the dominant work-habit of the Hyperbian wee folk.

These people had been scurrying around their valley-filling chores for a long time, from well before the time Geoffrey found himself suddenly out of Cumberland and into Hyperbia – he knew not how. Since arriving, Geoffrey had often walked among these people, chatting with them, watching the deft hand of Carymba in her helpful moves. But he had never thought about them. All those wee people he had met in passing. They were friendly enough even with a strange newcomer like himself. Yet, in a sense, the busy craftsmen were just part of the scenery; they were the sort of thing which one sees and never notices, nor considers beyond the mere fact that they are *there*.

Today, for Geoffrey at least, was different. He really did not know why he had awakened so early, gotten up far before his time, prepared himself in his usual way for the day – as a gentleman's gentleman, everything had to be just so in order to face the day publicly. He had found his breakfast early at the Inn-by-the-Bye and wandered to this spot on the hill, overlooking the valley and its busyness. He did not know why, but he was there, sitting with time to spend. And this time found his eyes and habits pricked by the movements below.

Those wee people in the valley were special people – their mingled flavor of easy regularity and regular ease which presumed nothing and offered friendly space, a softness of life which was comfortable overflowed their togetherness. Geoffrey remembered his old home, Cumberland, as he watched them: Cumberland was different – or, rather, this Hyperbian valley is different. Before, in what he had known so well, arrangements of propriety and the like were assured by the proper ordering, day by day, of all the people and all their opinions. The grumpy outsiders there called it a pecking order – and it was; here, it was only the grumpy outsiders – Geron and Orgello, his mentor – who want a pecking order, These working people simply go about their labors equal in consideration, respecting and valuing their differences in talent and experience. Master and apprentice work side by side productively, congenially, happily. It was as if the rigid hallways of Cumberland were there to assure regularity and the soft accompaniments of Hyperbia were there to ensure affirmed quality in living and working together. The contrast was strange to either side.

As he watched, Geoffrey found his attention drawn to a small corner of the glen, to the place where the stone carver was at work. The master had been there for some time, tugging and shoving the heavy stone around in order to get it ready to begin the day. Back in Cumberland, Geoffrey remembered, that would be the chore for the apprentices; it is simply the labor of getting ready to set up the work to be done. But what he saw here was one man, working alone, struggling to get the stone in place. After this work continued for a while, a pair of much younger men came hurrying up and pitched in to set the stone aright. These tardy fellows, Geoffrey soon decided, must be the apprentices to the master stone carver. An apprentice is the young person who goes to learn from someone who knows what he – or she – is doing so that someday the title of master craftsman might be their own.

Geoffrey recalled that, back in Cumberland, after such a scene there would be soon a terrible noise, a ferocious scene over the inconvenience of such late arrivals: the apprentice should have been there first. Indeed, the other apprentices in the valley had greeted their master craftsman at the master's arrival. Geoffrey watched to see what could happen here. He could not hear them – a good thing if this were anything like it would be in Cumberland! – but he could see everything that happened.

The two young men rushed in, as we said, and took hold of the stone with the older master and soon had it set all correctly. Geoffrey could see the men talking together, all with smiles and the normal calm gestures which accompany most of the talk of all the wee folk in Hyperbia. One of the young men went and brought their tools so they could start working on their task together.

Later, at lunchtime, the master stopped and called for lunch which they proceeded to eat together. Where, wondered Geoffrey, was the anger which the master ought to have had? Deep in his thoughts and concerns over this behavior and way of thinking that was expressed in those gestures by the stone cutters – for it was all very, very strange to one who had so recently come from the ways of Cumberland, or any other place like that – Geoffrey did not notice that company was coming to join him. Carymba even sat down and watched with him for a while before speaking and surprising Geoffrey into noticing her presence next to him on the hill.

'Those boys are not late very often. They work well for the master. We find that work goes better when we do not worry too much about ourselves and give each other room to love. Everybody just does it that way. It is the mind we share here' commented Carymba.

'I like that' replied Geoffrey. 'I think I even understand it a bit. I will learn! Now, how about finding some lunch? This morning has been full for me, having started ridiculously early!'

And, as Geoffrey began to stand up, Carymba laughed and opened her basket ... .

For the sermon of 6 April 1980, titled "Remember How He Told You", based on Luke 24:1-11.

XV

It had been one of those funny kind of days, one where everything was set on edge, where nothing really fit together as it should. It seemed to have been that way for everyone who gathered about at the Resting Time at the Inn-by-the-Bye as the day closed out in its strangeness.

'For me, today's strangeness began when I was getting dressed. My shoestring broke – and I could not find another set of strings; so, I tied it together. Then it broke again, in a different place. So, I had to fix it again. The other shoestring broke three times. My feet look like a disaster. The Inn was all out of shoestrings and the whole day has found me falling all over myself. It has been disgusting!' And, for Geoffrey, who is always so perfectly attired as a Cumberland-style gentleman's gentleman, the event was *very* distressing.

'That is nothing, Geoffrey. Why, I ran out of eggs this morning. Then I ran out of milk. The flour had gotten all wet and was like a great lump of dried paste. I had fifteen customers wanting breakfast at that time!' Marthuida complained, too, and went on and on … for the broom had broken, the duster had lost its feathers, the brass polish ran out – leaving Thyruid in a horrible temper all day (he simply cannot stand to have any of his precious brassware *unpolished*), there was a leak upstairs and the drain plugged up. The Inn-by-the-Bye had suffered a most miserable day.

Yves had been one of the disappointed hungry breakfast customers. Before that, he had already stubbed his toe and fallen, hurting his ankle, his knee, his hand and his pride … not necessarily in that order.

The tales continued around the circle. Everyone, it seemed, had been trying to get through a perfectly impossible day. It was as if days like this one came along every now and then to remind those otherwise happy Hyperbians that the things they ordinarily assume are true are really only close guesses that do manage to work most of the time. They were reminded well this day for no one there admitted to anything going as expected; nobody could find anything which had *not* given them trouble all day long.

As the talk of the day spread around the circle and everyone unloaded the burden of frustration, casting it all upon the central fire as an offering in smoke, one among them sat quietly by, listening. This was Carymba, the hobble-styled wee girl who was always watching, always listening, always being there – perhaps to offer a prompt hand or a simple smile, even a gentle word. She always did seem to be just there, with a knack for sensing what no one else can see.

Carymba was out at the edge of the group, largely unnoticed, as usual; but then, no one was paying any attention to anything or anyone except for the problems they were remembering for themselves, their own deep frustrations from the day. Everyone had been talking past each other, not with each other; and once more the strange frustrating power of the day took over again, unbeknownst to anyone – except for the nimble-hearted Carymba.

Finally, Carymba edged herself into a visible spot in the circle. 'Guess what?' she called into the rumbling mist of increasingly foggy complaining about the miserable day. The call cut through the mire cleanly, leaving a stunned silence. 'Guess what?!' she repeated; and still there was no response … until the muffled gruffness of Thyruid rumbled slowly across the circle; 'What?'

'I think you are being foolish. That is what. You met a day – it was a very difficult sort of day – and tried to cram it into your own habits. No wonder you were frustrated. Like Geoffrey there: he found it was not a spit and polish day and tried to keep up the ruse of spit and polish. And Marthuida dear, could you have done something different for breakfast today? The plumbing will be fixed: be patient. And dear Yves, so big and yet so little: your pride was all that hurt. Your best medicine would have been a big laugh and a roll in the meadow ... but you would not. Why?' They all sat there, dumbfounded. No one had ever heard such nonsense before!

'Let me tell you about Anna Marie, an old friend in my hills of the East. She lives in a cliff-hugging hut. She once showed me her wisdom about days like today, that they happen to give sense to all the other days, not be nonsense. She taught me that years ago; and it is still true today. Days of shining difference may be frustrating – and will be frustrating – unless we let them lead us where they will, into corn meal mush and bare feet, into laughter and ... the kind of life we are meant to share. Things are all different than they seem. Days like today prove that fact. Can you see what Anna Marie and I are saying?'

But the others were not sure. It was hard to be ready for taking today, this miserable, stumbly day, as giving meaning to normal days. It is easier to mumble about bad dreams and go on ... as usual. And, for most, that is exactly what they decided to do. But some, a few ... wondered: ... just maybe ... just maybe ... .

For the Sermon for 13 April 1980, titled "Sharing In Jesus", based on Revelation 1:9-19.

XVI

It had taken a while; she had had to look for a long time; but, finally, Betsy had found herself a corner, her size of a corner. This was a rarity in a land far more accustomed to taking the wee folk into their nooks and crannies than to accommodating anyone the size of Betsy, even as a child. Now, at last she had found one, out by a curl in the End Ridge, near the fading scratch line where Ribbert had led Yves and her back to the tune Carymba sang, near where the voice had sung to her. Alone, Betsy would not go over End Ridge to the Other Side. She had been there once already; she had been lost and found again. Today, it is enough to sit in her corner and think. That is what she wants to do today, does Betsy.

The curl in the End Ridge proved a good place for a girl to sit and be alone. It was not like being forgotten – Carymba, for one, always seemed to know what she and Yves were doing, always sensed when trouble or being troubled loomed about them, always helped. Silently, Carymba was trusted to do whatever was needed; that was a great comfort to Betsy, particularly as she was sitting in the curl at End Ridge, so close to her haunting memory of the voices singing like unseen mermaids to her and to Yves. Secure and tucked away from all the daily distractions, Betsy sat to ponder. There was nothing special on her mind; rather, this was one of those occasional days which she took for herself to sort out all the things that had happened to her in this, her life.

Ever since she and Yves had found themselves in Hyperbia, this strange but pleasant land which was becoming home for more reasons than by default, by the fact that they were here and not going anywhere else, life had been one big hurry-scurry rolling along series of events, rushing over one another in an impatient urge to reach ... well, wherever they were going ... she knew not where. The only time she avoided all that was on her days of retreat, days of putting this mad rush of happenings into some sort of pattern which could be understood by a little girl. Sometime, even, these days of retreat were fuller than the others, all by themselves.

So it was that Betsy settled herself into her little curl-away corner. The flush of people, wee people and even brother Yves, came cascading across her mind like a miniature Niagara. But, even as they flashed by, her corner seemed to fold them all under the strange, very strange allurement of the place. Sneaking into the tumbling mirage of disordered memories came a thread, an alien thread from – she was not at all sure from where. Betsy settled herself a bit more into her nature-made seat and into the depths of her thoughts, even toward the images of her non-thought and beyond toward the imageless absorption into ... again, she did not know what.

The thought of maybe being hypnotized by that persistent tread, felt though not seen, not even by the eye of her imagining mind, flickered like a wind-bothered candle before her eyes. She was awake, aware of all that was happening, in control of herself; yet she was meeting the memories of a song sung low, coming from the Other Side; more, she was meeting afresh the sense of that song sung low from the Other Side, sung low for her.

Nestled into her corner, Betsy felt the song; she was feeling it more than hearing it, if one can hear such a song at all with mere ears. She wondered about the song. And, more than just wondering, she found it directing her, filling her, embracing her. She wondered, in a sort of worried fashion, if it were calling her to itself, across End Ridge. Was it like a siren, beckoning her from reasonable and comfortable living toward destruction?

Betsy wondered; yet, she sat still easily, firmly, right where she was. Her eyes were moved to gaze back across the meadows, back to her Hyperbian home. She looked back, and was filled: There, before her eyes, was where the song directed her, back home again.

In her childlike way, Betsy began to see that things were different. This song was so right that the half-stepped ways of good people were suddenly seen as an off-beat, mis-rhythmed, not quite syncopation. There was something more: there was, she was sure, and the strange song, felt although unheard, had sung it to her.

Betsy rose and walked back to the Inn-by-the-Bye. Her pace was the same; but she felt it and knew it to be different. How different it was would only be known, even by her, when the new song in her blood expressed itself in the meeting of life day by day, night by night. Even the flush and the rush of the wee folk took on a new ordering in her sight.

'It is strange' she thought, turning to her brother. 'Hi Yves' she called. Is there time to play some, now?'

For the Sermon of 20 April 1980, titled "We Must Obey God", based on Acts 5:27-42.

XVII

'Carymba, how do you ever keep yourself as stable and easy going as you do? You hobble about, seeing people all the time; or you sit in your corner of the place, watching people with eyes that see all. You say little, except when you take everything everyone is saying and flip-flop it over on top of them! Then, they look at you and wonder what you are talking about. You seem nice enough, they say. But they just do not understand you. One said the problem with you, Carymba, is that you do not live the way they do. They would have you like everyone else. How do you ever keep yourself stable and keep yourself going?'

'Well, Geoffrey my friend, I guess that the best answer is that I do not do so well at keeping myself stable. In fact, I myself do a very poor job of it all. It is simply that, some time ago, I was privileged to see and hear things differently. I took you up to my hills to see part of that. Do you remember?'

'Oh, my! How could I forget that?! The plains and the meadows misted together in glorious review. Even the climb seemed short from the top'. 'Well, Geoffrey, that is part of what I mean. Do you remember when Yves and Betsy went over End Ridge and were lost?'

'Yes. And you were the only one with an idea of how to find them'. 'Ribbert, that dear, helped immensely. He had found me over there once, aided and sent by his mother; she also knew the secrets of the Other Side. Over There, you hear things, even see things, such things as change the way you view the world about us here. I have been both places, to the hills on the one side and to the Other Side on the other. In the middle lie these meadows and these dear people. How can you help but like them? They are so helpable, so blind, so deaf, so heavy of heart – and they don't even know it! No, I do a poor job. It is what I see, what I hear that matters – that does the good job, not me. How about going for a walk in the glens, Geoffrey?'

'That would be fine, Carymba. But I do think I would prefer not climbing the hills today'. 'Of course. That is a job for the early morning, and it grows late now. We will find the "mermaids singing each to each" instead'. 'Mermaids?' 'The wee folk see them better'.

And with that, Carymba turned with a twinkle and started off toward the lead glen, over on the right. Geoffrey merely shook his head and wondered what she was doing. 'What has this to do with the hidden chuckles of a girl so very different from the lives of the tradesmen and Innkeepers whom she tries to touch?' Thus did Geoffrey muse as he came along to see he knew not what.

They walked on and on, down the glen. Geoffrey surprised himself by recognizing the path to the top; it was still steep, still high, but not so imposing as it had been. 'That is the path we took to the top, isn't it?' asked Geoffrey. 'Yes. That is it. Come along' responded Carymba, never easing her pace down the glen. 'Towards the mermaids, I suppose' muttered Geoffrey to himself. 'I see what they mean. She just does not make sense most of the time'. Carymba simply ignored him as she followed the glen along the way onward.

The glen had begun as a sudden neck, pushing itself in the low way between a pair of little hills. The hills became bigger shortly; the glen became more pronounced, more sharply making its way as an increasingly narrow corridor winding between the now-awesome heights. They had long passed the trail to the top.

The glen became tighter; Geoffrey dropped behind and followed Carymba whose eyes and pace were always ahead, always onward. 'There must be something somewhere; she always ends up somewhere. But this makes no sense to me … ouch!' The glen had contracted to its narrowest place; they had to turn sideways to squeeze through the narrows.

Geoffrey had pinched himself out of his reverie, quite unexpectedly. 'Be careful! It is tight here. … Oh, I am sorry, Geoffrey. … Are you all right? I have been too absorbed in the trek. I forgot …'. 'No, no: I am fine. I just surprised myself. That is all. You would think I could pay attention to where I am going. But, no: my mind was miles away'. 'Back at the Inn-by-the-Bye, perhaps?' "No. I was just daydreaming of another time, another place. Where do we go now?' 'Come along and see'.

The glen began to open up a bit. The area grew wider; the hills became more subtle in their ascent on high, the peaks a little softer in their crest. It was midafternoon now, and the trail evened out to a shoreline and an endless glittering of blue.

'Let's sit down a while, Geoffrey. This is the place to which we were coming. Even the hill people, my people do not come here. The music of the Sea does not fill them as it has me'. 'I hear nothing' said Geoffrey, sitting down slowly, carefully. 'Then listen' the "mermaids are singing each to each"; they sing to us as well. Listen'.

Gently, the rhythms of the waves threw back the melody of wide-blown maidens of the Sea. Geoffrey listened, carefully. And he heard songs that had never touched his soul before. He thought: 'I still do not know how she does it; I still do not understand the way she comes; I still do not, cannot, even guess her heart's soaring way. But I do now know it is real, it is right, it bears us where we have not been and to where we would go'.

'It grows late, Geoffrey. We need to pass the narrow place while it is light. We must go back. I come here to know my songs and my stories, to obey them. But now we must go back. Maybe you know some of your answers now'.

'I am coming ... slowly. It will be late getting back; but as yet I am not hungry. And yes, the answers are there, though not stated. Maybe they cannot be stated'.

For the Sermon of 27 April 1980, titled "Tell Us Plainly", based on John 10:22-30.

XVIII

'Here it is, midday, and there is no one around. The quiet is surprising; the silence is so loud that my ears are roaring'. Marthuida was sitting in the Inn-by-the-Bye, resting and musing; usually, she did not have much time for resting and musing. At midday, there were usually customers to care for; today was quiet. All to be heard was her own breathing – and, if she listened carefully, that of Thyruid, sitting over against the wall, under the brass-framed window, lost in his daydream. 'Thyruid usually is not so quiet, nor so dreamy. What is so funny about today? I do not know. I simply do not know. This quiet – it is so strange'. Marthuida shuddered in spite of herself.

'I wish I could figure out what is going on around here'. The booming voice of Thyruid cut through the quiet, shoving what had seemed so heavy aside, proving its density to be as fragile as porcelain. The booming voice of Thyruid startled poor Marthuida out of her deep preoccupation with Quiet.

'Why, Thyruid, you startled me' she said as she gasped after her breath. 'It was good for both of us. We were too quiet. Where is everyone? Is no one around today?' Thyruid's grumble was rougher than normal today. He was accustomed to having people around: 'What good is an Inn with no customers in it?'

'*We* are here, at least. And talking does push back the quiet' offered Marthuida timidly, glancing at the quiet as if were about to pounce on her again. She was still unsure about the way this day was going. Things were *so* quiet.

'Thyruid, how long has it been since we have spent a whole morning alone? without any customers?' 'A long time. This quiet ... it does not pay the bills!' 'Now Thyruid! I would like to have some business, too. But it is pleasant being here with you, just you. I guess I have become accustomed to having others around as well; but you are nice'.

'There has got to be a reason, a simple reason why no one is here. Perhaps the road has taken to turning the other way when that curve comes up all of a sudden like. Maybe there is a new place … with better brass than mine …'. His eyes passed over his brass trimmings proudly. 'Oh, Thyruid: you worry too much'. 'Too much, you say. Too much! How do you think we make a living here? We need customers!'

'No, Thyruid – you need people, not just customers. You even turn customers into people; or at least you try. When you have a crowd around, you are happy. Now, *I* am your crowd'. 'And a quiet crowd you make!'

'Maybe I should go looking for people. Maybe they are tired of this place. What do you think, Marthuida? I am getting nervous … in all our years here, it has never been so quiet. There is work to do, but no one to do it *for*. How long have we been here now … twenty years?' 'No. It is twenty-five years tomorrow. Time goes fast, fast as a cup of water'.

They gave each other a long-puzzled look. Memories of days gone by swept across their minds. Their eyes glanced quickly about their Inn-by-the-Bye and all the years and all the people, all the laughter and all the tears which had flowed together here – all that was before them. Always they had flowed mist-like about the brimming mugs and the cups of water. The memories cascaded and drew an unthinking dampness about the eyes, a tear of remembrance mirrored in each other's lamps.

'After all this time, we need a house full of people to share this spot. We have an *Inn*: now, let us get the folk in here once again. If folk are not here, it is not because we lack hospitality – never have we wanted for that. No, they must not know a good place at all. Maybe they need some encouragement. Yes, that is it: encouragement!'

Thyruid had been talking more to himself and the walls than to his precious Marthuida. And his excitement at the mere thought of a bustlingly busy Inn raised his voice all on its own. 'You – all of you – come

153

to the Inn. Come tomorrow: … why, tomorrow marks twenty-five years here for Thyruid and his little Marthuida!'

Thyruid bellowed out his excitement; his voice echoed around the meadows, speaking back to him in a hundred little voices, mimics of his own booming cry. They came back weakly, back to the Inn and to Thyruid; they came back weakly to the empty Inn … empty save for the master and the mistress of the place.

'Oh, wait, Thyruid. Wait. Someone will come. Someone …'. Marthuida saw the loneliness in the Innkeeper's heart. A host must have his guests. And that is what Thyruid has become since he came here: a host. But the yard of the Inn-by-the-Bye looked like Hamlin after the unpaid-piper left: empty. Empty of everyone. Empty of laughter. Empty of joy. The hour grew late; evening pressed the empty, lonely afternoon towards yesterday.

Thyruid sighed and turned heavily toward the back room. Twenty-five years he had been a host. And now, the people ignored him, ignored the cry of his voice. Poor Marthuida could only watch and wait; she hurt, her ample heart hurt to see her Thyruid so low. He always gave his best.

Together, they shuffled through the routine of straightening up the Inn. The hours of puzzled sadness had dulled their expectations. And the failing echo had nearly finished their day. All they expected now was more of the same, more of the frustrating same. And so it was that they did not hear the low rustling of many little feet – and four big ones – slipping over the meadows and into the yard of the Inn-by-the-Bye.

'Surprise!' The unsuspected chorus rang out from the now-dim yard. Thyruid was silent. He turned and looked out and saw his guests … and, for the very first time in twenty-five years, he was silent. He just looked at the mob of wee folk, with Yves and Betsy crouched down behind them, holding an enormous … 'what is that thing?' thought Thyruid. 'It looks like the Inn all over again … could it be another Inn, a competitor?'

It was a cake, a fact that soon impressed itself upon his startled mind; all of these, his friends, had made it. 'M … Mar … Marthuid … da … get some mugs … lots of those mugs … let it flow … let it flow. And plates, too … hurry, get the plates … and the forks … and a knife. Yes, a knife … and … and …'. He just stood there smiling, tears streaming down his face: his people were here and he was host again in Hyperbia.

'Maybe they did hear my call … maybe'.

For the Sermon for 4 May 1980, titled "Trustworthy And True", based on Revelation 21:1-5.

XIX

Slowly, surely, the light began to come. It had been one of those infamous nights which last forever amid tossing and turning, eyes open or half-open, seemingly forever. Light came, bringing to a merciful close the night which seemed to be all awake; even in the times when sleep did come, it came timidly, afraid of the restless host. Light came, bringing a wary beginning to a day of unknown happenings and to a still restless young boy.

Yves did not know whether he should be relieved that *that* night was over, or saddened that day had actually come with its own special needs. Minds of little boys, like those of other people, are slower than usual at such decisions when the mantle of sleep, ragged though it be, still clings like yesterday's cobwebs about the head.

Yves rolled over – it seemed to take forever to accomplish that feat, and even that forever seemed too fast: it was one of those miserable mornings, known best to those who prefer for the day to start after noon. But this was not the usual way for Yves, a fact which made it only more miserable. Yves sat up slowly and gazed across the way; all was blank as his energies were all consumed in the almost hopeless task of getting himself put together *enough* inside to admit to another day.

Finally, he got up and stumbled off to find the suddenly-there crook in the road to the Inn-by-the-Bye. Barely aware of more than the mere facts that there were both light outside and emptiness in the pit of his stomach, Yves shuffled his way into the green before the Inn and plopped himself down on his belly, peered into the door, yawned cavernously and, stretching with the greatest vigor yet shown this morning, groaned out his presence.

'Well, Yves! What may I do for you?' bellowed Thyruid in his customary way. 'Is there something to eat?' mumbled Yves in timid response. Thyruid disappeared quickly into the back, returning shortly with an Yves-sized breakfast. That, of course, was far larger than any of the wee people could consume in whole week. Such was Yves fate in a land of wee people.

'Where is Betsy this morning?' thundered Thyruid. 'I do not know' was all Yves could muster; to himself he thought: 'Why must he be so loud, so close, so early? Ooh ... will day never come to my head, too?' And, in peace, Yves ate his breakfast – with seconds on milk brought by plump and pleasant and not nearly so loud Marthuida. 'That is better' thought Yves, responding to the gentle Marthuida who did not thunder her greeting, did not rattle his still fragile arrangements with the new morning. By now, Yves was finding his eyes operating without too many conflicting cobwebs. Yet, the legs preferred to wobble and the mind to wander itself over untutored inner landscapes.

The feet of Yves began not wander with a careful aimlessness – careful because he did not want to step on the wee folk; aimless because any planning of events even to the next five steps lay beyond the range of his morning-bound and limited concentration. All in all, this was proving to be a most improbable day ... except that poor Yves was graced with a rare looseness as the cobwebs which held back his ability to think also set free his relation with the moments of the morning of the day.

With all that Yves did not see – for he did not really see any of the wee people; his feet just missed them by accident or habit – it is amazing that he did see that one sad lonely little figure who struck his eye and caught hold of his mind. This wee man was a ways away when Yves noticed him and was drawn to him as one veiled by cobwebs is to one veiled by something else, by cobwebs of sadness and loneliness. Yves came up and sat down beside the wee man – whose name he never knew.

There came a magic moment together; the wee man began to talk. He spoke of blossoming catacombs, of fountains springing in the desert where rocks are broken, of hills new clothed in lime green, shedding after hard nights the cloak of unknowing stupor, stupidly laid over him in the lamentable past. He spoke nonsense, for that is what he saw. He spoke nonsense into the ears of a lad whose mind was bound back by the stubborn cobwebs of morning so that Yves could smile warmly and answer.

'Ah, yes. The shrouds of yesterday fall briskly in the new day. It helps to see when the eyes are slow; and when the ears are dull, we hear sharply. The sights come backward-like, and so do the sounds. Welling up and flooding down, they meet and ... and ... well, the aloneness of veiled mornings becomes the sharedness of mornings unveiled'. And the wee man smiled ... for the unsuspected dawn flooded with light behind his veil, rushing forth toward tomorrow, a great tomorrow.

'Do you know the Inn?' 'No. I do not think so. What Inn?' 'The Inn-by-the-Bye ... where folk gather. We can only glimpse behind the veil for a hint; now, we must remember from the usual side. Come on, the supper will remind you ... gently ... of the glimmer behind the veil'.

For the Sermon for 11 May 1980, titled "It Seemed Good To Us", based on Acts 15:1-6, 22-29.

<h1 style="text-align:center">XX</h1>

'What is all that noise out there?' hollered Thyruid in a voice very much louder, much noisier than the source of his complaint. It was early, though, and he had barely started his chores – he was just now in the middle of his daily brass polishing – so he was hardly ready for very much company. He was accustomed to handling a very few early morning customers – one or two, perhaps – but not so many as to really interfere with his regular morning ritual of chores to prepare his pride for a new day, a new round of customers. Today, however, he was spared that luxury as the green before the Inn-by-the-Bye was half full already with more coming in all the time, and all of them were talking, talking so excitedly that one had to wonder if anyone among them was bothering to listen.

'My heavens, Thyruid! There are so many. We must get to work!' Marthuida, always the practical one, began to scurry about to find room for the "so many". 'That road must be busy this morning, turning so many toward the Inn'. But Thyruid was slow in response; he just looked and looked, for it was so early – and there were so many. 'Thyruid! Come on! We have work to do!' And the host of Hyperbia's Inn-by-the-Bye shook himself out of his reverie of surprise, rattled a smile onto his face, stepped out – almost tripping on the threshold – and bellowed his greetings: 'Good morning, my people, my friends!'

The greeting rang out above the swirling chatter of the many wee folk gathering and brought their attention to the beaming host. Surprise had passed away and the habits of hosting, the habitual taste of graciousness washed through Thyruid.

'My good Innkeeper' spoke up one of the leading guests, having turned to see the beaming face and clean white apron of the Innkeeper, 'we know we are early here today … and that we are, shall we say, unannounced in our arrival. But we have felt the need to gather and to consider some

159

things going on out in the wider parts of Hyperbia, particularly in the hill country. And where better can people gather graciously than in Thyruid's Inn-by-the-Bye?

Well. If Thyruid had not been won over by the overwhelming urgency within himself to be the best of hosts for whoever came to his door, such a kind introduction would surely have won the heart. And so, with double warmth and just a hint of blush, Thyruid raised aloud the question of breakfast while Marthuida was moving about, aiding in arranging the large number so they could be fed. Thyruid turned to join her and, almost by magic, the trays and the beverage – in wee folk sized mugs – appeared and spread quickly among them all. Breakfast followed presently as they were happy with the usual Hyperbian breakfast of gruel-mush and suet-fried cakes. (It may not sound good to us – but what would you like if you were one of the wee folk?)

Ordinarily, a good meal will leave a crowd happy and mellowed, satisfied with the way things feel. A full stomach usually will ease a crowd down to have a good and ordered meeting. There are exceptions, of course; those exceptions normally happen when the people are excited. And, today, the people from the hills were *excited*; they had things to talk about so that breakfast served only to freshen their zeal. The roar now rose to overwhelm even the booming tones of Thyruid. 'What did you put in that breakfast, Marthuida?' asked Thyruid. 'Nothing special … just the usual. It has never done *this* before' she replied.

'All right! All right! Settle down, or we will never get to talk over all the noise'. The same leader shouted forth, calming down his people. And, somehow, his voice was heard in the midst of all the noise. The quiet that followed was as deafening as the racket that preceded the call. The interest was there and was great. The issue was urgent in their hearts. 'Thyruid, my friendly host, would you be so kind as to listen to us and to offer your wise suggestion when we have gone on a while? We all trust the wisdom of the Innkeeper of the Inn-by-the-Bye'.

'Why, of course, I guess' answered the surprised and pleased Thyruid.

'You know that there are old customs in Hyperbia. And in the hill parts, among the hill people, those customs hang on longer, stronger. Some say that those customs are very necessary to our living, to our identity as Hyperbian folk; without our ancient ways, we would fall apart they say. Others, mostly the young, say that is ridiculous. Listen to what they say'.

And Thyruid sat and listened along with the rest of the assembled people as the two sides argued back and forth the values of tradition and the values of cutting free. The day wore on and on, and Thyruid sat and listened, sat and listened … and squirmed just a bit. Finally, it was nearing supper time; they had talked right through lunch and poor Thyruid's wisdom was being severely tested by the rumbling of his stomach – for he had become quite hungry.

'All right! All right! Let me speak!' said Thyruid. And all were quiet. 'I have heard your talk and considered it all. We in the valley and the meadows have had similar problems in the past. And it seemed good to us to blend the two. For our traditions have a spirit of openness about them, although we do not always look at them that way. Those traditions are meant to give some meaning and order to our lives together. They set in perspective some things which are important so that we keep our dignity and respect for one another. And for ourselves.

'From your own words, your family is very important: uphold that truth. And your helping spirit – keep that. And that which is sacred: keep it sacred. But much of the rest is just convenience and may well be relaxed. Keep the main threads firm and relax the rest. That is what seems good to me.

'And now, let us look to dinner. I am hungry, aren't you?'

And Carymba, watching from the side, smiled for her people and for her wise friend from the valley's Inn-by-the-Bye.

For the sermon of 18 May 1980, titled "One", based on John 17:20-26.

XXI

'You do not have any idea what you are talking about! None whatsoever! You have been burying your head in the sands of forgotten time, ostrich-like'.

'What do you mean by that? Let us remember well the heritage of this place; by being here, the heritage is our own. It owns us'.

'I do not go overboard on my attachment to the past. And that is not the problem anyway. These fools, these newcomers, these ... these intruders ... they have disregarded the rules and the standings of Hyperbian folk from forever; they have disregarded all the natural Hyperbian signs of importance and are dragging us down from the grandeur of our fathers. Mind you, they are leading us all to disaster! Something must be done!'

...

The argument continued long. It had been going on for years and years. Without the argument and the old pride which cannot see, there would be no kingdom of Grump for Orgello to rule – or for the hero-worshipping Geron to people. Really, Orgello was only concerned with himself; he wanted to make real the "improved" memories he bore – but that was impossible ever since the other little people had come into the meadow lands of Hyperbia. Still, Orgello was easy to misunderstand. His bitter conceits burrowed behind his fantastic, playful panoramas of a yesteryear that he wishes had been and still was.

...

'Tradition lies hard here. The growth from our past is very important, for it makes us a people. come, let us walk about and see'. Carymba thus finally entered a sane voice into the screaming match of the year. (These arguments flair up every now and then, bringing to light the weak fabric of Hyperbian life together.)

Mocha, who is said to look only forward, and Otto, the temperate traditionalist, agreed readily. But Orgello simply threw up his hands in despair: 'Either it is my way, with my understanding and no other ... or it is nothing at all. There is no alternative, no room for talk or hope with their folly. Why talk? All truth is with me. If you want the truth, come to me!'

And off he went, Geron following carefully, stomping their silliness into the dust as the kingdom of Grump swallowed its prince and populace once more. The others watched them go – and sighed with relief; talk was impossible, mutual acceptance was impossible when ... 'he will not even admit that we exist, that anything exists outside his kingdom of Grump' – Carymba finished the thought of them all.

Carymba began her steady hobble by crossing over the dust trail to the kingdom of Grump and moving on across the rolling meadows. Two others, Mocha and Otto, followed. The three walked along in quiet for a while, until Carymba broke the silence: 'Notice the green here; the glow is not this sharply brilliant very often. I always see it in moments of piercing promise, moments when pieces of our heritage throw themselves forward, recreated in hope for tomorrow or the next day'.

'And the shadows the pebbles spray across the sky: are they not refiguring the images left in the dust aglow underfoot?' Mocha surprised himself with that idea, for he had seen those patterns in the Hyperbian sky every day – but only now did Mocha see the changing-ness of it all. The linkage of tradition to today and tomorrow came to him just now.

'Well ... yes. These things do come from today. But the need is to remember well yesterday and all the linked days before that. All of them'. Otto insisted on the past; it was dear to him. Even the insight born from Mocha's stubborn mind did not satisfy Otto. 'We need to remember; that is necessary if we are not to lose ourselves'.

'And find ourselves in the loss, perhaps?' needled Carymba, her eyes sparkling in fun. 'Do look at the patterns up there, Otto. Mocha is right; those shadows are thrown up by old, old pebbles; those bits of rock have witnessed all our yesterdays – and Orgello's, too (those, that is, which are real, rather than products of his wishing for his own sorts of glory). They throw images out from the dust, but not all the images. Only some can go up from yesterday, carrying on till today – and new ones come to join with them. Tomorrow, we will find the same sort of changes again'.

'What are you talking about, Carymba?' inquired Otto. 'I am not at all sure I understand you. I have never heard of such things before'.

'Yesterday was good. You know it; I know it; even Mocha knows it. If he did not know, he would not have blushed right then. Yes. And these pebbles know yesterdays beyond our memories. Those memories were good in their own way, in their own day: the pebbles know. But only some of those memories make shadow patterns today. Some are useful; some are not. The light seeks out the useful to create the oneness of today. ... Now, we are people'.

'Yes, we are' agreed both Otto and Mocha.

'And, as people, we are part of this land, our Hyperbia'.

'Yes'.

'Part of yesterday's memories builds that togetherness which is today and tomorrow. Some parts do not'.

'True'.

So ... let us turn in to the Inn-by-the-Bye and find our growing oneness in the promise of the pebble-shadows and the special green of today's promising glow. ... Marthuida! Give us three mugs!'

For the Sermon for 25 May 1980, titled "On All Flesh", based on Acts 2:1-21.

XXII

An early breakfast sat before his eyes, barely seen. The eyes were not seeing well yet, for the hour was early and poor Geoffrey always woke up slowly and with great difficulty. His room in the Inn-by-the-Bye, however, set directly over the kitchen – and the host and hostess, Thyruid and Marthuida, began their day early, every day.

So it is that Geoffrey is awakened by the clatter of the kitchen of the Inn-by-the-Bye, by the chores and by the fine aroma of a fresh day's breakfast. There is no point in trying to sleep; it is an impossible idea anyway. So, Geoffrey finds himself daily sitting in a chair, off to the side of dining room at the Inn, gazing at his breakfast and not really sure how to coordinate himself into enjoying it.

And on this particular morning, the barely roused Geoffrey found himself met by his good breakfast – Marthuida is a master in the kitchen – and by the always awake Carymba. As his mind stirred slowly, his first wondering was how anyone could be that awake, and at such a time! Of course, Geoffrey could not realize that some people waken quickly and stay sharp almost all of their waking hours. Poor Geoffrey always had to clear his fog and so could not possibly imagine what it would be like not to have one's head enwrapped in a heavy cloud every morning.

Geoffrey was still operating on habit and reflex. When Carymba bounded in brightly and sprightly, poor Geoffrey knew not what to make of this morning-sprite's cheerful urging: 'Geoffrey! Have you forgotten this day?' He looked blankly; what day? was all that he rumbled, turtle-fast, through his sluggish mind. Carymba giggled lightly: 'Oh, Geoffrey! We have only an hour and half ... and it takes an hour to get there. Come on, Geoffrey! We need to keep moving!'

'With that guy, you mean *get* moving!' laughed Thyruid, good naturedly. 'You should know better than to schedule anything with Geoffrey before

165

noon!' Thyruid's eyes sparkled and shone, nearly as brightly as did the well-polished brassware … which had just come out from under Thyruid's busy polishing cloth.

The surprise and the slow realization that he must get himself moving finally brought Geoffrey's cooling breakfast to his mouth. Ten minutes later, he had finished. For Geoffrey, the pace was blistering; for Carymba, the clock just sped along for she had in mind the walk into the hills. Fifteen minutes more and Geoffrey had managed, barely, to prepare himself to meet the outside world. A proper gentleman's gentleman, even without a regular position (other than with Yves and Betsy, who really did not know what to do with a gentleman, let alone a gentleman's gentleman) had to take time to prepare just to meet the day.

Finally, they did get off, although Geoffrey was certain they need not go so fast, nor so steadily as Carymba's steady hobble dictated. Even after noon had passed, Geoffrey preferred the slow movements of a fine gentleman to the steady march of Carymba when she had someplace to go.

The meadows soon turned into little hills, which grew in turn into ever bigger hills. Carymba led him skillfully along the paths his careless eye had never noticed. 'Come along, Geoffrey; we will be late. Really, you will like the people once you see them there. You will even like the place'.

'Are you sure you know where you are going? I would think we were lost; everything looks the same to me'. 'Yes. Yes. Geoffrey. Relax and look. You will see there is a great deal of difference to be seen along this little path. It is not well worn because few from the hills go to the meadows and fewer from the meadows go to the hills'. 'With good reason! Why should anyone want to climb these hills?'. 'We are doing just fine. There is not far to go'. And with that, she turned their steady pace to the steepest hill yet. Geoffrey groaned; Carymba wondered why she had brought him along … then remembered … .

After the climb, which seemed to go on forever in Geoffrey's mind, they came to a flat spot with a cup like recess in the middle. 'Here we are … and on time, barely' sounded Carymba with satisfaction; Geoffrey sighed in true

166

relief. They had arrived … Carymba must have been right – there is a path which does something besides wind around the same hill all the time.

But, as Geoffrey looked around, all he could see was this cup-like are, half filled with people. He had been in places like this before – even bigger ones, fancier ones – and they had offered nothing which would have been reason enough for an hour's forced march up these hills. Politely, though, Geoffrey smiled and followed Carymba into the arena, feeling at once both comfortable and strange, for everyone knew everyone except for him. Yet, the air was pleasant in their midst.

The general expectation was for a pleasant gathering. Geoffrey, relatively new to Hyperbia, having come suddenly from his employ in Cumberland, came to meet the hill folk, the old friends of his new friend, little Carymba. He expected to meet lots of people – and maybe remember a few. Carymba guided him about, introducing him, inviting that pleasant chatter which graces friendly gatherings. Pleasant and congenial, indeed, everything went along as everyone expected.

The day wore on pleasantly for everyone, even for Geoffrey whose fog had lifted, and uneasiness vanished by the time the afternoon wore long.

Carymba was the first to notice a shifting sense in the air, in the place, in the new electric-like ring to the setting. She sniffed approvingly and watched in her special way. These folk had always been friendly; now something more is happening. They had gathered here for years; now the gathering is meeting a strange embrace. Hearts are fired and directions of view are shifted.

'We are finely together now' – the comment rose from Geoffrey, the one who usually does not see. They all agreed; the action among them now filled them. They have become finally finely together and in common with the embrace which eased with them, did not force them but fulfilled them all, each one. Carymba knew … and then rejoiced quietly at the gift.

'Now, Geoffrey, we must return. Leaving here now changes nothing of what has changed. … Take me back to the valley, to the meadows'.

For the Sermon for 1 June 1980, titled "The Wise Song", based on Proverbs 8:22-31.

XXIII

Rumblings echoed their loud exchanges of ominous greetings from the darkened and wind-swept North land. Hyperbia and her gentle, gentle folk cowered before the threatening scene. Like a giant black cat, the North flashed its lively eyes, hissed and roared as giant, tearing black claws tore across the ways.

Like a cornered prey, Hyperbia huddled back, hoping to endure the rushing leap of the storm upon her. Huts were battened; the Inn-by-the-Bye was barred shut, tight against the coming rage. Almost all the wee folk had found their corners wherein they might cower. The few wee folk left out glanced North … and scurried home. Yves and Betsy, so large in a tiny land, found shelter behind a ridge. All eyes, all ears kept attention on the North.

The longer those eyes watched, the blacker advanced the sure fury, and the ghastlier glimmered the flashing glare of those blinking lights of terror, striking out of the tumbling mass approaching. The closer those ears listened to the raging fury, the louder came the screaming, haunting howl of the coming unknown. At first, it was like an angry, stalking cat; now it was more like ten cats, giant cats, fighting fiercely for the right to devour the awaiting gentle land. The people trembled and held their doors closed tight, barred their windows … yet they still peeked out the cracks, always to the North, the now ominous North.

Yves and Betsy had never needed a house. As children, they had never thought of such a place until it was needed. They were far too large to fit into the huts and cabins of the wee folk; even the Inn-by-the-Bye was much too small. That had never been a problem … before tonight.

Huddled into their corner, the children looked at each other and shuddered. All their attention was on the North … and on their lack of shelter now that it was needed. The children peered out over the ledge, timidly glancing at the North, the North. The look they took did nothing to assure them, for they saw the storm approaching their gentle land. The swirling, snarling darkness was coming upon them; and they were afraid: they had nowhere to go. They could only wait and watch – or wait and hide ... and tremble.

The wee folk were little better off behind their walls and their battened and bolted windows and doors. The rage rattled their huts and shook the bravest heart. Ribbert, bold and brave, quit his window crack for a more forgetful stance. The Innkeeper and his wife with his guests huddled together in pale silence, listening to the groaning. Meadow tradesmen and hill folk alike: they all trembled as the fearsome guest – or guests – descended on their poor, gentle land.

Geoffrey could remember nothing like this in the more brazen Cumberland. Thyruid knew terrors of his own before ...: they were nothing to compare with this rumbling, tumbling, frightful unknown. The land of Hyperbia had always been a peaceful place. This kind of rage from the North wrenched their unwary habits. In brief: everyone was afraid. The walls offered no more relief from the grip of fear than did that puny ridge which marked the place of shelter for the big children, Yves and his sister Betsy.

From the North, it came closer. Really, this was not an 'it'; it was a 'they'. A massive horde or raging beasts swirling, twisting, snarling, whining, driving the fierceness of their primeval anger against each other and against the lands trampled beneath their slashing claws. Yves alone peeked as the rage came upon the helpless meadows; all the others trembled and hid ... but listened sharply for the Northern Rage.

Snapping up on the right came a horrid black hand-like movement, sparkled with an arching yellow – horrid – and with flashing sparks of crimson ... a tide crushing against the horned evil on the left, spitting fire and venom in vile return. The crash of monsters, wild and mighty. controlled by hungers and angers unknown to even the bitterest, nastiest of the wee folk – that crash moved forward.

Rumbling out of the center came a third – darker, larger, fiercer, angrier, more glaring in white hot erupting terror than the others. The three lurched forward, exploding onto the meadows. They moved relentlessly toward Yves in the frenzy of their destroying rage. He watched where every ear was turned, awaiting the meeting of the waring beasts with his own little place of hiding. Betsy was rolled in a ball beside him, trembling with a fear that now held Yves motionless.

Shelter was meaningless before these beasts. Everything in Hyperbia looked North, to the coming end, to the waste which lay behind the screaming, raging destroyers at war with each other … but burying all else in their fury unspent.

Every thought was toward the North. North was the way that mightily demanded attention. But North was not the way of importance.

Besides Yves and Betsy, one more knew no roof in Hyperbia. One more lived in open communion with the gentleness and the fierce presence at work in the land. One more – Carymba, the little crippled waif. And she alone looked not North to the raging warriors of the darkness, but South, the other way, toward where the Delight danced in the pleasuring to be had about the land.

Carymba walked, hobbling with the roar dwindled to a purr in the reflection of Delight. She came to Yves, before his fear-wrenched eyes … and she smiled. She pointed the other way, away from the raging, fearful Unknown. 'Look' she said. Yves was frozen as the monster darkness neared. 'Look' she said, again. Yves stuttered … and saw her point behind him and once more he shuddered, fearing the meeting of more monsters with the Northern ones upon his head.

But Yves looked anyway. And he poked Betsy, curled up in fear at his feet. 'Look! Look!' he pointed away. And Betsy just barely peeked one eye out of her hiding, toward the South.

Three turned from the rage toward the delight beyond them ... and the Northern Rage stood still. Three stood up, looking South ... and the Northern Rage retreated north, tamed by Delight taken in by three.

In the South, there was a song. Only three heard it ... the others were too busy being afraid of the North they heard, even after the Rage had ended its roar.

For the Sermon for 8 June 1980, titled "A Man Of Authority", based on Luke 7:1-10.

XXIV

'No. No. Definitely not. I would not even consider such a thing. That would be ridiculous and would do me no good. Why would you ever even think to suggest such an idea?'

'Settle down, John. You would think I had asked you to sell your soul to the devil, down at *his* forge in the glen. Just because you do not want to get involved: that is no reason for flying off into a … a tirade like this. Settle down, John.

'Settle down you say! First you tell me to work with that misplaced lowlander who could not hold a job in the hills if he had to. And now you tell me to settle down. Who do you think you are, anyway? A big deal of some sort? Well, you are not that; you are just plain old Ribbert. Nothing more than that'.

'John, you have no idea what you are saying. I suggested to you that you would find value in this man from the meadows. He moved into the hills because he liked the skills he knew were here … or thought he knew. Not many have ventured into the hills from the meadows. Life is easier down there. One, however, comes to work at your trade – and you are the best iron worker in the hills. But your can only see a lowlander. You may be hill folk, a high-lander, but you certainly are not high-minded'.

Ribbert turned away. He was not accustomed to speaking much. And he was not accustomed to being so angry. John, the master iron worker in the hills, the finest craftsman at his trade that any one could remember, was also stubborn, easily angered – as hot as his own forge fire at times, and perfectly willing to listen to no one, not even his own mother.

John had always been that way. Perhaps that violent independence contributed to his fine skill. John was not mean. He was easy to get along with if everything went his way, if everyone took his advice as gospel, never raised a question – except for a piece of clarification, provided it be done with sufficient humility – and never offered anything different. *Then*, he was as pleasant as anything and as sweet as he could be. Usually, people treated John that way; it was easier even if it did confirm him in his foolish, prideful anger.

Today, John had another problem. First, Ribbert had had the audacity to suggest something to John – and it was not even an order for iron work. That would have been bad enough, in John's eyes. But now Ribbert had had the nerve to turn away from him. The anger level in John's heart reached the heat of his prime forge fire. John took after Ribbert.

Both men were strong and determined. They were hard workers and were proud in what they did. When John grabbed Ribbert by the arm, Ribbert spun around to face him. Anger flared; muscles tightened; like a pair of rams in mating season, they prepared to attack each other ... and all because John was so thoroughly independent.

The engagement came in a whirl of arms and legs and bodies hardened by the tempering of hard labor, sharpened by the flashing fire of hot anger. They wrestled each other, pulling, twisting, holding each other. They rolled and bellowed about, echoing the exertion of their anger about the hills. Others, who knew both men but nothing of the cause of the battle, watched, aghast.

Hour passed by hour. The battle kept its freshness. Hour passed by hour. The battle raged ... although the combatants shared a growing weariness which neither would confess, to which each would not permit himself to succumb. John had never admitted anyone to even a trace of authority over him; he had to be autonomous. He had to see himself as he had always been. Ribbert likewise could not permit the attacker to hold any edge. The wee folk watched their fellows in titanic struggle and puzzled over the most unusual contest.

Night came; they fought on, matched in strength, in skill, in growing weariness, in stubbornness. And light came again; they fought still, too stubborn, too sure to stop, either of them.

The hill folk watched. They had few fights here and a match such as this, engaged with such continuing intensity, puzzled the peaceful folk.

The lowlander, whose case had brought the occasion for the struggle, fled. He was afraid. Returning to the meadows below, he met several at the Inn-by-the-Bye and told them of his adventures in the hills and the fight which had erupted before his eyes. He told them he was afraid.

A voice entered: 'Who was fighting?' 'Ribbert, who had befriended me, and an iron worker named John'. Then the crowd at the Inn rumbled among themselves about those strange hill folk; they must be barely civilized, to be acting like that.

Two sets of eyes caught sight of each other and left, quietly, quickly. The almost hidden path into the hills carried them along until they could see the weary but still-active warriors in firm combat.

They came to a pause: "Ribbert! John! Stop that fighting this moment! You met to do good and you fight out of pure stubborn foolishness!' The hill folk looked and gaped; Ribbert and John stopped and looked, too.

'John, you go to the meadows, to the Inn-by-the-Bye. Ask for a man named Gilbert of Hoya. You will bring him back in peace and teach him your trade. He needs you and you, in your shame, need him. Ribbert, as for you: come here!'

The men, fresh from unresolved combat, looked at each other and shook hands; each went as directed, without question for a strange air hung suddenly upon the hills. John sought out Gilbert as a helper, to teach him the finest of iron work. Ribbert climbed to the perch from which the voice had cried to them in their combat.

'Ribbert, this is Sola, a man young of spirit, a retired tradesman from the meadows. He will help you prepare a place for Gilbert, near the forge of John. All right?'

'We will take care of it all. Shall we start, Sola?' 'Yes'. 'Farewell … and thanks, Carymba'.

For the Sermon for 15 June 1980, titled "The Gospel Preached", based on Galatians 1:11-24.

XXV

'Betsy … it is getting light out. We should get up and see if we can get some breakfast. Thyruid and Marthuida will be up soon. Marthuida will have some breakfast for us.

'Oh, Yves, I would rather sleep. This morning, I just do not feel very adventuresome. All of this time we have been here, we have gone and looked, gone and played; we have run to the Inn-by-the-Bye for our meals; we have been lost and found. I always wanted to be big! And now we are big – but still children. All the grown ups are wee folk. Oh, what is the use! … leave me alone, Yves!'

'No, Betsy: I cannot just leave you alone. We must go and find our breakfast. That is just the way things are'.

'Well, why *must* they be that way? Why can't we just sit here and rest and not worry about all that stuff? The world ought to be kinder to little girls!'

'Quit pouting, Betsy. Life here is good to us … good enough anyway. We have not gone hungry. We have room in which to play, to laugh, to cry, … to do all the things children should do. We have many friends among the wee folk'.

'Oh yes, I know, Yves. But it should be easier. At times, I think Orgello has a point; his way, things would be orderly …'

'everything in *his* place! Now, come on. I am getting hungry'.

The road to the Inn-by-the-Bye appeared, carried the children along, turned suddenly with the curve that was not there a minute ago, and dropped them onto the green before the Inn. 'Good morning!' The voice bellowed from the Inn with more seriousness than usual as the children bumbled in, flopping themselves down before the Inn, upon the broad and empty green.

Betsy, already grumbly about everything in particular and nothing in general, never noticed; she was too concerned with her own pique to take note of the seriousness in Thyruid's rumbling greeting. Yves, however, did notice it … with concern. 'And good morning to you, sir. What do you have for breakfast?' Yves tried to be cheerful; he had awakened cheerful though first Betsy and now Thyruid were slackening his eagerness for the new day. 'The usual. Just wait a minute' returned as Thyruid's abrupt answer.

Shortly, the wee man brought out the platters of children's portions; he and Marthuida had learned to use their big trays rather than many plates for Yves and Betsy. He did not have his usual flash, however, but sort of shuffled over and merely set the trays down offhandedly. 'What is the problem, Thyruid?' asked Yves; Betsy had not noticed any problem and said so. 'But he is not as … as …. as Thyruidish as usual complained Yves.

'Oh … maybe it is just one of those days … I guess that is it. … Well, not really … it seems that nothing is hanging in place very well. Marthuida and I make the usual plans, go through the usual routine. We have a business as usual approach. But the spark of Hyperbia seems to be missing. Somehow, we ought to find it again'.

The children pondered over breakfast. Then, Yves turned to his mopey sister and said: 'Betsy, let's go look for the spark of Hyperbia, the one Thyruid said was missing!' 'Ok, Yves: but what is it?' 'I do not know. That will be our first problem. Thyruid! What *is* the spark of Hyperbia? We want to look for it; we need a new adventure to fill today'.

'That is hard to say, Yves. Perhaps you two will be able to find it and to learn what it is once you find it. We had it once … but not now. It has been a long time. Years ago, everyone worked together and built up a closeness. Then we got busy, or disappointed; sharing that pity instead of care.

Carymba came down from the hills … and she helped for a while. You two came and stirred us up for a while. And so did Geoffrey, our little gentleman's gentleman. Maybe we have become too settled and look for some sort of super magic to move us out into yesteryear. I do not know what it is. But we sure do not have it, whatever it is. Maybe, if you look, you can find it'.

'You are the Innkeeper in a magic land … and you are seeking a special super magic! Ha! But we will look. Come on, Betsy'.

And the two big children looked high … and they looked low. They wandered around the meadows, looking carefully as the wee crippled waif Carymba had taught them. The looked over End Ridge … and sat to listen for a while: maybe they would hear something. The song was soft and light and spoke of pearls from the sand; they did not understand and went on, taking the song and the melody with them.

They looked to the hills but saw no help there. They wandered in the valley, out toward the Sea. They talked to hill folk and to meadows tradesmen. They talked to Geoffrey and to old Sola. They even went out to the kingdom of Grump; it was worse there for they had never lost the spark since they had never had it. Grump relied on the fathers alone.

Evening came and the two returned to the Inn, tired and sad. They had looked for a spark, the likes of which they did not know, among a people who only knew it was missing, whatever it was, whatever it had been.

The children sat down and ate; everyone was quiet with them until Marthuida asked what they had found. 'All we found … *all* … was a song from the Other Side, a song about pearls in the sand'. Then old Sola looked up, raised his big old voice and sang the same song the children had heard. The song had been forgotten, but no more … the price was too great to lose a second time.

Night settled well, nestled about that song.

For the Sermon for 29 June 1980, titled "Peoples' Sayings", based on Luke 9:1-24.

XXVI

'People sure do talk a lot! I have been sitting here, out of the way like I am now, quietly listening to these meadow craftsmen in their work. Their jaws should be tired, their tongues exhausted before they even stop for a lunch break. It is worse than the Gossips' Convention they held in the capital of Cumberland each year. At the least, it is *as* bad. The noise, the confusion of tongues and of tales, all wagging in eager delight over half truths and overly stretched inferences, and even stranger stories passed off as real: it is hard to believe it at all'.

'Come along, Geoffrey. We might be able to find some lunch at the Inn-by-the-Bye' interrupted Carymba. Off they went to the Inn by way of the well-known path, the curve which is suddenly there, the turn into the green before the Inn and into the comfortable setting of Thyruid's common room.

Settled into a corner table, to the side and out of the way, Geoffrey ordered a light lunch for himself and for Carymba, his friend. 'I cannot get over that land of … of … of babel out on that meadow'. 'Easy, Geoffrey … let's relax and enjoy our lunch. Marthuida prepared it … and she is a great cook. *That* you must admit!' 'Ok. How was your trip into the hills this past week? I have not talked with you since you came back'. 'Oh, it was fine. I saw many old friends … we reminisced a lot'. And, over such small talk, friendly and kindly, the two friends ate their lunch.

As Geoffrey and Carymba sat in their back corner, the center of the room became filled with men, excited men. The two listened as one of these newcomers raised his voice and spoke.

'My friends! We have just come down from the hills. The ferment there, which we saw, would frighten the very boldest of you. Mother turned against daughter, father against son, brother against brother. The very air is

179

tense … like the brooding feel one has when a mighty storm hovers, ready to pounce upon the land and rend asunder what we treasure so dearly. The talk there is that a strange person has been moving among them, stirring up the young to throw away the values of their parents. One man told me it was like a magic piper drawing people away, like they were enchanted. It is a fearful thing. Believe me!'

The folk in the Inn were spellbound by the story. They could hardly believe, they could barely imagine such a thing – although Orgello himself lived by believing that this society in Hyperbia, on the meadows, had come about by so many being enchanted-down from the pristine oppression of his grandfather's day. People found themselves taxed. If it had been good news, that they would not have believed for it would seem so strange. The word of an ominous threat: *that* they were ready to believe, and be safe in their belief.

The storyteller continued. 'Now, I did not see this enchanter myself. I have to rely upon the older folk who told me of their terror. They were afraid for their lives, for their property. They are crying for someone to arise and protect them from this terrible threat. That is the hills, of course. *My* fear is that the enchantment will flow to our beloved meadows and blacken our hopes here'.

'Friend! Permit me to ask of what sort this enchantment is! If we know its sort, we can be wary for ourselves, free from the constraint of a strong-armed crutch'.

'*Who are you*?!' demanded the speaker, peering into the depths of the Inn's dim corner. 'My name is Geoffrey, of Cumberland, a gentleman's gentleman – once. Now, I am becoming a part of our Hyperbian place. And your name, sir?' 'Hrumph! What do you mean by challenging me? Do you think I do not know what I am saying? Do you think I do not know what is important?' 'Well, Mr. Hrumph, it seems that my friend here with me also just came down from visiting in the hills and … well, perhaps they were different hills'.

'My name is *not* Hrumph! And who is your silly friend, anyway?'

'Her name is not Anyway, Mr. Hrumph; she is a lady named Carymba'.

'Enough, Geoffrey. Let me tell the sayings of those people, the hill people. They are my people. I was raised among them before I was brought to live and walk among these people, here in the meadows. Now, Mr. Hrumph, how long has it been since you came to the meadows from the hills?'

'A few days. What difference does that make?'

'I thought so. The hill folk were relieved when I was there just yesterday. It seems the real Troubler of Greenhill had given up his designs and left a few days before. Families were relaxing and building together for peace. Now they were freed of fear. They know you, Mr. Hrumph, as Dumart – although I like your choice of names better than your mother's earlier choice. And you, my people, do you forget so easily the songs that are sung to you? Can you turn to the babbling of a nameless wretch, afraid of what is given for you? Weep! It will cleanse your folly. Weep! And return to your joy!;

For the Sermon for 6 July 1980, titled "Seven Thousand", based on 1 Kings 19:14-21.

XXVII

'What is the matter, Yves, my friend? You look as though all of Hyperbia is pushing you down! You are all alone over here in this rare corner, away from where the people are likely to be. To tell you the truth, I wandered over here to find some quiet myself. But your gloom has distracted me; I cannot find quiet without the brightness of your usual face, my friend'.

'Geoffrey, really it is nothing. I just wanted to sit out here and think a bit … about things. Do you know what I mean?'

'I think so. May I sit down and think with you?'

'Sure. Why not? Do sit down'.

And so, they sat together, in quiet, just thinking. Geoffrey was thinking about his friend, Yves. For a while, until it became obvious that such was useless, Geoffrey had played gentleman's gentleman to Yves and Betsy, his sister. Geoffrey had become quite fond of them, but they really did not need a gentleman's gentleman; nor did they want one. In time, he had adapted to the new land and the different way of acting. The change had not been easy, and the games with those children, as large as they are in a land of wee folk, and to a wee person … well, they had helped Geoffrey get used to it all. Now this friend, Yves, seemed awfully sad, awfully alone. Geoffrey thought and thought: 'how can I help Yves be happy again?'

Yves sat as he had sat before, simply being glum. He was so blue that he had forgotten what had made him sad in the first place. And most of the time he merely left it as forgotten. But every now and then, he would sort of look up and remember. It felt like the old enemy who had made him sad just stood there, waiting for him to lift his head, waiting to hit him over the head with a big wooden mallet, swinging hard to drive him further into gloom and make the bell ring … like the old time carnivals where a man can test his strength. Yves remembered seeing one of those carnivals once … but the memory only made him sadder, if that were possible.

Geoffrey looked at his friend and his heart ached for him. 'How did you get so sad, Yves? I hurt to see you so sad. What can I do?'

'Nothing, Geoffrey: nothing. Let me forget'.

'You are not forgetting. You are being beaten by your sorrow … whatever it is. Your enemy within is beating you. … Perhaps telling me will help'.

'The tale is too long, Geoffrey. You would not be interested. I cannot even remember all of it'.

'Perhaps, if you go backwards through the story, I will find a place which I recognize, and you will not need to tell the whole story. You can try it, anyway'.

'Ok, I will try'. said Yves, settling uncomfortably to his task. 'You found me sitting here. My … my mother would have called it my sulking. Hiding in a corner: I used to do that all the time when I was little, before Betsy and I found ourselves here, in Hyperbia. I have been sitting here for a while; I forget how long now, but a while. And after a while, I forget why I am sulking. And then, I look up and get clobbered by it again. I still do not remember the reason; I only know that I do not want to remember.

That makes your question harder, Geoffrey; I do not want to remember and you are asking me to remember. My mother used to do that, too. I am not sure she ever understood. Maybe you don't either. Anyway' – Yves shuffled to find a position less uncomfortable for his reverse-tale, 'I kept looking down like this; I did not get clobbered by my sadness-maker that way. It is easier to sit in the marshmallow and cotton-candy mist of unknown sadness than to keep getting hit. It is like being in a dark hole without a light. You cannot see, but you get used to that after a while. Oh, what's the use!'

'Go on, please. There must be another step. Perhaps some light will help me see'.

'Well, I got here, as I recall, from feeling hopeless. There was nothing that would make sense or right of anything. I remember being very confused about everything. I was alone, feeling very alone. No one would understand. It was painful, which was what brought me to forgetfulness, this blackness that wraps itself around me like a sticky, enclosing blanket. There is a comfort in forgetfulness; I can just be sad'.

'How did you ever get such a black view on things?'

'It was easy. Everyone was against me. Everything I did was wrong. I tripped over myself. I tripped over my thoughts as well as over my feet. Even I did not laugh at my jokes. Even I cackled at my failings; everyone else did so I did too. But it did not feel funny. Not to me, anyway. … Why is it that I feel like I keep ducking that memory that kept hitting me? It seems like it is quite ready to clobber me, but I have managed to step aside while we are talking … . Oh well, where was I? … Yes, I felt poorly for myself. The others just laughed. They did not care'.

'That is pretty bad. How did you get there?' Poor Geoffrey, he was still looking for some little clue to help Yves.

'It is hard to remember now. A bunch of things, I guess. I tried to help Betsy and did not. I tried to help, doing some work with a tradesman on the meadows, like Carymba does and failed, making his work harder. I just did it wrong. I tried to follow Carymba, to learn from her, and got lost. I broke a tray down at the Inn-by-the-Bye … one of the good ones, Marthuida's favorite. She cried when it happened. Things like that'.

'Yves! Help! I hurt my ankle and cannot walk! Help!' The cry came from not far away. Only Yves in all Hyperbia was big enough to help her, really. Yves forgot his forgetfulness – and Geoffrey, too – and ran to his sister, Betsy.

Geoffrey sat as he had been sitting and smiled ... and Hyperbia became a bit lighter that day.

For the Sermon for 13 July 1980, titled "Harvesting", based on Luke 10:1-12. 17-20.

XXVIII

'Thyruid, I tell you, truly I tell you that your action is needed. Can you not see the need? Look across that green' – she gestured broadly – can you see only customers there? Are there no hearts crying?'

'Poppycock, Carymba! You are always full to overflowing with a bunch of nonsense. Do you not realize that this is an Inn? that customers pay the bills so that there is an Inn where they can gather? Because I am who I am; because this place is an Inn; because Hyperbia is Hyperbia and the order of things is as it is; because all of that is, I see customers out there. If I do not see customers, I am in trouble'.

'No one is there now, Thyruid. But when they are, do you see *only* customers? Remember the day they held off to surprise you? Were they only customers then? Remember the night of terror, when even the mighty Inn trembled in fear, and the Innkeeper with it? Were mere customers enough then? enough to ease the screaming terror from the North?'

'Yes, yes, Carymba. Settle down, please. I used to agree with you. Then I thought that guests were guests – and friends about the hearth. But times have been tight lately. I have costs, too, and pressures which no one can know. I see now that I would have been wiser to have been more prudent over the years'.

'You have been talking with Sylvester, haven't you?'

'Yes. How did you know? What do you care?'

'I just know. Remember, Thyruid, remember why the Inn became so beloved. And consider well the advice of Sylvester. He is a sly one'. And, with that, Carymba hobbled off toward the meadows, lost in her thoughts. She was troubled and saw others troubled as well. Hyperbia was not as it had been. The meadows had a different flavor than they used to have. Even Geoffrey was worried: no one needed or wanted a gentleman's gentleman … and the alternatives he had met here of late were settling uneasily.

Sylvester, you see, was new. He had come down from the stormy Northland, easing in with a callous smile and a cautious step. He steered clear of Orgello and his kingdom of Grump; he did not need them. But the rest of the meadowlands were fair game for him. Here, foolishness reigned. This way of life is foolishness according to the self-evident standards of the Northland … and of the kingdom of Grump. Sylvester would have been happy on Orgello's blanket of gloom; but, in his eyes, the chains of prudence and fear stood in need of being shown abroad. That is why came to talk with Thyruid: the Inn-by-the-Bye was a good place to begin.

Carymba had left Thyruid with a call to remember. Since the Inn was empty, Thyruid propped his head in his hands, leaning upon the counter, and thought. Remembering was difficult; there was so much fresh stuff in the way that the old ways to be remembered were clouded over. That was the wish of Sylvester. So, Thyruid brooded, an angry spirit upon the face of the deep.

Behind the shadows of the kitchen stood Marthuida, unsure of what to do. Such a change had come over her husband, Thyruid. She could hardly imagine such comments and attitudes coming from him after all these years. Marthuida was worried.

'Thyruid …'. Marthuida's voice echoed in the empty Inn. 'Thyruid, this Inn was made for guests. These walls were warm for friends, both old and new. We have never had just customers. What is a customer, anyway? Who would come here as only a customer? This dust … it is our dust. What are you doing, Thyruid?'

Thyruid stood there and thought Sylvester's thoughts. He forgot Papa and Mama, the Boss and the little old woman with the rough work hands and the strange look, the one who had sent them to work here and not to forget the cup of water … ever. Thyruid forgot the urgency of his work in the hard-nosed "common-sense" that Sylvester had fed him. At least it seemed like common-sense to Thyruid at the time. He had not ignored his wife; the want of an answer came from his deep, deep preoccupation with himself. Thyruid was forgetting everything, even his empty Inn; he was forgetting himself with his new preoccupation with prudence.

Carymba walked across the fields and the meadows. The craftsmen were not very busy today because they were all talking together. 'Carymba, come here!' came the call from one group of gathered craftsmen. Carymba came to the group and more gathered around her for they were all confused by the day. 'Carymba, do you know this newcomer from the North named Sylvester?'

'Yes. Why? Has he been troubling you, too?' 'He has been around, talking to a lot of us. And, well, we are confused. What he says makes sense, in a way. How can you argue with a man who says he is warning us about the efforts of others to take advantage of us? To help the other guys, he says, we have to look out for ourselves ... each of us. Still, the whole thing does not set quite right. We know Thyruid has been listening to him, and it has become really worthless to go to the Inn; there is no joy there anymore. The same kind of tension can be felt out here now, too. What do you think we ought to do, Carymba?'

'Do what you have always done, following the teachings of Priastes. What did you do with Orgello and Geron? All their old friends decided to go to the Inn-by-the-Bye; it was better there, our way, than in the fear-filled way they had known too well. Sylvester will destroy you with his prudence, if you let him. Your only strength is your kindness shared richly, freely together. Without that impulse of kindness, you are mere slaves to one another, to yourselves, to your fear. Your only defense is your kindness; show it to Thyruid, too. We need that Inn'.

Together with Carymba, the craftsmen came to the Inn-by-the-Bye even though the magic road, the Bye, was not working today. Thyruid had almost forgotten kindness in favor of his new-guessed prudence. Almost, but not quite, had he forgotten. He remembered just enough to smile a real smile, and to forget about customers for the sake of guests, friends about his Inn. The road turned back to the Inn-by-the-Bye when the cup of water was remembered.

And Sylvester stopped by Grump for a visit on his way back to the North once more.

For the Sermon for 20 July 1980, titled "Thanks Be To God", based on Colossians 1:1-12.

XXIX

'Betsy has that dreamy look about her this morning. When she has that, she always gets into interesting adventures. I think I will tag along with her'. Geoffrey started after the already-begun Betsy. 'Wait up, Betsy! Can I come along with you today? I am kind of lonely and would like to walk with you?'

'If you want to come along, then come along, Geoffrey. I have no place to go today, no plans in mind except to wander around. Maybe I will go over by the hills. This is a dreamy kind of day for me. How has it been for you?'

'Oh, I have really not been too busy, and have nothing in mind myself. I saw you and your dreamy look, and I thought we might enjoy the day together. … You lead, and I will come along. If you want to talk, we can talk; if you want to be quiet, well … that is fine with me, too. So, … let's go!'

And they trailed off, wandering along, going slowly, watching things. In a thick part of the grass, Betsy suddenly threw herself down on the ground and stared closely into the grass. Geoffrey looked, too, though the ground was a lot closer to him than to his child-friend. Looking into the array of greens, Geoffrey commented: 'No. I have never really noticed how many greens there are in the grass. But yes, I do see the greet of the deepest forest right next to the sharpest yellow green. And yes, I see those tiny little flowers, nuggets of gold peeking out from behind the blades of grass like shy, wee, very wee fairies hiding their promises from all those who look most closely, most carefully'. 'I think anyone must care for these little flowers in order to see them. Maybe they are shy and simply hide from most folk' replied Betsy. 'I must admit, I never noticed them before' agreed Geoffrey.

He would never admit it out loud, but Geoffrey was soon becoming tired of that particular patch of green and gold. It was very small and there was much else to see. It was better to wander and daydream, he thought. Just then, Betsy shouted out: 'Look! Down there!' At that point, Geoffrey's wandering mind was visibly snapped back to the moment – except that Betsy was so engrossed with her patch of ground that she did not notice. 'Where?' ... 'There!' Down in the lighted root area, things were moving. (Remember, this is Hyperbia, and here the light glows up from underneath, giving a green tint to all things.)

Geoffrey too dropped down on his knees and gazed at the tiny creatures: 'I have never looked so closely at anything before. ... We must walk on them all the time. How could we help it?' 'Look, Geoffrey: see how they work carefully down in among the crumbles of dirt. I wonder what they are doing?'

After a while, Geoffrey once more wandered off in his thoughts, leaving Betsy to her watching. He mused: 'This may have been a poor choice for today. Perhaps she will get up again ... soon'. And off his mind meandered through fairy tale mountains of powder puff firmness.

As suddenly as she had plopped down, Betsy jumped up and started off toward the hills. Geoffrey almost forgot to follow ... then wondered if he should, then jumped up and dashed after her as he saw once more that dreamy look which promised adventure. He ran, stumbled, fell, rolled over a few times, lost a bit of his over-filled dignity but not his hat, bounced to his feet once more and chased after Betsy. 'My! Don't I wish she had shorter legs! This is hard on the likes of me'.

Up the first hill, Betsy stopped again, as suddenly as before. She stopped and stooped over, looking on the other side of a stone; Geoffrey was still puffing behind her and could see only the clod of sod inching up a good-sized stone ... it must have been head high on Geoffrey. Betsy smiled and said 'Hi'; Geoffrey, still coming, wondered to whom she had spoken but had sense enough to slow down, keep quiet and just watch and listen. (He did learn something at the clump of grass!) 'Who are you, sitting here so quietly and alone?' asked Betsy. 'I like to do that, too, somedays. May I sit down?'

No answer was heard but something must have been agreeable, for Betsy did sit down, looking toward the hills, away from Geoffrey. Puzzled now, Geoffrey lay down in the grass, back a bit from Betsy, to see what was going to happen. After what seemed to Geoffrey to be an awfully long time, a small voice next to Betsy, from behind that stone, said 'Hi'. Betsy looked down and smiled. 'The hills are beautiful today. ... I like sitting here with you. ... It is comfortable and relaxed here'. Then it was silent once more.

'My name is Marro. What is yours?' 'Mine is Betsy. Marro ... that is a pretty name. It fits you, I think'. Geoffrey stayed put even though his curiosity was about to wear him out: 'Who is Marro?' he wondered over and over again. 'Are you from the hills, Marro?' 'Yes'. 'They are lovely. I have never been up there though. What are they like?' Eternal silence followed – Geoffrey was sure of that; he wanted to say about the view that he had seen from up there; he wanted to mention the few hill folk he had met with Carymba; he wanted to say more and more; but he kept his silence; somehow Marro was more important than all that, even though he had never seen her. 'Oh ... it is a place to be from, a place to which a person might return, a home, I guess'.

Geoffrey thought of all those greens and the tiny, tiny flowers and those tinier yet things moving in the dirt. 'What was it that Betsy said? ... That you had to care for them to see them? Was that it?'

Betsy asked: 'Do you like the meadows?' 'I am not sure'. The reply sounded terribly sad to Geoffrey; he listened more carefully – perhaps his ears would help him see. Betsy continued: 'Have you been here long?' Marro replied 'This is as far down from the hills as I have been'. 'Oh. Then you do not know anyone down here'. 'Just you ... now'. 'Are you hungry?

I know a good place to eat'. 'That sounds good'. 'Come along, then'. And they got up to go.

Finally, Betsy remembered Geoffrey. 'Oh, Geoffrey! meet my new friend Marro. Marro, Geoffrey cares too'.

'To the Inn, then!'

For the Sermon for 3 August 1980, titled "Praying", based on Luke 11:1-13.

XXX

About the low-burning fire, on the green before the Inn-by-the-Bye, as the evening Resting Time was sliding into the night, a few lingering people sat. Yves and Betsy had long ago gone to bed; Marthuida had long felt like closing the Inn for the night; Geoffrey had tumbled off to bed; most of the tradesmen had said good night; even Thyruid, firm host that he is, had felt the night had come. For that very reason he had been letting the fire die away in its slow progress from flame to glow to cloudy heat to cooling embers. Thyruid and Marthuida finally gave up waiting and asked if there were any more needs from the Inn. 'Not tonight' was the reply – and they closed the Inn and went to bed.

Left in the still air of the enclosing night were Carymba, Sola and Ribbert. The three lone figures sat quietly for a long time as the heavy night air held close the distilled smoke from the now-glowing embers. Carymba sat on the far side of the fire, having laid herself back against a large, smooth stone, warm in the glow of the dying fire. Ribbert sat abruptly on the side, resting his head upon his hands, his elbows supported by his knees. Sola, not as flexible as his younger friends, sat propped upon a chair. Silence hung with the smoke over the central fire; thought was occupying the time for all three of them.

Earlier that evening, during the course of the free talk which filled that welcome hour of gathered neighbors and friends and, on occasion, some guests, someone had come, wondering at the habits of this place. It was the wandering peddler who had raised the point. This man typically went to-and-fro about the land. He knew the sea, but not the mermaids for they had not sung to him. He knew the hills. He had even been down the beach to the ends of the world. He had looked across End Ridge but had despaired of finding either wares or market there – so had never gone over End Ridge.

These Hyperbian folk, the meadow dwellers and the hill folk, were not like anyone else, not anywhere else he had gone; that is what he had said to them. Geoffrey had agreed; Cumberland was certainly different. The peddler agreed; it must be true even though he had never been to Cumberland, nor did he have any idea where he might find it. (The peddler was a little disturbed, however, by the idea that someone had been someplace that he had not been.) Yves and Betsy had agreed, too, for their home had been different, when they had been there. Hyperbia was a nice place, though. That is what they said. (The peddler had never seen anyone as big as those children anywhere but here; he wondered where *their* world was.) The peddler had wandered off then, going elsewhere, he said. Business was better in other places.

The gentle folk had been bothered by the peddler. He was nice enough, at least on those rare occasions when he wandered into their midst. Yet he was different. He brought a different edge into their company. The difference was different than that brought by others from beyond Hyperbia, like Geoffrey and Yves and Betsy, or Thyruid and Marthuida a few years back.

The peddler was a man of the world, a wide traveler, if you believe half of what he says. He must travel a lot for he sells little here and is gone most of the time and does not look nor act too poor. He would not learn the ideas he spouts around here. The folk grumbled about him for a while. But they did not understand him very well; so, the put him off, taking up instead their usual talk and wandering along, just like any night.

All that had happened earlier in the evening. It was getting late now as only the same three friends remained sitting around the dimming coals. 'That peddler is a sly fox. I do not trust him. He knows what he is doing in his talk and in his show. He can control a world like he was describing'. 'I agree, Sola. But what can we do?'

'I say we keep him out, that we beat him at his own game. We cannot let him take over the mind of the meadow lands'. 'Precisely, Ribbert, and that is why we cannot beat him at his own game, as you say. Even to play his game is to lose'. Silence hung over the cooling embers. Just as the light was finally giving out, Sola said: 'Yes, we will respond by our own game.

Let us find some rest for the night'. And the three friends slipped off into the night.

Marthuida had overheard them, as she could not sleep, and her open window looked over the green. Thyruid snored quietly in the heat, as his wife wondered to herself what they meant. 'I will watch and see' she thought to herself.

Over the next few weeks, a careful eye could see the little edge of concern for themselves that was rising among the folk, particularly those who had laughed off the word of the peddler. That seeming-wisdom he had spouted so easily set a little roughly as it worked in its forgotten-ness. As wariness ate away at the shared gracious, masters looked harshly at tardy apprentices; one took greater care of his accounts; another watched his neighbor closely. Each suspected the same uneasiness in their fellows. Marthuida noticed the testy-carefulness of once warm friends over the fire; she puzzled.

In the hills, Ribbert worked as always. On occasion, he saw John and Gilbert of Hoya: the iron work was going well. The peddler was far away and Ribbert knew what he was for and what he was against. His business was as open and free as always. Although some neighbors began to wonder, Ribbert held firm his life-long practices. 'You will lose your business if you keep going like this. It will not work anymore. Keep up with the times, Ribbert'. With such advice, he was greeted by his peddler-bound neighbors. He laughed at them: 'I would more likely loose my heart than lose it'.

Marthuida heard of it – and smiled. She also heard of the steady, limping handy placings of Carymba: just like always. And Sola: well, the retired man kept his way going firmly, witnessing by flesh and blood to the power of his position.

Marthuida chuckled to herself and hoped to find the peddler confused at his return. Now, she understood that strange talk about the dying fire.

For the Sermon for 31 August 1980, titled "For Discipline", based on Hebrews 12:7-13.

XXXI

Brusquely, the coolness of evening swept down. This was a different sort of evening for this time of year. Yves and Betsy had known the pleasant land, the warmth of Hyperbia, the gentleness of the land. The cool gusts which were battering their ease this evening were unfamiliar at best; unpleasant would be a better description. Even the old timers found such a coolness strange for the meadow lands in late Summer – although the hills would occasionally feel this kind of coolness. Carymba remembered a few nights; Ribbert, a few more.

Now, the friends of the meadowlands were huddled about the fire before the Inn-by-the-Bye. Usually, they gathered here for friendship; this time, the interest was in the warmth of the fire to their bodies. No one was very comfortable – except, perhaps, for the side turned toward the fire and, perhaps, what was cuddled toward their closest friends. Back sides were icy. Good cheer was at a low force. Friendliness and kindliness were excused from the general atmosphere. People had trouble thinking of anything except their own discomfort. They were not accustomed to this sort of trouble.

Late that evening, old Mother Bosworth wandered in. Her entry marked this a rare evening for she hardly ever went out, not to the Inn-by-the-Bye nor to any place else. Some say she just does not to be around people because someone had once told her she had to be nice to them – and that is something she did not want to do: definitely *not* that! No one had ever asked her why she stayed away; they might not have understood if she had told them. All they knew was she did stay away and had for so long that everyone *knew* that this was the reason.

As she approached the Inn and the open fire, the old woman cast her eyes quickly about the circle of backs closed to her; some of them shuddered extra, feeling colder than before. Old Mother Bosworth felt the cold, too; she knew in her heart that she was only reflecting the cold she felt from the many. 'It has been this way for years' she sighed to herself. 'Those folk will never change. They will always see me in their odd way rather than in the way that I am'.

'Give me room here' scolded the old woman. 'Do your think you can control all the heat around here? Let an old woman ease the chill in her bones'.

Icily, a slot opened, and she entered. It took a while because everyone wanted someone else to make the room. 'Who', they thought to themselves, 'would want to sit next to Old Mother Bosworth?' 'Not I' said each to themselves. Finally, Yves and Betsy separated a bit and waved the old woman into the gap between them. She glanced at their size: quite enormous in her eyes. She hesitated; but she was cold and this was an opening to a warmth her joints longed to know once more. Between the great big children, she sat. The gap left was soon taken up by Yves himself. Old Mother Bosworth found herself smothered a bit but warming, even if the fire seemed distant. The wee folk sighed, glad that Old Mother Bosworth was hidden away from them, warm and quiet.

Betsy watched the poor hospitality of her little friends, a coolness for the old woman whom she had never seen before. Betsy did not understand; glancing at Yves, she could tell he did not understand either. The tiny woman was innocent enough between them. Some of the little eyes caught Betsy's eyes and felt the sting of her disappointment in her glance.

The minds she saw turned to a past that Betsy could not have known. They remembered the oddities of the woman, her aloof quietness, her keeping to home all the time, her slowness to welcome them when she came into their land, the hard bargain she always made for her goods. She was always ready to complain. She never noticed the nice things in their lives. She never came out to meet them. And, besides all that, she moved here as a curious old woman and lived her life to herself. Betsy could never have known all that was stirring behind the shaded eyes.

Betsy looked away from the hard eyes of her friends and looked down to the stranger beside her, between herself and Yves, her brother. Old

Mother Bosworth looked back. Her eyes were soft to Betsy's soft. For the old woman, that felt different; she had not known that feeling for a long time. She smiled; and, to her surprise, her face did not crack. In fact, her face felt good for a change. She even blushed a bit and looked down quickly, glancing around hastily, but with nothing to fear as no one saw but Betsy. Everyone else was too busy, lost in their unthinking.

'Betsy is too young to understand all the things which are important here'. Thus thought all those minds which had sensed Betsy's questioning look. In their own minds, there was no possible doubt that Betsy could not understand. A young girl like she was simply did not have the experience, the knowledge, the wisdom of time to see how things were, how important the customs of the place were. The Hyperbian meadowlands were what they were because everyone was friendly; anyone who did not want to be friendly could not be welcome here. And that was precisely the problem with Old Mother Bosworth: *she* was not friendly and never had been. And that was that.

That cold evening was a strange one. The more the friendly folk huddled together for warmth, the colder they felt. They even commented to one another about that biting cold that night, and how futile the fire seemed. Neither Yves not Betsey felt half so cold; they were chilly, of course, but not bitten sharply like the others. Old Mother Bosworth simply nestled in between the large children and sat there nice and warm and happy.

For a long time, they all simply sat there, the cold friendly folk around the circle, the warmer children and the toasty unfriendly old woman between them. The fire glowed in the center, the same on all sides. Then, finally, Marthuida was cold enough to raise herself and approach the children – and Old Mother Bosworth. 'May I join you?' 'Sure, there is plenty of room!' And one more was warm.

Betsy was young enough not to know and young enough simply share; now, Marthuida was, too. A crooked little smile sat among the cold ones, wondering if anyone knew where the friendly ones sat.

For the Sermon for 7 September 1980, titled "Be Slow and Gracious", based on Proverbs 25:6-22.

XXXII

'Now, Thyruid: take it easy. There is no need to get yourself so bothered. Nothing terribly terrible has happened. Everything will work out just fine, *if* you keep your head cool.'

'Get our of my way! You are not going to bottle me up like this, Marthuida. You are not!' And Thyruid burst around his wife, stormed out of the kitchen, through the common room of the Inn-by-the-Bye, out the door and stood in the fullness of the mid-morning glow. He glowered through the light and across the green, past where the youngsters sat. The gloom of impetuous anxiety, of headstrong fear bridled his senses so that he stumbled over Yves great feet and fell on his face.

This did nothing good for his dignity, nor for his ill-humor, and he sputtered angrily about the feet which had come to be in his way; his upset had distracted his eyes and now turned aside his usually guided judgment. In the face of Thyruid's angry outburst, Yves looked surprised ... then sat up tall and stared down on the wee man he loved as his first host in Hyperbia.

Muttering to himself, Thyruid wandered off. 'Nothing is right. Everything is wrong. Nobody understands what they are supposed to do. Mostly, they do nothing; and what they do do, they bungle. This whole place is all oofgebungled!'

Back at the Inn, standing about the green as the fuming Thyruid stormed across the meadows, all watched. Yves and Betsy watched him go, puzzled because they had never seen Thyruid this way and could not understand his strange fury. Geoffrey just scratched his head and shrugged his shoulders and went back to his brunch. He mumbled: 'I do not think I provoked him. There is nothing I can do anyway. Besides, my breakfast is late already ...and it is getting cold with all this ruckus'.

A few old folk, who had seen Thyruid's rare outbursts of temper before, chuckled to themselves: 'He looks very foolish when he gets this way. I have to laugh!' said one. The others agreed with a healthy chuckle of their own.

Carymba heard it all and glanced back to Marthuida, holding her plump fingers tightly woven together so that they turned red beyond the white signs of her over-gripping. A questioning glance brought Marthuida's confession that Thyruid's anger boiled over when the new wine shipment was delayed. He felt that it was so important that he tend it in its ripening months ... and there is now a pressure of time on those months. 'I told him this would do no good ... but he would not listen. And off he goes'.

'Whom does he seek?'

'Who knows? Perhaps he is going down the Bye to tell the wine makers to hurry their grapes! O Thyruid, why can you not just relax!?'

Turning to the Inn, Marthuida prepared to meet the rest of the day. 'Geoffrey, would you help? Perhaps an old ... er, a *former* gentleman's gentleman could manage the tables while I manage the kitchen. Only go slow on the wine. Serve more milk ... there is plenty of milk'. Before Geoffrey could even agree, Marthuida was in the kitchen; the hour of lunch was nearing for those who had had breakfast at a normal hour. Geoffrey smiled: 'Of course I will help' he said to himself. 'Could there be anyone out here who is interested in some food ... with fine milk ... a beverage of the highest quality?'

Geoffrey had grabbed an extra apron and was tying it on so that he looked *something* like Thyruid – until you looked, that is. The crowd all stared for a moment ... for Geoffrey was younger and lighter than Thyruid ... and the old Innkeeper had never set his apron over the gentleman's gentleman's formal wear that Geoffrey always wore. Nor were Thyruid's shoes ever so shiny. Geoffrey's old habits still lived, but did not fit with the oversized (for Geoffrey) apron. The sides almost met in the back and the ties went an extra turn around his waist.

After staring and chuckling at the re-formed Inn-meister, the many came in and began to shout their orders with less order than usual. And the usual was not very orderly at all. Geoffrey had to scramble to keep up ... and to keep his sense of humor.

Poor Yves, poor Betsy! They could not fit into the Inn for they were very big for Hyperbia. And Geoffrey, the rattled novice, forgot all about them until their voices boomed in through the door in a sound as big as they were themselves. This reminded the Inn-meister (as Geoffrey had begun to call himself, all of a sudden) that they, too, wanted lunch.

Soon, the nimble Geoffrey caught up with the rush and the expert preparations of Marthuida. Everyone was eating. The till was filled. And only milk was drunk. Everyone was enjoying the day ... even Geoffrey, who found the chance to chat with many of the wee folk. The host of the Inn-by-the-Bye, even a stand-in as was Geoffrey, sees the crowd differently than the crowd sees itself. That is because of the fact that the host is responsible for all and for the Inn. Following the lunch, many stayed well into the afternoon; this was just habit for the friends of the Inn's hospitality. This was a good place to visit and, often, the early afternoon is not such a good time to work.

In the hours of the lingering of the company, a pair of figures came to the door, hungry and tired. These were Carymba and her sort-of escort, Thyruid. The Innkeeper returned much more withdrawn than usual ... much as many people do when they know how foolish they had been. Carymba had found him in the hills with his fury about spent; she had eased him home quietly. The Inn always approaches when it is needed, even for a wayward Thyruid, the Inn's keeper.

The pair slipped into the Inn, not knowing what to expect. In the midst of all the talk, only Geoffrey noticed them. He sat them quietly in a half-hidden corner booth, assured them of an order, brought it and let them eat their late lunch in peace. The crowd broke up, never noticing the two latecomers. The two ate in obscurity. Then Geoffrey brought the apron for the man it fits. Thyruid would need to be ready for supper. 'Just remember: serve milk instead of wine … until the right time. All right?'

'All right, Geoffrey. … And, thanks'.

For the Sermon for 14 September 1980, titled "Refresh My Heart", based on Philemon 1-20.

XXXIII

'Chert, why have you come down to the meadows? Weren't you the one who was going to "always" stay in the back of the hill country, back where the murmur of the sea is a part of your life? This is certainly a long way for you to wander, my old friend. Even so, it is good to see you again. I have not been in your part of Hyperbia for a long time. Let me see: Why, two years must have passed since I was there. Tell me, how are you doing these days? How have these years treated you?'

With that, Carymba, the wandering waif, took up her mug and drank deeply. She looked down, offering relief to the shy and quite nervous Chert, relief from her friendly inquiry into his rather surprising presence.

Chert knew full well that his appearance in the meadows would be deeply surprising to anyone who knew him. Back home in the hills, he had always been quiet. His chosen home spot lay in the far back corners of the hill country; very few ever found themselves so far out, so close to the edge, as they called the cliffs by the sea. He, however, had his reasons for coming down.

For now, Chert would only admit that Carymba's friendly and known face was a welcome greeting. In her smile, he could find comfort. He was not, however, ready to talk too much of himself or of his pilgrimage to the meadows. 'Oh, I just decided to look around a bit. So, I came to look. Say, do you mind if I sort of hang around with you? You do know your way around and all. I just thought that might be nice'.

Carymba looked at him quickly, to catch the look in his eye. But he had also been looking down the whole time – out of shyness, as Carymba knew well. 'I guess that would be possible. Of course, I am still the wandering sort. ... I have no house to call my own ... no home except Hyperbia herself'.

'Perhaps I can help you. Do you need a house?' 'Not really'. 'Then I will not make you one. But I *can* assist you. I *will*, if you like'.

There was no question that Chert was going to be with her for a while. Carymba remembered enough of his honest and persistent resolve to know that much beyond any question. She had always managed well enough herself; but now she had a new adventure, a helper. She must see how it will go.

Chert had always been a solid man, wholeheartedly reliable if a bit of a loner. In both respects, he had a reputation of outdoing the strongest personalities in all Hyperbia. Carymba was about to find out more of the strengths of Chert. Some people notice strengths and do not waste their time on weaknesses; Carymba is one of that kind of people.

'Well, Chert, shall we go see what is happening in the meadows today?' 'Fine'. Chert did not talk very much; Carymba is patient. They walked along, as was Carymba's habit, greeting the tradesmen and meadow craftsmen. Chert nodded his greetings as Carymba never tired of introducing him to a list of names that, he was sure, would take him years to remember. If that made him uneasy, it firmed his resolve and he never showed it; 'there will be time to learn some of those names' he told himself.

Carymba's hand came easily to help or hold something for one craftsman after another. Her touch was always welcome. Chert watched: 'I know many of these trades myself. Back where I lived, you had to do many things and do them fairly well. I was better than most'. Chert watched but did not enter in to help. He was still unknown in the meadows and could feel the questioning glances. He kept himself close to his old friend, Carymba.

The two wandered and greeted weavers and binders and smiths, candlemakers and many others: all busy, all friendly. Eventually, the two came over near the quarry, where the mason and his assistants were working. Carymba looked in and Chert with her. The rigging was caught in their working setup and they were struggling with the rock. The rock was not being very cooperative at all. Both visitors recognized the difficulty but Carymba, for once, could do nothing. She felt helpless where aid was needed. Chert lost his shyness and came to the necessary chore with a quickness Carymba had only seen in a cat or an escaping mouse.

Now, Chert knew what to do and had the skill and strength with which to do it. There was no time to worry about propriety. Nimbly, the rock was set back to where the others could hold it easily. Monkey-like, Chert scrambled to the rigging and re-strung it to hold the piece in the moving. With the setup corrected and secured, the stone was moved, lifted and place for the fine working. 'That should do, I believe. Are we set right?' 'Yes. That is what we had in mind. Thank you.' 'Surely. Good bye'. And Chert walked off, Carymba following.

'You were not working the quarry when I last saw you, Chert. When did you learn the tricks? You did a beautiful job and really saved a tragedy'.

'I started a quarry near the edge. Most of the work was just common sense or feel for what was going to happen with those heavy rocks. Before I began on my own, I *did* work for a master mason at his own little quarry. After I left him, he was not happy. In the end, I lost my work to him. Still, I took what he had shown me and improved on it. My rigging was better; my dressing was better. I was … I *am* a better mason. But I lost my quarry, my stone'.

'Did that bring you to the meadows? and to coming along with me? I like your company and all, but you were always to yourself in the hills'.

'The ruling was that I had not gone the regular route to become a mason. I had to surrender my work until I was prepared in their eyes. I will not go back'.

'What about that quarry back there? They certainly know part of your skills'.

'I could go there. But I could also go with any of the others we saw. I have done all that in the past. Most of it was done well'.

206

'Come with me tomorrow. I have an idea'.

The next day, they went around again. From the Inn, through the meadows, to the quarry: at each stop, Chert lent the hand, not Carymba. After the surprise, they all agreed that Chert was handy; more, they agreed he was a deft hand; more yet, they agreed that he was skilled at all the trades.

That night, Carymba came up to the fire with Chert behind her. 'You now know my friend from the hills, Chert. You have seen the turnings of his hand. He needs a place. I would hope for a room, Thyruid, and a task, my friends. Refresh me with the meadowlands' hospitality'.

'I will begin with a tower room, Carymba'.

'Chert, would you show me how you did that rigging?'

'And could you show me ...' 'and me ...' 'and me ...' '...'

'I think, Carymba, that there is room in the meadows for your friend, Chert'. That was Geoffrey, who had also found room once before. 'Sometimes, all of us just have to see about the room which can be there'.

For the Sermon for 21 September 1980, titled "Turning And Turning", based on Exodus 32:7-14.

XXXIV

'Betsy, I want to tell you about what happened this morning!'

'All right, Yves. I will listen'.

'Well, I went over to the hills and who do you think I saw over there?'

'Oh hi, Geoffrey! How are you? I heard you were not feeling well lately. I hope you are better now'. 'I am feeling better now. Thank you, Betsy'.

'Betsy ... I saw old Sola and had a nice talk with him ... what are you doing now, Betsy?'

'I was listening. Really, Yves, I was listening; there was just something floating in the air, and I was watching it as it floated along. Don't let me disturb you. Keep talking'.

'Anyway ... where was I ... oh yes ... Sola was talking about the troubles here a generation ago. They brought about ...'

'Oh, Betsy, Yves: Can I get you some lunch?'

'Yes, thank you. Perhaps some of Marthuida's special biscuits, some eggs, and some milk'.

'And you, Yves?'

'The same, thanks. Now, Betsy ... are you listening?'

'Of course, I am listening, Yves! What do you think I am? Say, what are they doing over there?'

Yves gave up. Sola really had been interesting. He told of the times when Orgello's grandfather was old and the meadows were unhappy under his rule. But there had been three bad years in the hills and some of the hill people had begun to come down to the meadows, in spite of the Old Man. Sola had been here then, a young man from the meadows. He began to work with a man who had come down from the hills, a true master craftsman.

Work at the trade filled up the days. For the evenings, there was no Inn then; the Old Man, as they called him, would never have permitted one. So, many of the hill families would gather at the home of Sola's boss. There, the disgust with the Old Man turned to sterner thoughts which eventually found Orgello retreating to his kingdom of Grump, rather apart from the mainstream of life in the meadows. 'The story was ... is ... a good one' thought Yves. 'But Betsy will not pay any attention'. In silence, he ate and then wandered off.

All this time, Betsy had been talking to anyone and to everyone. One after another, like a bee in a flower garden, she had passed along the lines of greetings and small talk. When Yves had walked away, Betsy hardly noticed. Only in passing did she wonder *why* he was going. 'Oh, well, there are others here' she thought as she shrugged and looked around.

Betsy was still looking around when one lady came up to her. 'Betsy, can I talk to you?' 'Sure! Sit down!' Betsy looked at her and listened. The lady began to tell of some problems she had been having. Normally, one does not talk that way to a child, but Betsy is *so* big that the wee folk often forget that she is a child still. Besides, Betsy is always nice and pleasant – and soon forgot what had been told to her. Both traits were desirable to these wee folk who wanted to talk out their problems without having them return to them across the back fence.

The shy lady began to talk quietly and, for one minute, Betsy listened. At least the sound went in her ears and the sight in her eyes – both at the same time. Then, once more, it was: 'Oh hello, Marthuida. Those biscuits were very good this noon'. 'Why, thank you Betsy'. ...

The lady paused, then went on where she left off until once more Betsy called out 'Hi, Sola. Yves said he saw you thins morning'. (And Yves thought she had not heard at all!) 'Hello Betsy. Yes, Yves and I had a nice chat'.

'That is alright, Betsy. I will talk to you later'. Then, the poor, shy lady left.

The whole lunch time went that way. Betsy had a marvelous time until everyone left. Then, she wondered about Yves: 'What was he trying to tell me? He certainly was not very clear about it all. I will have to tell him to clear up his speech and keep to his point. He certainly needs to improve on that score!' Then, she wondered about the other lady: 'She sure did not want to talk very much. I wonder why she asked to talk to me; she hardly uttered a word'.

Now, it was all quiet and Betsy had nothing to do. She was bored. She went around behind the Inn and peeked in the kitchen window. Marthuida's plump hands were busily working at her baking. 'Hello, Marthuida!' 'Oh, hi Betsy. Sorry I cannot talk right now. I have to get this all done before supper time'. 'Sure'. Marthuida worked away, busy and not able to look up from her chore. Betsy was bored again. She went to the front of the Inn and looked in the window there, finding Thyruid. 'Hi Thyruid!' 'Hi Betsy. I cannot talk now. I need to work on my books. Can you be quiet so I can concentrate easier?' 'Sure'. Betsy sat up and looked around. She was bored

Betsy walked about the area before the Inn and beyond. Everyone was busy now. No one had time to chat. She was bored. Very bored. She saw Yves over by the hills, talking. She went over to see him. He was with Sola again. 'Hi'. 'Hi Betsy'. 'How are you doing?' 'We are fine. We are talking now. You can stay, but be quiet, please'. 'How dull' she thought. Having nothing to do, she sat. She even listened long enough to realize they were talking about long ago. Then, she quietly ignored them. She tapped her foot and gazed about, looking for anything to ease her general boredom.

'Settle down, Betsy. You are bothering me!' Thus scolded Yves; Betsy left. Nobody wanted to do what she wanted to do. But then, even Betsy was not too sure what it was she wanted to do. So, she found a place to pout. And she pouted, though for no good reason. 'Are you happy with that pout?' It was Carymba. 'No. I guess not. It is just that there is nothing to do'.

'Correction: there is a lot to do. Pay attention to someone sometime, for a change'. Carymba sat down with Betsy in the afternoon quiet and they talked until supper time. Betsy even listened, really, and kept to the general topic. Come supper time, the two of them went to the Inn-by-the-Bye. Betsy looked for Yves – an easy task if he were anywhere near. 'Perhaps he will explain to me what was so interesting with Sola today'.

For the Sermon for 28 September 1980, titled "The Steward", based on Luke 16:1-13.

XXXV

As the morning glow began to glimmer from the sod and from the worn pathway, casting its most haunting early shadows of pebbles and rocks across the questioning sky, a lone figure came walking slowly up the glen from the Beach Road. He had been traveling all night and was unsure of his steps, tired as he was. Just as few from the meadows or the hills had ever even seen the sea or the beach, few from down that way had ever been to the Hyperbian meadows. This stranger came today for the first time.

All the wee folk were still asleep as he came toward the end of the cliff-shrouded path and stumbled by the foothills. As the glow richened toward day, his weary step was no longer alone. Many were rising. Many were beginning to go toward the Inn-by-the-Bye for their breakfast. Thyruid and Marthuida were dressed and beginning their day. The brass polish was out and the yawning Innkeeper was trying to start his morning ritual. Marthuida was piecing together the probable for breakfast.

The stranger paused and watched while his shadow was still lost among the castings from the rocks. The activity of the meadows came quickly as the habitual response to light spread across the scene. He was surprised by it all, having been alone for so long and having never been here before. Many folk sped by within speaking distance. But they did not notice the stranger; neither did he reveal himself.

For him, the light brought with it the weary knowledge that night had passed unslept. The bustle of activity brought with it the knowledge that he was strange and lost. The combined effect was the knowledge of hunger. 'I wonder if I can find something to eat around here?'

Before him now was noticed a path; he walked down that path as there was no more activity around him. He walked and found, all of a sudden, a sharp turn which had not been there a moment before. The turn in the Bye revealed the upcoming Inn-by-the-Bye, full of customers.

'Hello, friend' came the voice behind him as he paused to wonder at the crowd for breakfast. 'Would you join us for some breakfast? Marthuida is a *good* cook. I am not sure which meal she prepares best! Oh yes, Marthuida is the Innkeeper's wife. I am Carymba. My limp slows me to meals … so it is well that Marthuida always prepares plenty. Come along!' The stranger had jumped when first greeted; he was not ready for all this in his own mind. Yet, he was seen already … and there was no choice but to go on.

As if by magic, the stranger moved behind Carymba, curving smoothly through the assembled folk. Breakfast did look good. His stomach felt even more empty. He had to admit that he was hungry as he had to admit that the food appealed to his eyes and his nose. Those fine aromas from Marthuida's kitchen and from the trays of food handled so cleanly by Thyruid can do that sort of thing – and did, once more.

'Over here. Let us sit down and have something to eat. Thyruid! Some breakfast for my friend and myself! Oh … I forgot to learn your name. Did I remember to give you mine? I am Carymba, the resident gadabout'. 'Well, … my name is Michael. The food certainly does smell good!' 'And it tastes better'. Carymba had already noticed his reserve.

After breakfast, most of the meadowland folk went back to their work. As they left, Yves and Betsy came into the green. Michael saw them for the first time and jumped in fright. New to the Hyperbian meadows, he had never seen *anyone* so large. Carymba was concerned with the sudden washing of color from Michael's face. It was like he had seen a ghost.

Glancing quickly behind her back, Carymba knew the problem. She gently reassured Michael, saying that Yves and Betsy were just big children: he need not be frightened.

Still nervous. Michael wanted to retreat. He was not able to eat and run, however: Carymba had been too kind for such a maneuver. 'What kind of work do you do?' she asked. 'I … uh … I travel'. 'From where do you travel?' 'I … uh … well, I come from the Shores'. 'Did you hear the mermaids singing?' 'No. Where were they?' 'Down by the sea. They sing to me'. Poor Michael was confused. 'What do I do now?' he thought to himself.

'I have never been down to the Shore. We had a visitor from there once. He was a real troublemaker. He confused a lot of our people for a while. But his ideas did not take'. 'Oh?' 'Yes. He wanted people not to trust each other and to try to get the best of each other. Soon it was clear to enough of us that he was only concerned about himself and no one else. He has not been back for a long time'.

'That is how it is back there. Perhaps that is why I left. I certainly did not know I would come here. I did not even know "here" existed!'

'Do you want to stay?'

'Why not? You all seem friendly. Even the big ones are not too threatening!' Michael smiled toward Yves and Betsy.

'If you do, you can live among us or in the kingdom of Grump. They – in Grump – live as you seem to have lived. Here, we go another way. If you like, I will introduce you to Chert. He is from the hills and has mastered many of the trades. He can help you get started'.

'All right. We will go that way. Where is this Chert?'

I am a retired minister from the Christian Church (Disciples of Christ) living in the hills of the Northern Panhandle of West Virginia. I began writing these stories in August 1981as a part of my background reflection toward sermon preparation. I continued the discipline for nearly twenty-five years. Changes in my circumstances twenty-two years into the process eventually brought the series to an end. I came to refer to my stories a fairy tale exegesis. I now live in retirement with my wife of fifty-two years, two dogs and several cats.

Made in the USA
Monee, IL
06 July 2021